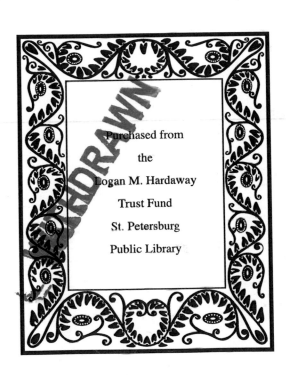

How I Met My Countess

HOW I MET MY COUNTESS

ELIZABETH BOYLE

THORNDIKE
CHIVERS

This Large Print edition is published by Thorndike Press, Waterville, Maine, USA and by BBC Audiobooks Ltd, Bath, England.
Thorndike Press, a part of Gale, Cengage Learning.
Widows of Standon Series #1.

The text of this Large Print edition is unabridged.
Other aspects of the book may vary from the original edition.
Set in 16 pt. Plantin.

LIBRARY OF CONGRESS CATALOGING-IN-PUBLICATION DATA

Boyle, Elizabeth.
   How I met my countess / by Elizabeth Boyle. — Large print ed.
      p. cm. — (Widows of Standon series ; 1) (Thorndike Press large print basic)
   Originally published: New York : Avon, c2010.
   ISBN-13: 978-1-4104-2594-2 (alk. paper)
   ISBN-10: 1-4104-2594-0 (alk. paper)
   1. Large type books. I. Title.
PS3552.O923H69 2010
813'.54—dc22   2010001696

BRITISH LIBRARY CATALOGUING-IN-PUBLICATION DATA AVAILABLE

Published in 2010 in the U.S. by arrangement with Avon, an imprint of HarperCollins Publishers.
Published in 2010 in the U.K. by arrangement with HarperCollins Publishers.

U.K. Hardcover: 978 1 408 49100 3 (Chivers Large Print)
U.K. Softcover: 978 1 408 49101 0 (Camden Large Print)

Printed in the United States of America
1 2 3 4 5 6 7 14 13 12 11 10

To Diane Tice,
for her kind and generous spirit,
as well as her support of quality
education.

And to Tia, her granddaughter,
for being such a sweet character —
in life and in this story.

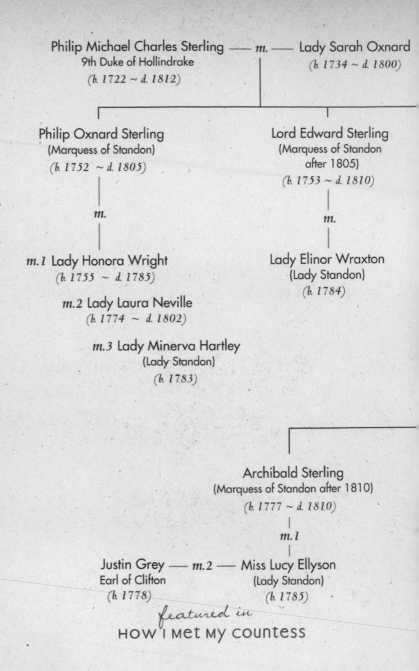

Philip Michael Charles Sterling —— m. —— Lady Sarah Oxnard
9th Duke of Hollindrake   (b. 1734 ~ d. 1800)
(b. 1722 ~ d. 1812)

Philip Oxnard Sterling   Lord Edward Sterling
(Marquess of Standon)   (Marquess of Standon
(b. 1752 ~ d. 1805)   after 1805)
                                                      (b. 1753 ~ d. 1810)

m.   m.

m.1 Lady Honora Wright   Lady Elinor Wraxton
(b. 1755 ~ d. 1785)   (Lady Standon)
                                                      (b. 1784)
m.2 Lady Laura Neville
(b. 1774 ~ d. 1802)

m.3 Lady Minerva Hartley
(Lady Standon)
(b. 1783)

Archibald Sterling
(Marquess of Standon after 1810)
(b. 1777 ~ d. 1810)

m.1

Justin Grey —— m.2 —— Miss Lucy Ellyson
Earl of Clifton   (Lady Standon)
(b. 1778)   (b. 1785)

featured in
HOW I MET MY COUNTESS

For more of the Bachelor Chronicles
Family Tree, please visit ElizabethBoyle.com

the BACHELOR CHRONICLES ♥ ♥
sterling family tree

Lady Mary Sterling
(b. 1755 ~ d. 1759)

Lord George Sterling
(b. 1758 ~ d. 1761)

Lady Geneva Sterling
(b. 1770)

m.

Mr. Robert Pensford
(b. 1765)

Lord Charles Sterling — m. — Lady Rosebel Redford
(b. 1757 ~ d. 1801)   (b. 1760)

Aldus Sterling
(b. 1778 ~ d. 1806)

Aubrey Sterling
aka Captain Thatcher
(Marquess of Standon after 1810,
Duke of Hollindrake after 1812)
(b. 1780)

m.

Miss Felicity Langley
(b. 1793)

featured in
love letters
from a duke

CHAPTER 1

Mayfair, London 1815

Major Thatcher should have been the envy of Society when his grandfather died, for upon the man's passing, Thatcher had been bestowed with the title of Duke of Hollindrake and all the lands, houses and great wealth that came with it.

But no one really envied him all that much, for he'd also inherited the care, feeding and headache of the previous three heirs' widows.

The Dowager Marchionesses of Standon.

It wasn't such an odd thing, to have one or two dowagers lying about, elderly widows who kept quietly to themselves while they waited out their eternal reward.

Not so the Standon widows. For not only were they young, they were of no mind to just wait patiently for their reward.

Now most everyone agreed that the first two dowagers — Minerva (having been wed to Thatcher's uncle Philip) and Elinor (his uncle Edward's bride), daughters of an earl and a baron, respectively — were every bit as haughty and aristocratic as their lofty title implied. That didn't mean they weren't capable of being, shall one say, difficult.

Difficult was not the word used to describe the third dowager Lady Standon, the former Miss Lucy Ellyson, the widow of Thatcher's older brother Archibald. On the contrary, Lucy, Lady Standon, left most of London speechless.

Or aghast. Depending on the day of the week.

But today was a Wednesday, and with a summons in hand from Thatcher's wife, the now infamous Duchess of Hollindrake, Lucy alighted from her carriage in front of a house on Brook Street and knew that today, of all days, she needed to be on her best behavior.

To that end, she'd worn her favorite green silk, doing her best to look the part of a well-heeled and respectable lady. Glancing down at the expensive fabric, she shook out the wrinkles creasing her skirt and concentrated on what she was going to say.

Your Grace, I hardly know what that innkeeper is referring to. Damages to the entire wing? Why, when we left, the fire was well contained.

Lucy paused midstep. *No, no! That will never do.* That was akin to admitting that the fire was her fault. And there was no proof.

At least not the sort that could condemn one.

She took another deep breath and began mentally composing yet again.

Ah, Your Grace, how lovely you look! Letters? What letters? From Minerva? I daresay she has quite mistaken the matter. I am certain I wrote beforehand to let her know we would be using the abbey in Lancashire for the entire month of December. How was I to know she'd arrive with her own party of eight and we'd all be snowed in together for an entire fortnight? Actually it proved to be quite a snug, jolly Christmas.

Yes, that sounded as if they had all gotten along splendidly.

Which couldn't be further from the truth.

Good heavens, how she was supposed to have known that Lady Gillmore was allergic to almonds? Or that Lord Wainewright would take offense for having his cheating at cards pointed out? Or that Mr. Mackey was intended for Miss Gillmore?

Lucy shook her head. Spoiled little chit! Why, the young lady should be thanking her for revealing what a scoundrel her nearly intended turned out to be. She — that is to say, Lucy — had certainly not given that bounder any indication she'd wanted him in her bedroom.

In truth, it had been a shocking and rather unpleasant surprise to find him waiting for her. Lounging on her bed in his altogether.

If she'd welcomed his advances, would she have screamed and chased him out with the fire iron?

Not that Miss Gillmore and her parents had believed her. Or even Minerva.

No. All because she was *that* Lady Standon.

Behind her, Thomas-William, her father's former servant, was muttering as he unloaded the luggage to the curb. He paused and shot a wary glance at the plain door before them. "Are you certain this is the right place, Miss Lucy?"

"This is Brook Street, is it not?" she replied as she tugged at her yellow gloves and checked to make sure her bonnet strings were properly tied.

"Yes," he answered, piling her hatbox atop a trunk.

"And this is the house number His Grace's butler told us where we might find the duchess?"

Thomas-William shot a skeptical glance

at the nondescript town house, his dark eyes narrowed. "Yes, it is. But I don't like this, not one bit. What with her summons and all this shilly-shallying about."

Lucy threw up her hands. "Well neither do I, but what am I to do? She is the duchess."

Unfortunately . . . she would have liked to add.

"I don't put it past her high and mighty to be up to something," Thomas-William was saying. One could argue that he'd muttered this to himself. Then again, he'd been with Lucy's family so long that he had no compunction about speaking his mind quite freely, especially to her.

"You are much too suspicious, Thomas-William," she chided, not that she hadn't had her own qualms over the duchess's sudden summons — er, rather, *her gracious invitation,* as dear Clapp, Lucy's elderly companion, had urged her to refer to this great inconvenience of having to pack up everything she owned and bring her entire entourage to London.

But now that they were here, and Lucy was about to beard the lioness in her own den, so to say, she took another deep breath and got back to crafting a litany of explanations and the accompanying apologies that might be necessary to extract them from whatever dreadful reckoning lay ahead.

Because without the Duke of Hollindrake's favor — which in translation meant the duchess's good graces — Lucy didn't know what she would do with her disreputable collection of dependants and servants.

For without a home of her own and very little money to speak of, she had no roof over her head other than the ones provided by her unlikely position as Lady Standon.

Lost in thought and her own anxieties, she barely heard the door open, nor took much notice of the man who came down the steps in a great hurry, for she'd gotten quite used to the efficiency of the duke's servants.

But still, she mused, it was about time one of the footmen arrived to help poor Thomas-William.

What she hadn't imagined was that the fellow, in his expedience, wouldn't notice the great pile of mismatched luggage in his path, or that he would go tripping over it, landing in a heap near Thomas-William.

As he hit, the man let out a great oath, one that should never touch a lady's delicate ear.

Then again, Lucy hardly cringed, for she'd heard such language most of her life, and now she had an entirely new set of worries.

"Oh, dear heavens!" she gasped as she eyed the large man lying all akimbo. Whatever would she do if he had a broken bone?

She could only imagine the duchess's dismay over having one of her footmen put out of commission because of Lucy's luggage.

Oh, yes, that would be the last and final straw, she had to imagine.

But to her relief, the fellow righted himself quickly, shaking out his coat and drawing his shoulders in a taut, proud line.

"Thank goodness," she sighed, for he appeared quite in order. "Oh, yes, my good man, so sorry for that," Lucy called over to him. "Do you think you can manage those three boxes over there? They aren't as heavy as they appear."

Then she gathered up her courage, turned from the latest scene of her crimes and went blithely up the stairs, as if she had been invited for tea and not this mysterious summons.

But even as she got to the top step, she had the uneasy feeling of being shadowed, and being her father's daughter, she whirled around. And while she had half-expected to find the footman standing there, holding her luggage as he ought, instead she came nose to nose with a man who had every aspect of a ghost from her past.

Except he was quite alive. Very much so.

For it was no footman who had come to their aid. No Hollindrake servant who'd tripped over her luggage. There, standing on the steps, looking at her with an expression she couldn't fathom, was the last man she'd ever expected to see again.

Him. Himself. The Earl of Clifton.

Then again, she'd never been able to read much behind those inscrutable blue eyes of his. Nor could she control the way her heart thudded, or how her insides fluttered, like a row of trumpeters.

It's him. It's him, Lucy. It's him.

No, the sight of him made her forget that it was Wednesday, the day she was meeting with the duchess. It prevented her from remembering that she was a lady now, a marchioness even, a dowager to boot, and most important of all, she forgot she was supposed to be on her best behavior.

"Good God, Gilby, is that you?" she gasped, feeling her knees shake beneath the silk of her gown.

Her, Lucy Ellyson, quaking like a debutante. This was a remarkable day, indeed!

"Mi-ss Elly-son," he stammered in a voice that held none of the old familiarity that

16

had once existed between them.

They just stood there and stared at each other, the years that had separated them naught but a blink of an eye.

I'll come back for you, Goosie. I promise. How could I not when I love you so?

And I'll hold you to that, Gilby, she'd teased back. *For if you don't, I'll come find you. I'll make you remember.*

But he hadn't.

"I'm sorry," he managed to say. "I suppose I should use your married name, but I fear I don't know it."

She shook her head. "Lucy will still do, my lord."

"Lucy, then," he acknowledged.

Again they stared at each other, and for her part, she drank in the sight of him, her heart pounding as she gazed at his still handsome face.

Once she'd known every line of it — for she'd memorized it before he'd left, had held that visage in her heart all these years — but now? There was a light in his eyes she didn't recognize, couldn't fathom.

And that sent a frisson of worry down her spine. *It's not him.*

And it was in that disquietude that she realized she needed to say something and stop gaping at him.

Stop searching for the man she loved.

Had loved, she corrected before she asked, "What are you doing here? I hadn't heard, that is to say, I didn't know you were . . ."

She snapped her mouth closed before she made a complete fool of herself.

Especially when he stepped back from her, leaving an aching chasm between them.

It was always there, Goosie. You just chose not to believe it, a voice so like her father's whispered to her.

"I'm here on business. And you?" he asked, in the polite and simple phrasing of an old friend or an acquaintance happened upon.

An acquaintance! she thought with some pique. When once they'd been inseparable. Spent an unforgettable night entwined together . . . so close she would never have believed that anything could have torn them apart.

Yet everything had . . .

"I've come to London on business as well," she managed to reply, so taken aback by his cool demeanor. "But what brings you here, to this house?" She tugged at her gloves, then looked into his eyes again.

And hoped . . .

"An old matter," he said, taking a speculative glance up at the door behind her. "But it has come to naught —"

She glanced over her shoulder and wondered what sort of business the earl would have with the duchess, but before she could come to any likely conclusion, what he said next finally sunk into her ears.

". . . I went by the house in Hampstead some time ago, only to discover that all of you," he said with a nod toward Thomas-William and then back at her, "were gone."

"You came to see me?" Lucy's heart sparked with hope, but only momentarily.

And for a second, a brief, tiny flash, she thought she saw that old light, that bold spark of desire in his gaze.

The one, she'd once sworn, burned only for her.

But like so many things about the earl, that too had proved to be wrong.

"To see your father," he corrected. Then he paused and glanced away, obviously more than uncomfortable at this unlikely meeting.

As if he wished it would end.

Or worse, had never happened.

He glanced again to her father's former servant. "Good to see you, Thomas-William. As hale as ever, I expect."

"Yes, my lord," the manservant said in a tight voice, not returning the rest of the greeting. Then the older man shot Lucy a glance. The one that usually warned her she was wading into deep waters.

But for the life of her, she couldn't fathom what had him in such a fix until he tipped his head toward the carriage.

The carriage and its contents.

Or rather its occupants . . .

"Oh, good gracious heavens," she whispered.

"Is something wrong?" the earl asked, as sharp-eared as ever.

"No, nothing," she said, tugging once again at her gloves. "I just realized that I'm . . . well . . . most likely taking far too much of your time."

"No, no," he said. "I'm glad to have seen you. It saves me the trouble of trying to find you."

He did want to find me, the trumpets blared again, though in premature celebration, of course.

"I was most sorry to hear of your father and sister's passing, especially when I learned of it from the new tenants. This chance meeting gives me the opportunity to extend my consolations to you," the earl said, returning his attentions, what there was of them, to her. "Their loss was a terrible tragedy for you I am certain, especially

Mariana — for she was too young to be taken." He paused, as most everyone did when they spoke of Mariana's death. She'd been the flirtatious one in the family, the blithe spirit who'd seen good in all, the one who could have been a duchess — and a good one to boot.

Then the earl spoke quietly, the words for her and her alone, spoken so low that quite honestly she thought she might be imagining them. "It was quite a blow to come to the house and to find strangers living there."

Not that Lucy was really listening.

"_. . . to see your father,_" he'd said.

He came to see your father, Lucy Ellyson Sterling, not you. You are a peagoose to think the Earl of Clifton would come back for an ill-bred, madcap girl like you . . . especially after all this time.

The voice ringing in her ear sounded suspiciously like that of Lady Geneva, the Duke of Hollindrake's very proper and all-too-starched aunt, the one Sterling who had taken it upon herself as a personal endeavor to constantly chide her, correct her, write her scathing notes regarding reports of her conduct.

And don't moon at him so . . . , Lady Geneva would have added.

Something inside Lucy sparked, her infamous temper flaring to life. Perhaps it was just a bit too much chiding of late from her Sterling in-laws, or perhaps the duchess's summons had her far more on edge than she cared to admit.

Or more likely, it was the sight of Justin Grey, the Earl of Clifton, standing before her, with his half-hearted condolences of *"a terrible tragedy."* That was all he could say? Their deaths had taken away everything . . . everything she'd loved.

For she no longer counted him in that list.

She flicked a glance at him and did her best imitation of Lady Geneva. "I am so sorry you were inconvenienced. If I had but known where you were or how to contact you . . ."

Would have what? Written? Begged him to come help her?

Only to renew all the old heartbreaks from before? To rediscover the ugly truth when her pleas fell on deaf ears, to realize once and for all that she'd been naught to him?

"No, no, Miss Ellyson, it is I who should apologize," he was saying. "I should have come sooner to make my regrets known."

His regrets? Which ones? The ones about kissing her? The ones regarding his promise to return? Or was it just his regret over that night in his inn when they'd . . .

22

Lucy stopped herself right there. This was hardly the time or place, and she'd come to some sort of understanding over his place in her heart years ago — at least she thought she had until a few moments ago when he'd tumbled back into her life.

And here she'd been worried about him breaking a bone!

Thank goodness he hadn't, for it left him hale enough to leave. And leave soon. For the growing panic on Thomas-William's nearly apoplectic features said only too clearly that she should send the earl on his merry way. Yet there was still one piece of the puzzle that she had to know.

For she was her father's daughter, and as he'd always said, *"Information is what keeps you alive."*

Lucy pasted a smile on her lips and asked, "And what was it that brought you here to Brook Street, of all places?"

Of course there was always her father's other favorite adage.

Know when to stop asking questions.

"I was looking for Lady Standon —" the earl began.

"Lady Standon?"

She'd have been less surprised if he'd professed his undying love for her — and had actually meant it this time.

23

Instead she shot a panicked glance over at Thomas-William, who was even now scanning the luggage as if deciding which pieces to grab if a hasty departure became necessary.

The earl nodded, his blue eyes fixed warily on the door behind her. "Yes, do you know her?"

"I-I-I-" Lucy looked helplessly down at Thomas-William.

But thankfully, the earl missed the point of her distress entirely. "My thoughts exactly. The lady just sent me packing with a flea in my ear."

"She did?" Lucy replied warily, then rallied and tried to sound nonchalant. "I mean, whatever did you want with Lady Standon? She's quite the terror . . ." Lucy shuddered, making a good show of it. "Or so I've been told."

Thomas-William shook his head and got to work gathering up the hatboxes, tossing them back in the boot of the carriage.

Wonderful man, Thomas-William. He knew how much she loved those hats.

Clifton paused and studied her for a moment. After all, he'd been a student of her father's as well, and thus he knew all the old adages too. "Some old business. Of no matter. Must be all a mistake anyway,

24

though quite unlike Strout to make such an error —"

"Strout?" she muttered faintly. Oh, heavens, she hoped Thomas-William could manage the smaller blue trunk. Her best gown was in it.

"Yes, Mr. Strout," he repeated. "But of course you'd know him. How foolish of me. He did business for your father, didn't he?"

She could only nod.

"Well, I can't see Malcolm having any association with that harridan. Not that I can imagine how he'd ever have met her," he said with a nod toward the door.

"Malcolm?" she echoed. Dear God, she was starting to sound like a parrot. What she needed to do was change the subject and do so quickly.

"Yes, you did hear about him, didn't you?" the earl managed. The pain in his voice tangled around her heart, so much so that she nearly reached out for him, like she might have done once before.

Instead, she folded her hands together in front of her and uttered polite, simple words. "I did. I was most sorry to learn of his . . . his . . ." Of his what? Death? She couldn't say that, for it was hardly the truth. Murder, really. Shot as a smuggler on a beach near Hastings.

When Malcolm had been no such thing, had been so much more.

Just like his brother . . .

She stammered over how to finish, and finally rushed to say, "I would have written, but I didn't know where to send —"

"Yes, well, I understand," he said in a formal, tight voice that cut through her yet again.

Oh, heavens, Malcolm's death must have ripped him in half, as it had . . .

The situation grew from bad to worse, for a terrible awkwardness sprang up between them, and they both looked left and right and not at each other.

Then Clapp, dear old fretful Clapp, came to her unlikely rescue. "Lucy, is this the place?" she called out from the carriage window. "Or must I stay out in this draft all day? You know this wind is likely to have terrible consequences."

So is standing about mooning over the Earl of Clifton, Lucy wanted to add. Instead, she said, "Please, Mrs. Clapp, stay where you are. I'll have this matter sorted out forthwith." She shot an apologetic look at the man before her.

Her Gilby.

The Earl of Clifton, she corrected herself. Never again her dearest Gilby. Hadn't she

26

given up on that foolish dream years ago? Hardly thought of him at all.

Well, not if once a day wasn't often.

"I'm afraid I must —"

"Yes, yes, you must see to your employer," he said, taking a glance back at the carriage and coming to all the wrong conclusions. Of course he thought her poor, and thought that now that she had no one left, she must make do in the world on her own.

Goosie, men like him never look at girls like you. Not in the way you fancy, her father's warning echoed up from the past.

The earl smiled politely at her. "I am heartened to see you well placed, Miss Ellyson."

Not Lucy. Not his Goosie. But Miss Ellyson.

She planted her feet firmly on the steps to keep her boot from connecting with his shin.

"If you ever have need of anything, you or Thomas-William," he continued, "please do not hesitate to contact me. I owe a great debt to your father."

Not to her. To her father. Lucy pressed her lips together, the old hurt threatening to do something worse than causing a scene by booting him off the steps like a vagrant.

No, definitely worse than that. Like making a regular watering pot out of her. Right here on Brook Street. In front of a good part of Mayfair.

With that, he took her hand and shook it quickly. Then, just as hastily, he let it go, before tipping his hat slightly to Thomas-William and crossing the street to where a lad stood holding the reins of a great black horse.

As he strode away, in that commanding pace of his, Lucy tried to breathe. Tried to still her racing heart.

Call him back, Lucy. Tell him the truth. Set him straight. Tell him who you are. A widow. A marchioness, even. A real lady, worthy of being his . . .

And then what? Watch him take everything else she loved away? Have him rip into pieces what was left of her heart? Besides, the nobleman who had just turned his back to her was more a stranger than the man she'd once known.

Her hero. Her Gilby.

Bah! He was, as her father had always said, *one of them.*

The earl tossed a coin to the boy, got up on his horse in one smooth motion and rode down the street without taking a single glance back at her. Which was good, because before he was even halfway down the block, the door to her carriage opened up and a small figure tumbled out.

"Lucy, who was that?" the six-year-old lad asked, as he made his way to her side and took her hand in his small one.

Her other scandal. Her beloved little Mickey.

She squeezed his fingers. "An old friend."

"Is he a toff?" the boy asked.

"Mickey, you know how I feel about using such language! You sound like a coachman."

The boy set his jaws together, for she knew he thought growing up to be a coachman a far better thing than being a gentleman. "Well, is he?"

"Yes," she replied, trying to keep the sigh out of her voice.

"A lofty one?"

"Yes, an earl. Actually he's a hero, Mickey. He helped Wellington in Spain."

"One of Papa Ellyson's gentlemen?" Mickey asked, glancing back at the departing man with awe.

"Yes," she said. "Yes, he was."

"And he was your friend?" he asked, not quite believing her.

"Yes."

"Is he still a friend?" Mickey sounded hopeful, for he was forever pestering the Duke of Hollindrake for stories of Spain, and now, perhaps, here was another man to regale him with tales of outwitting Napoleon and battles hard fought.

"I fear not," she told him.

"Too bad," the boy said, kicking at a loose stone on the cobbles. "That's a fine piece of cattle he's riding. And I rather liked the cut of his jib."

She didn't correct his speech this time; instead she smiled down at his dark, fathomless eyes before she stole one last glance at Lord Clifton as he turned the corner and was lost from her sight.

For she rather liked the cut of his jib as well.

Though she hadn't thought much of him the first time she'd met him. Quite honestly, she hadn't liked him a bit.

Arrogant and proud and too lofty for his own good.

How Lucy wished she could still claim that sentiment, for it would be far easier to reconcile herself to that vision of him than to the truth — for it held all the pain threatening to break her heart all over again.

CHAPTER 2

Hampstead, seven years earlier

"Where the devil did it go?" George Ellyson complained as he made his way around his "map room," as he liked to call his large, well-lit study.

The room took up half of the third floor of his house, with skylights overhead that flooded the room with illumination despite the cloudy day and the rain pattering against the panes. In the corner, a Franklin stove warmed the entire space, giving it a cozy, comfortable air.

But this sanctuary under the eaves, which seemed more suited for a quiet scholar or a gentleman scientist, was Mr. Ellyson's domain, and right now he paced about it like a lion with a thorn in his paw, thumping his cane down with each step to have yet another way, one suspected, to emphasize his ill humor over his lost map.

Justin Grey, the Earl of Clifton, glanced

over at his half brother, Malcolm, and shrugged.

This is England's mastermind of intelligence?

Master of a grand mess, he could almost hear Malcolm thinking.

The two men did not have the same mother, but they shared their father's determined spirit and a resolute temperament — qualities that now saw them venturing across the Channel to the Continent to conduct, as their illustrious taskmaster, Mr. Pymm, liked to call it, "England's other business."

But first, they had to pass muster with the man before them.

Thump. Thump. Thump. Mr. Ellyson and his cane progressed down the long wall of cubbyholes, where he kept a vast collection of rolled-up maps of all sorts. City maps, coach routes, old parchments that revealed faint, shadowy lines, paths only sheepherders might recognize, but for a man trying to slip past Napoleon's guards and troops in the Pyrenees such knowledge could prove invaluable, life-saving even.

"Perhaps if —" Malcolm began, but he was cut off with a wave of the cane and an expletive that would have turned a sailor's ears blue.

"Let me think," the man blustered. "Where the devil did that gel put my map?" This was followed by a litany of cursing that had both the earl and his brother cringing.

Words that could curl a man's ears, let alone send the "gel" who'd lost this map running for the timbers.

Clifton pitied the chit when she showed up. But then again, if she was a servant in this house, she was most likely used to Mr. Ellyson's harangues.

So he and Malcolm continued to learn several new turns of phrase as they stood at attention, for they hadn't been invited to sit.

Perhaps, Clifton mused, this lesson in profanity was also part of their initiation into service. A rite of passage every gentleman endured with Mr. Ellyson, if only to gain the privilege to serve their country.

"I'll send her packing," Ellyson railed, shaking a finger at both of them as if they might have some share in this missing map. "I will."

"Sir, if I may —" Clifton asked, stepping forward, his hand reaching out.

"Don't!" Ellyson snapped, the cane flying up and at the ready. "Don't touch the maps."

Clifton backed up and retook his place

next to a grinning Malcolm. Growing up, it had usually been Malcolm about to be caned, not Clifton.

So no doubt his brother was enjoying the rare sight of the lofty Earl of Clifton being chastened like an errant lad.

Never in his comfortable life had the earl ever been as disconcerted as he had been over the last hour. From the moment the large, imposing Negro servant, the infamous Thomas-William, had opened the door of Mr. Ellyson's residence, staring down at the pair of them on the front steps as if he hadn't known whether to let them in or carve them into pieces, a cloud of doubt had encompassed Clifton's spirit. The good twenty minutes they'd spent left to wait on the steps outside in the rain like a pair of bill collectors hadn't done much for his temper either. As if *he* had to be deemed worthy enough to be shown into this madman's lair.

He was the Earl of Clifton, demmit, and that should be enough.

Even now, as their coats dripped on the carpet and they waited for Mr. Ellyson to find his map, a blistering argument from downstairs between two of the servants drifted up to their ears.

At least Clifton hoped the discord downstairs was between servants, for he'd never heard a lady raise her voice thusly — a harangue that nearly outdid Ellyson's own tirade over the state of his papers.

"Demmed gel, I'll have her hide if she's been sorting them again," Ellyson muttered as he thumped his way across the room to the door, yanking it open. "Organizing females, gentlemen, are the bane of a man's life," he warned before he turned and shouted out the open door, "Lucy! Lucy-girl, get up here. Now!"

The last word was punctuated with a loud *thump.*

Ellyson turned to his guests and glanced at them, blinking owlishly through his spectacles. Then, as if finally taking note of them, he did his best to sound congenial. "Going to Portugal, are you?"

"Yes, sir," Clifton replied. Not to sea, as most of the Greys had done before him, not even to command troops, as a few of his more "reckless" forbears had done. No, he had chosen to break with the family's noble tradition of valiant (meaning obvious and highly visible) service to the King and England by skulking off to serve as a spy.

He could imagine the graveyard at Clifton House was full of skeletons rolling over in protest at such a plebeian choice. A Grey prowling about like a commoner? Taking part in underhanded and unscrupulous acts? Why, it wasn't to be borne!

And yet here he was, not even sure himself why he'd come this far. Of what lay ahead . . .

Suddenly aware of the deep silence in the room, he glanced up and found Ellyson studying him. The earl hadn't felt such an inspection since his first day at Eton . . . or that he was utterly failing, either.

He shifted slightly, trying to draw his shoulders in a tauter line, pull himself up to his full height.

This did not impress the man before him.

"Harrumph. Pymm must be out of his mind," Ellyson muttered. "But who am I to argue with him?" The man went back to thumbing through his rolls of maps, muttering unintelligibly to himself.

Clifton cringed. For this was George Ellyson. *The* George Ellyson. The man reputed to have been England's greatest agent of the last century, until he'd been shot in the leg in Paris. A man of dubious origins and even more questionable honor, but nonetheless, he was regarded in some circles as the most brilliant mastermind who'd ever lived.

And now he served his country by ensuring that the agents who went out into the field were ready. It had been no easy measure to get this far, Clifton knew, but without Ellyson's final approval, he and Malcolm wouldn't be given leave to venture a single foot off British soil.

"I assure you, sir," Malcolm offered, "we have the will and the nerve."

Ellyson paused all his anxious pacing and wandering movements. He stilled and turned slowly, casting his sharp, narrowed gaze toward Malcolm. "Do you?"

Clifton's brother shifted, ever so slightly. "Certainly."

"Ever killed a man?"

Malcolm shook his head. "Of course not."

Ellyson glanced at them both, the chill of his eyes sending a shiver down the earl's spine. "Can you?"

It was a question that took Clifton aback, for he hadn't considered such a notion. *Can I kill a man?*

When neither of them answered — for truly, how did one answer such a thing? — Ellyson went back to his pacing. "Bah! Running back and forth to the coast is child's play. My daughter Mariana has done as much. You're off to Portugal, you fools, not Hastings. Nerve, indeed!" Ellyson glanced at the door. "Demmit, where is that gel? Lucy!" he shouted just as the door opened

37

and a young lady entered.

While the Earl of Clifton had been expecting a scullery maid or even a housekeeper to respond to Mr. Ellyson's shouted orders, the minx who arrived in the man's study was as much a contradiction to his expectations as George Ellyson was.

Her glorious black hair sat piled up atop her head, the pins barely holding it there, the strands shimmering with raven lights and rich, deep hues. It was a color that made one think of the most expensive courtesans, of Italian paintings and exotic bordellos.

Yet the illusion ended quickly, for beneath her shining crown of hair, the miss wore a plain muslin gown, over which she'd tossed a faded and patched sweater. There were mitts on her hands, for the rest of the house was cold, and from beneath the less-than-tidy hem of her gown, a pair of very serviceable boots stuck out.

This was all topped off by a large splotch of soot decorating her nose and chin.

She took barely a glance at Clifton or his brother before her hands fisted to her hips. "Whatever are you doing shouting like that? I'm not deaf, but I fear I will be if you insist on bellowing so."

Crossing the room, she swatted Ellyson's

hand off the map he was in the process of unrolling. Plucking off her mitts and swiping her hand over her skirts — as if that would do the task and clean them — she caught up the map and reshelved it. "I doubt you need Paris as yet."

There was a presumptuous note of disdain in her voice, as if she, like Ellyson himself, had shelved their guests with the same disparagement that she had just given the errant map.

And in confirmation, when she cast a glance over her shoulder and took stock of them, it was with a gaze that was both calculating and dismissive all at once. "Why not begin with ensuring that they know how to get to the coast," she replied, no small measure of sarcasm dripping from her words.

Ellyson barked a short laugh, if one could call it a laugh. But her sharp words amused the man. "Easy girl, they've Pymm's blessing. We're to train them up."

"Harrumph," she muttered, putting one more stamp of disapproval on the notion.

Clifton straightened. It was one thing to be dismissed by a man of Ellyson's stature, but by a mere servant? Well, it wasn't to be borne. He opened his mouth to protest, but Malcolm nudged him.

Don't wade into this one, little brother, his dark eyes implored.

"I need to start with Lisbon," Ellyson said, "but demmed if I can find it."

"Here," she said, easily locating the map from the collection. "Anything else?" Her chapped hands were back on her hips, and she shot another glance over her shoulder at Clifton, her bright green eyes suddenly filled with amusement.

Until, that is, her gaze fell to the puddles of water at his feet and the trail of mud from his boots.

Then she looked up at him with a thunderous glare that said, *You'd best not expect me to clean that up.*

Clifton could only gape at this bossy termagant of a chit. He'd never met such a woman.

Well, not outside of a public house.

Still, he couldn't stop watching her, for there was a spark to this Lucy that dared to settle inside his chest.

She was, with that hair and flashing eyes, a pretty sort of thing, in an odd way. But she held herself so that a man would have to possess a devilish bit of nerve to tell her so.

Then she shocked him; at least, he thought

40

it was the most shocking thing he'd ever heard.

"Papa, I haven't all day, and I've a roast to see to, as well as the pudding to mix."

Papa? Clifton's mouth fell open. This bossy chit was Ellyson's daughter?

No, in the world of the Ellysons, Clifton quickly discovered, such a notion wasn't shocking in the least.

Not when weighed against what her father said in reply. "Yes, yes. Of course. But before you see to dinner, I have it in mind for you to become Lord Clifton's new mistress. What say you, Goosie?" he asked his daughter as casually as one might inquire if the pudding was going to include extra plums. "How would you like to fall in love with an earl?"

Lucy glanced over her shoulder and looked at the man standing beside the door. Very quickly, she pressed her lips together to keep from bursting out with laughter at the sight of the complete and utter shock dressing the poor earl's features. He had to be the earl, for the other man hadn't the look of a man possessing a title and fortune.

Oh, heavens! He thinks Papa is serious. And in a panic over how to refuse him.

Not that a very feminine part of her felt a

large stab of pique.

Well, you could do worse, she'd have told him, if the other man in the room, the one by the window — the earl's brother, from the looks of him — hadn't said, "Good God, Gilby! Close your mouth. You look like a mackerel." The fellow then doubled over with laughter. " 'Sides, I doubt Ellyson is serious."

Lucy didn't reply, nor did her father, but that was to be expected, for Papa was already onto the next step of his plans for the earl and his natural brother and therefore saw no polite need to reply.

"Sir, I can hardly . . . I mean as a gentleman . . ." the earl began.

Lucy turned toward him, one brow cocked and her hands back on her hips. It was the stance she took when the butcher tried to sell her less-than-fresh mutton.

The butcher was a devilish cheat, so it made ruffling this gentleman's fine and honorable notions akin to child's play.

Clifton swallowed and took a step back, which brought him right up against the wall.

Literally and figuratively.

"What I mean to say, is that while Miss Ellyson is . . . is . . . that is to say, I am . . ." He closed his eyes and shuddered.

Actually shuddered.

Well, a lady could only take so much.

Lucy sauntered past him, flicked a piece of lint off the shoulder of his otherwise meticulous jacket and tossed a smile up at him. "Don't worry, *Gilby*," she purred, using the familiar name his brother had used. "You don't have to bed me." She took another long glance at him, from his dark hair, the chiseled set of his aristocratic jaw, the breadth of his shoulders, the long lines of his legs, to his perfectly polished boots — everything that was wealthy, noble and elegant — then continued toward her father's desk, tossing one more glance over her shoulders. "For truly, you aren't my type."

Which was quite true. Well, there was no arguing that the Earl of Clifton was one of the most handsome men who'd ever walked into her father's house seeking his training to take on secretive "work" for the King, but Lucy also found his lofty stance and rigid features troubling.

He'll not do, Papa, she wanted to say. She considered herself an excellent judge of character, for she'd spent a good part of her life watching the agents come and go from her father's house. She knew them all.

And as much as she found it amusing to give this stuffy earl a bit of a tease, there was a niggle of worry that ran down her spine.

This Clifton would have to set himself down a notch or two if he was going to stay alive, at the very least, let alone complete the tasks he would be sent to do.

No, he is too utterly English. Too proud. Too . . . too . . . noble.

In that estimation, she saw his future and it wasn't good. Well-intentioned gentlemen were the bane of the Foreign Office. With one glance, she dismissed him. For this Clifton, this noble earl, would never return to England, no matter the effort her father extended to train him properly.

He'll never come back.

Well, I don't care, she told herself, crossing the room and putting her back to the earl. She opened a drawer and handed a folder to her father, who, throughout this exchange, had been muttering over the mess of papers and correspondence atop his desk. "I think you need these," she said softly.

Her father opened it up, squinting at the pages inside and then nodding. "Ah, yes. Good gel, Goosie." He turned back to Clifton. "Whatever has you so pale? I don't expect you to deflower the gel, just carry her love letters."

"Letters?" Clifton managed.

44

"Yes, letters," Lucy explained. "I write coded letters to you as if I were your mistress, and you carry them to Lisbon." She strolled over, reached up and patted his chest. "You put them right next to your heart." She paused and gazed up at him. "You have one of those, don't you?"

CHAPTER 3

A few days later, Mr. Ellyson poked his head into the kitchen. "Oh, excellent! You're going out. Perfect timing, I must say. Lucy-girl, be a dear and take his lordship along with you."

Lucy glanced up from beneath the brim of her bonnet and sent her father an exasperated look. For she knew exactly what he wanted.

That didn't mean she wanted it.

"Today? Now? You expect me to drag Lord Fancy-pants about?" She shook her head. "He's not ready." Pulling on her gloves, she reached for her market basket, hoping to hasten her departure all the same.

"Lucy!" he warned. "Don't you dare leave this house without the earl."

Demmit all! She'd been nearly out the kitchen door before Papa had arrived. If only Bess wasn't in her bed sick. Then Mrs. Kewin, their cook, wouldn't have asked her to check the cellar for more onions, delaying her trip to the village. "Send him off with Mariana," she said. "She'll do the task admirably."

"No, no, I want you to take him on his first outing," her father said, coming all the way into the kitchen. "I've made all the arrangements." He went over to the teapot on the table and laid his hand on the side of it to see how warm it was. "Ah, Mrs. Kewin, you're a dear to know when I want my tea every afternoon," he said, flashing a rare smile at the elderly woman. Then the old devil settled down at the table and poured himself a cup as if nothing were amiss.

But the cock of his brow and the turn of his lips revealed all. He'd outwitted his daughter and thought it a fine thing.

Mrs. Kewin, hardly undone by her employer's rare flattery, looked from one Ellyson to the other, then ducked around the corner into the pantry.

Coward, Lucy thought as she watched her disappear. She knew there was a row brewing.

And right she was.

Lucy faced her father, something few people were willing to do. That didn't mean she was going to launch into an attack;

rather, she took a page from her father's book.

Identify the problems of a plan straightaway and have a solution at hand.

"You know as well as I," she said smoothly and carefully, "that Mariana will do the job better. I'm as likely to kill that pompous nit as whoever you've got out there waiting for him."

The Earl of Clifton had proved to be every bit as high and lofty as Lucy had first suspected.

Ringing the bell for tea three times a day. And when it wasn't brought up promptly, he'd yank at the pull until it did arrive.

Couldn't the man fetch his own, like everyone else in the house?

Handing her his laundry because he didn't like the way the girl at the inn had done his cravats. Tracking in mud.

Didn't the inconsiderate lout know how to use a scraper?

Then there was the way he spoke to her, as if it was the last thing in the world he wanted to do, but alas, so very necessary, and therefore he had to reduce himself to the task.

"Miss Lucy, see to having this letter posted . . ."

"Miss Lucy, send round for . . ."

48

As if she didn't have enough to do as it was.

She ground her teeth together. Oh, she didn't like him. Not in the least.

Her father, having taken her suggestion into consideration, shook his head. "I want you to go with him. You'll see to the job admirably, your personal considerations aside. Besides, you know how your sister gets around blood."

Blood?

Lucy perked up. The image of a battered and broken Lord Clifton limping back to the house in defeat rose up in her imagination. Now that quite warmed her heart.

Perhaps a few bruises would even make the arrogant man a bit more palatable.

Or at the very least, bring him down a peg or two.

Her father mistook the smile on her face. "Yes, you see the wisdom of this. Remember how poor Mad Jack fared when Mariana took him out?" He shook his head and nodded to her. "I'm not much worried about his lordship, but I wouldn't like to see Rusty and Sammy harmed. They're good lads."

Rusty and Sammy? Lucy set the basket down. "You've got those two cutthroats lying in wait, and you're worried for their safety?"

"Oh, aye," her father said, reaching for another biscuit. "I know you think Clifton a tiresome fool, but I think he'll surprise you, Goosie. He'll make a good accounting of himself." Her father sat back. "He's just never had to stand on his own two feet before. But you can show him how, my girl. He's got the mettle, he just needs to believe it."

She snorted. What was there to believe in? Lord Proper-And-By-the-Book against Rusty and Sammy? The pair had grown up in the Dials. They were two of the meanest, hardest criminals who had ever cut a path through the roughest streets of London before her father had hired them and given them somewhat legitimate work — the sort suited to their, *er,* talents.

The bell over the door rang, and Lucy didn't need to look to know who was pulling the cord.

Himself. Probably wanted his tea brought up.

She ignored the impatient jangle, as did her father. And, Lucy noted, Mrs. Kewin didn't seem in much of a hurry to reappear in the kitchen.

Earl or not, their cook wasn't fool enough to return until all the dust had settled.

Her father continued blithely on, ignoring

the bell and Lucy's growing agitation. "I have a suspicion he'll not take kindly to being tested. So you can see why I would want you there. You're a good match for him. You'll be able to talk some sense into him when he discovers that he's been sent into . . ."

Lucy stopped listening after she heard her father's assertion. *A good match for him . . .*

She shook off the implications of such a phrase. A good match, indeed! That implied she and the earl were suited for each other, or shared something in common, and nothing could be further from the truth.

The man was completely unsuited to become an agent for the King. He didn't belong here, using up her father's valuable time, looking down his nose at the rest of the household.

Handsome, rich and spoiled. That was all the Earl of Clifton was, and whatever notions he had of serving his King and country should have ended the first hour he'd walked into their house.

But it could all end now, Lucy, a wry little voice whispered in her ear. *Let him have a little taste of the very real dangers ahead and he'll be back in London before supper.*

Then Papa and Mr. Pymm would see what was so evident to her.

51

That the Earl of Clifton was no hero.

"Where the devil is that girl from the kitchen?" Clifton asked, standing before the bellpull. "This house is run in the most slipshod manner."

Malcolm glanced up from the papers he'd been reading. "You could go down and see to it yourself," he suggested, his tone implying that the very notion was quite amusing. "Probably shock Miss Lucy into some decent manners to discover you aren't as stiff-rumped as you like to appear."

Clifton turned to him, his shoulders going taut. "I am not stiff-rumped!"

Malcolm laughed. "You've been about as high and lofty as I've ever seen you since we got here." The earl paused. Malcolm continued, "I would even say you are deliberately baiting that gel. You are, aren't you?"

"I'm doing no such thing," Clifton said, tugging at his cravat, which he was now starting to believe she'd starched with sand. "It is just that Miss Lucy's manners could use some . . . guidance." He leaned against the wall next to the bellpull and folded his arms over his chest.

His brother snorted. "Oh, you're guiding her alright, but I'd mind just how far you provoke that bit of muslin. She's Ellyson's

52

daughter, through and through."

Clifton waved him off. "And whatever do you think she could do? She's naught but a slip of a girl."

"I don't know about that," Malcolm told him, shaking his head. "But I do know I wouldn't want to be on the receiving end of her wrath. Just a piece of brotherly advice." He closed the book before him. "How unfortunate she doesn't take after her sister. Ah, the enchanting Miss Ellyson."

Clifton shook his head. "I would suggest that Miss Ellyson is trouble in another direction."

"She's an adorable romp," Malcolm said, grinning.

Clifton had no doubts why Ellyson kept his elder daughter here in Hampstead. Lithe and elegant, with a mischievous sparkle to her eyes, Mariana Ellyson, fairer than her sister Lucy, had an ethereal quality to her that would have set the collective hearts of London on fire.

"And well she knows it," Clifton said. "Not that either of them seem to be the marrying type."

"Odd, that," Malcolm agreed. "The fellows out here must be blind."

Or so well advised of George Ellyson's shady past that they stayed well away from the man's daughters.

"Still," Malcolm said, "I would think you'd find Hampstead a far better place to be than London, what with the Season in full swing. No one here trying to foist their daughter off on your unwitting hands. Why, you should be in the pink; we've made it this far, and in a fortnight's time we'll be off. Whatever is wrong with you?"

"Nothing," the earl said, glancing back at the bell and considering another tug. "Everything. Are you sure this is what you want to do?"

"Yes, of course. Rather like having something useful to do."

All this — joining the Foreign Office, going to the Continent — had been Clifton's idea. But now the magnitude of it was starting to weigh upon him. What if they didn't make it back? What if they failed?

What if he couldn't live up to the legacy of his forebears, heroes and champions all?

The dismissive light in Miss Lucy's eyes said as much each time she looked up at him. Said she no more believed him capable of being a spy than she had faith in their elderly cook to lead a battalion.

Vexatious, wretched minx.

He'd never met anyone like her. A mere slip of a girl capable of upending every bit of confidence he possessed.

However had she gotten so under his skin?

Because she's unlike anyone you've ever met . . .

No fawning miss. No smiling debutante. Lucy Ellyson's straightforward and all-too-pert opinions quite took him by surprise.

Why, if he was being honest, he might even admit that he found her a bit intriguing . . . what with that glorious head of hair and her open, all-too-honest eyes.

"I suppose I've been a bit of an ass," he conceded.

"A bit?" his brother teased. "Oh, don't look at me like that. You haven't been as lofty as father used to get, but you've been a bit of a cross-patch." Malcolm paused. "Perhaps you need to take up with that gel at the inn. Whatever is her name?"

"I haven't inquired."

Malcolm shrugged. "She seems quite willing."

Clifton shook his head. "Quite. But she's hardly my type and a bit old, don't you think?"

"Hmm, hoped you hadn't noticed she's a bit long in the tooth," Malcolm teased, leaning back in his chair, his eyes sparkling with mischief. "What about Miss Lucy? She is your new mistress, after all."

"Lucy Ellyson?" Clifton sputtered back, pushing off the wall. "Have you gone mad?"

To his dismay, Malcolm laughed even harder. "She does rub you wrong, doesn't she? You know, it is quite entertaining to watch the two of you. Circling like cats."

"Malcolm," the earl said in warning.

"And she's a pretty bit," Malcolm mused, sitting back in his chair, hands lounging behind his head.

"A pretty little snob, if you ask me," the earl replied. His brother laughed again, which did nothing to ease Clifton's discomfiture. "How is it you find this house so comfortable?"

Malcolm rocked forward. "Ah! For once I have the advantage. If you must know —"

"— I must."

"Then I would surmise it is because I am the illegitimate son. Puts me on equal footing around here."

"Now I see how it is. I've stumbled upon the English version of *Liberté, égalité, fraternité.*"

His brother laughed, not at all insulted at being called a Jacobian. "Watch out, or that Miss Ellyson will take it in her head to set up her own Committee of Public Safety."

"I'm surprised Pymm hasn't sent her over

to the French," Clifton argued. "She'd tie them up quite nicely, what with all her nagging ways."

"If I didn't know better," Malcolm said, returning to the book before him and nonchalantly leafing through the pages, "I'd say you enjoy needling her."

"I do not."

"Perhaps you are just getting her riled up to —"

Clifton shook a finger at his brother. "Don't even suggest such a thing. That chit is the most improper, ill-mannered bit of muslin I've ever had the misfortune to meet. She's the last woman I'd think to take to my bed."

Malcolm shrugged and went back to paging through the thick book, looking for the place he'd left off. Without glancing up, he said, "No matter, really. She's quite unimpressed with your lofty state. Probably wouldn't have you even if you wanted her."

The barb hit the mark. Because there was a bit of truth to what Malcolm was saying.

For here was Miss Lucy Ellyson of Hampstead Heath looking at him as if she expected him to fail before he got to the Channel. If, as her wry glances suggested, he could manage to get himself to Hastings, that is.

"I can do this, I'll have you know," Clifton said aloud.

"Whoever said you couldn't?" Malcolm said, doing him the favor of not looking up.

But that was where Malcolm provided him with a good foil. Full of good sense and no particular airs, Malcolm, like Miss Ellyson, was not impressed by lineage and inheritance. Perhaps it was why Clifton's mother had never objected to her son being brought up with his half brother. His father's natural son.

She'd claimed it would give Clifton a grounding in the common, ordinary world that would have escaped him otherwise. That had eluded his father all the man's life. Shielded the elder Grey from the changing, modern world that the new century had thrust upon England.

An unfamiliar society that included Lucy Ellyson and her pert opinions. And her obvious disapproval.

Clifton shifted from one foot to another, as that unfamiliar ill ease came over him. Just one thought of that gel had him at sixes and sevens. "Now where the devil is that maid with the tray?"

"Go get it yourself," Malcolm suggested. "Come to think of it, have you ever fetched your own tea?"

As loathe as he was to admit it, the earl shook his head.

"Do you both some good," his brother said. "Go on down. Try charming her."

Clifton had turned toward the door, but that last bit of Malcolm's statement stopped him in his tracks. "Do wha-a-at?"

"Charm her. Show her that you aren't a pretentious nit."

"I'm not a —"

"No, no, of course not," Malcolm said, a sparkle of mirth in his eyes.

"I cannot believe you are even suggesting that I go down there and charm that . . . that . . ."

"Pretty lady?"

Clifton wagged his finger in protest. "*Harridan* is more apt."

"Harridan? I suppose that is better than harpy." Malcolm slanted a glance at him. "Charm her, Gilby. If you can manage it."

Clifton ruffled at such an affront. "I can charm a lady." There was a loud snort from the other side of the room, which only served to insult the earl further. "What does that mean?"

Malcolm leaned back in his seat. "Well, little brother" — there were times when Malcolm liked to remind Clifton that while he might be the heir, he was still the younger of the two — "it is just that being a rake isn't really your forte."

The earl opened his mouth to argue, but there wasn't much to say. For there was some truth in it.

Well, more than some.

"Go practice with Lucy," Malcolm advised. "No, no, not another word out of you. I can see from your horrified expression that you cannot fathom why I would suggest such a thing. But tell me this, Gilby, have you not given a single thought to what that glorious mane of hers would look like if it finally escaped its pins?"

"No, I haven't," the earl lied. "Not once."

Malcolm laughed. "I didn't think so. That would be inappropriate, wouldn't it?"

Utterly, Clifton thought as he went down the back stairs. Completely and utterly inappropriate. Why, she'd look like the devil's own siren with those black tresses of hers undone and cascading down her fair shoulders.

Enchanting enough to tempt a man to breach the walls of hell.

Which would be quite the same as finding oneself tangled up with that termagant, he mused as he paused on the landing. And as he stilled, the rising tide of an argument inside the kitchen reached his ears.

Now, he'd always considered himself above eavesdropping, but apparently in his new profession such a skill was considered a talent to be possessed.

He took a careful, silent step closer, and not, he told himself, because it was Miss Lucy's earnest tones that had taken hold of his curiosity.

"You are utterly mistaken about him, Papa," she was saying. He could almost envision her hands on her hips, the steely, determined glint in her eyes. "You and Pymm both. Mark my words, he is a stuffy, arrogant, overbearing . . ."

Clifton didn't need to guess as to the subject of her protests. Nor was he surprised by her vehement defamation of his character. He'd have been more surprised to hear her praising his virtues.

Mr. Ellyson's bemused laughter filtered up the stairs. "Oh, enough, Goosie. I know you don't like him, but I insist you keep your opinions to yourself. And no dosing his stew," he admonished so severely that Clifton could envision the man wagging his finger at his daughter. "He is no Lord Roche."

"Harrumph," she sputtered. "I beg to differ."

Clifton's head swung up. *Roche?* That

61

horse's rump? The sting of being compared to that fool was enough to almost bring him into the conversation. And yet curiosity and a wild desire to prove Miss Ellyson wrong stayed his boots.

"Oh, certainly, Roche was a poor choice, I'll grant you that —" Ellyson began.

"And just as sure of himself as this fellow Pymm has forced upon us. Mr. Grey will do well enough, but the earl . . . well, Papa, I think you are quite mistaken on the matter." There was a noisy *harrumph* that finished her sentence.

"Come now, Goosie, you are too severe by half. Clifton has more mettle to him than you give him credit. He'll surprise you in the end. You'll see."

There was the ruffle of straw and ribbons, her bonnet most likely being shaken in vehement denial of such a claim.

Ellyson's laughter echoed up the dark stairwell. "You are just put off by his lofty manners, and that he hasn't flirted with you."

"Papa!" she protested. "That is ridiculous! I don't want that man —"

"Stand down," her father chided. "I think this has more to do with the fact that the earl is the first one of them who's come through here who hasn't fancied himself in love with you."

"You know I don't care about those things," she protested.

"Oh, I know. But one day you will, and that's the day I fear."

"Well, you needn't fear on my account over the Earl of Clifton." There was another one of those *harrumph*s that made her sound like Malcolm's grandmother. The blacksmith's wife. A beast of a woman who could bend iron with her bare hands.

"Good," Mr. Ellyson said, as if that settled the matter.

As if there was any matter to be dealt with. It was all Clifton could do not to go blustering into the kitchen and agree with the man's daughter.

Her father had nothing to fear on his account.

Lucy Ellyson, indeed. Clifton shuddered.

"For he won't have you, Goosie. None of them will. Not in a way that is honorable," the man was saying with a resigned sort of sigh. "I've raised you both to be ladies —"

Clifton's brow arched at such a notion. Lucy Ellyson a lady? He wanted to correct her father on that point, but he thought the better of it.

"— don't ever think for a moment that one of them will look past your bloodlines, such as they are, no matter what they say to charm you."

"I'm not the sort to be charmed, Papa."

Truer words were never spoken, Clifton mused.

"So there it is, Goosie. You can't abide the man, you've made that abundantly clear, but the truth of it is that Pymm wants him trained, and trained is what we will do."

There was a moment of silence before a resigned, feminine sigh broke the quiet.

"So you'll help?" her father asked.

There was a rustle of a basket being plopped down on a table. "Oh, aye. You know I will. And if Uncle Toad wants it done —"

Uncle Toad? She referred to Pymm, England's spymaster, the most feared man in the Foreign Office, as "Uncle Toad"?

Clifton didn't have much time to digest such a notion before Miss Ellyson was once again spouting off.

"— I have to admit I won't mind seeing that arrogant fellow set down a peg or two —"

"Goosie —" her father warned.

"Papa, you always say lessons in humility are the hardest to swallow. I daresay for the earl, today shall be most unpalatable." She paused for a moment before she added,

"Could turn out rather badly."

She needn't sound so hopeful, the little minx.

Clifton straightened. *Want to see me set down, do you?* His eyes narrowed, and a deadly calm came over him. Convinced that he wouldn't pass muster when faced with a challenge, was she? Oh, he'd show her a thing or two, this odious miss.

Coughing loudly, he finished his descent down the steps, knit his brows together in the most imperious line he could fashion and stepped into the kitchen. "I rang for tea, but no one brought it." He paused and surveyed the seemingly domestic scene before him, then arched a brow at Miss Lucy, as if to indicate that she should have seen to the matter.

Promptly.

She, in return and true to her character, scowled back.

Most likely wishing she could dump a scalding potful over his head.

"Ah, Clifton, good timing," Ellyson said. "I have a favor to ask of you."

"Certainly, sir," he replied, inclining his head slightly. "How may I be of service?"

"Goosie must go to the village for Mrs. Kewin, but alas, there is no one to go with her. Bess is sick . . . and Mrs. Kewin is busy . . . and Mariana and Thomas-William are off . . . off . . ." he stammered a bit before glancing at his daughter for help.

"Carrying baskets to the poor," Miss Lucy finished with the sweet, modest tones of a vicar's daughter.

Which she wasn't. And furthermore, while Mariana Ellyson was a generous and friendly bit of muslin, he'd wager his last year's rents that she was about as likely to be out doing charity work as she was out robbing coaches.

"Would you mind, my lord," Mr. Ellyson said, "escorting my dear girl up to the village? I dislike having my daughters venture out unprotected."

Clifton took one furtive glance at the old spy's daughter. The chit was good, for she appeared as innocent as her tones had implied, but there was a dangerous light to her eyes.

A challenge that dared him to refuse.

And what Miss Lucy, in all her pride and prejudice, did not realize was that he loved a good challenge.

Almost as much as he loved winning.

"Most certainly, sir," Clifton replied. "I would be remiss in allowing a young lady to go about unescorted."

At least not until I discover what it is you

66

Lucy found herself at odds as she left her father's house in the company of the Earl of Clifton.

"Would you do me the honor, Miss Lucy," he asked in a gallant manner, holding out his arm to her.

"Lucy, my lord. Please call me Lucy," she told him as he carefully settled her hand onto his sleeve and led her down the path as if she were a real lady and he was taking her for a fashionable stroll in a London park.

"But Miss Lucy," he averred, "I wouldn't want to impugn your reputation by having anyone assume —"

"Oh, good heavens, Lord Clifton!" she said, losing all patience with the man. "No one calls me 'Miss Lucy.' That is reserved for the vicar's sister."

There was a pause before he asked, "And someone might confuse you with the vicar's sister?"

This wry comment took Lucy aback. She glanced up to see if the man was teasing or just being insulting, but neither was in evidence on his handsome features.

"The weather is admirable," he commented blithely, as he opened the gate for her and they made their way to the lane.

"Yes, quite," she replied, suspicious all the same.

"Do you walk to the village often?"

Lucy glanced over at him. Was the man a simpleton? "Yes, my lord. Every day."

"Extraordinary!" he replied. "Take care here, it appears the road is uneven." He steered her through the alarming hazard of an overturned stone and a dirt clod.

Good heavens, I'm not made of porcelain, she wanted to exclaim, trying unsuccessfully to free her hand, but he'd clamped his other one atop it and held her fast.

Why, she made this outing nearly every day and most often alone, for there wasn't a lad or troublemaker within a good five miles who would think to give Lucy Ellyson anything but a wide berth and a good measure of respect.

And as she was used to her independence, she found it ever so disconcerting to be walking along in the earl's shadow, her fingers trapped on his sleeve.

Up this close he was taller than she'd realized — or rather wanted to think of him being — for he quite towered over her, and if it could be believed, he seemed, well, rather imposing.

Well, not completely imposing, she thought, glancing up the road and wondering where

Rusty and Sammy had hidden themselves, suddenly feeling a bit of ill ease.

What if her father was right and the earl did make a good showing against them?

She shook her head. Impossible. He was a spoiled, indulgent nobleman. That was all. Just another Lord Roche.

Her fingers flexed on his sleeve, and beneath her gloves there was nothing but solid muscles.

Something inside her fluttered at the sensation.

Are you so sure he's just a fool, Lucy?

"Have you lived in Hampstead all your life?" the earl asked.

"Excuse me?" Lucy replied, coming out of her reverie, her gaze absently fixed on his forearm.

"Hampstead? Have you lived here all your life?" he repeated, smiling at her as if he was speaking to a child.

"Most of it," she said, a bit disconcerted by the dazzling smile on his handsome face. "I was born in Rome, though I have no memory of the place."

Egads, whatever had possessed her to reveal that?

"Rome, you say? How unique," he declared.

Not so if your mother is Italian, she wanted

to say in sharp retort, but that would only lead to an explanation of her mother.

A subject Lucy avoided at all costs, and she was glad for the silence that fell between them.

At least for a moment or so.

"How nice of your father to allow me the pleasure of your company this afternoon," he said, picking up their lapsed conversation. "It afforded me an opportunity to speak to you . . . *alone.*"

Alone? The word ruffled down her spine.

Goodness gracious, whatever could this man want to say to her alone that he hadn't said already?

Perhaps he wanted to comment on how she'd had his shirts starched. Twice. Or was it three times . . . she'd lost count.

She smiled back at him, bracing herself for another overbearing request.

"Miss Lucy —" he began.

Here it comes . . .

"I fear we've gotten off to a bad start," he continued. "And I believe it is entirely my fault."

Lucy blinked. Had she heard him correctly? That sounded suspiciously like an apology. She glanced up and stared into his contrite expression, which held not a hint of sarcasm or mirth to betray his intent.

Egads! It was an apology.

She took another look at him. No, it couldn't be. She must have tied her bonnet on a little too tight, that or Rusty and Sammy had already knocked him over the head and she'd missed the event entirely.

"My brother tells me I've been a bit high-handed —" he continued.

"A bit?" she sputtered, then realized she'd said that aloud.

Again he smiled at her as if he hadn't heard her rude little outburst. The blinding glare of his straight white teeth and the sincere light of his eyes were capable of leaving a lady a bit off kilter.

Even a lady as unflappable as Lucy. At least she'd always thought of herself as immune to such charms.

"I mean to say, I don't think —" she stammered, trying to recover some sense of control. It was hard to think when he looked at her so . . . so . . . oh, bother, as if he found her quite delightful.

Which he doesn't, she told herself.

Yet, here he was, pompous Lord Clifton, apologizing.

"Yes, yes, I've been most high-handed. So Miss Lucy, as a gentleman, I extend my sincere apologies to you if I've offended you in any manner."

71

There it was again, that brilliant, boyish smile. The kind that beamed only for her. And demmit if Lucy's heart didn't beat just a little bit faster.

Oh, heavens. He would have to apologize right now. Just before she led him into her father's trap.

A niggle of guilt ran down her spine. And at first, she barely knew what it was, for she rarely felt guilty over anything. Not even cheating at cards.

But her guilt, as it turned out, had a short-lived existence, for the earl continued on with his apology.

"I would be most remiss if I offended a lady such as yourself, and a pretty one at that."

Lucy slowly tipped her bonnet and looked at him. Really looked. From that winsome, handsome smile meant to dazzle, up to the bright, concerned light in his eyes.

The man was devilishly attractive, much to her chagrin.

Sharp, dark eyes, the Roman nose of a gentleman, a smooth, solid jaw with a deep cleft beneath his sculpted lips.

Lucy fixed her gaze to the road beneath her feet as her heart once again danced with a haphazard tremble.

Oh, Lucy, don't be such a nit.

For despite all his sweet words and smiling glances, Lucy Ellyson knew without a doubt that whatever he was up to, he was flirting with her for a reason.

The Earl of Clifton was piling Spanish coins at her feet, false flattery enough to fill a pirate's hold, and if he thought his fine words could turn her head . . . nay, distract her . . .

Distract her?

Lucy's boots scudded to a halt, and the man mistook her momentary falter for something else.

"Am I going too fast for you, Miss Lucy? Do you need to rest?"

"No, no, I am most sound," she shot back, dispensing any further worries of guilt. *The demmed scurvy bast*— Why, he'd nearly convinced her he was sincerely sorry. "Thank you for your concern," she added, glancing up at this enigma of a man to find his dark gaze fixed on her. "But please, call me Lucy."

"Of course," he said with an elegant nod. "Lucy it is."

It was almost a shame that in a few minutes his smooth visage would be sporting a black eye, at the very least.

Terrible shame that. Perhaps you should

warn him that he is about to be jumped and beaten.

Then again, perhaps not. Lucy smiled up at him.

"My lord, truly there is no need to apologize, and I own I might have had a hand in our differences."

Well, she'd certainly had a hand in asking the laundress to starch his cravats a third time.

They continued on in silence along the cheery lane, wild spring flowers, brilliantly yellow, blooming happily beneath the line of oaks. Dappled sunshine fell upon them, and it was, if Lucy held such inclinations, quite a romantic setting.

Say something. Talk to him. Distract him, she could hear her father whispering at her. *Don't let him suspect a thing.*

"I suppose you miss London," she said. Most of the men her father worked with all complained about having to live in Hampstead, just out of reach of their usual haunts of White's and Tattersall's and Gentleman Jim's.

"Not at all," he replied. "I find life in London a necessary evil. I much prefer the country."

There was something so utterly honest about his response that it left Lucy rather

74

astounded. For she too had never taken to London and dearly loved the quiet of the Heath.

And worse, she discovered they had something in common.

"No, but you must miss the grand society and the entertainments," she insisted, not wanting to concede to any sort of commonality between them. "The Season is in full swing, is it not? Surely the delights of Mayfair and all those pretty ladies are a far sight more to your tastes than Gertie at the Bog and Heath."

He stumbled a bit and glanced down at her. "I beg your pardon?"

"Gertie. At the Bog and Heath. The inn where you and your brother have taken rooms. She always delights in entertaining father's students." Lucy lowered her voice. "But I fear she is getting a bit long in the tooth for working her trade."

She watched with some satisfaction as the earl's face colored a bit and he struggled to digest the conversation.

Most likely the first time he'd ever discussed a tavern wench with a lady.

"I-I-I, that is to say, I haven't made the acquaintance . . . nor would I discuss such a person —"

"Gertie," she supplied. "Her name is Gertie. Oh, you needn't be so squeamish around me, my lord. I am three and twenty and have a good idea as to the service Gertie provides —"

"Mind your step, Miss Ellyson," he said, hastily cutting her off and steering her around a pile left by a horse.

Oh, yes, she had him at sixes and sevens now. And so she continued unabashedly. "I do believe Lord Roche found her quite accommodating."

When I would not . . .

"Still, you might consider returning to London for the Season," Lucy continued blithering on like Mariana might, "so as to find a wife."

"A wha-a-a-t?"

She swore his shudder ran all the way down to his boots.

So the Earl of Clifton has a fear of matrimony. That might work in her favor.

"A wife," she supplied. "A countess. A lady of good bloodlines to supply you with an heir and a spare."

"Yes, yes," he said. "I know what a wife is for."

"Aren't you worried about leaving your title without an heir?" She paused and lowered her voice. "If you don't come back, that is."

He glanced over at her, a hint of annoyance flashing in his eyes.

Oh, she'd hit the mark with that one.

"I have an uncle who is in line," he said stiffly.

"Excellent. Is he married?"

"Yes."

"A sensible fellow, then?"

There was a long, measured pause from the earl. "Not particularly."

"How unfortunate. But perhaps he has heirs with the necessary qualifications?" she asked.

"Yes. Two sons." The answer came out like a dog snapping at a bone.

Lucy pressed her lips together to keep from grinning. Oh, she had him now. Then she composed her next sally very carefully. If only so it landed like a cannonball at his feet.

"So you'll marry when you return — that is to say if you return."

His brows knit together and his arm stiffened.

Lucy wondered if, perhaps, she might have pushed him too far.

"I'll return." He said this with a finality that should have been enough right there to end the subject — that is if this had been an ordinary polite conversation.

But it wasn't enough to stop Lucy.

"Of course you will, my lord. Most certainly," she said, patting his arm as if consoling him over a lost wager. And a paltry one at that. Then she continued, "What sort of lady will you look for?"

"Excuse me?" He stumbled a bit. Lucy waited for him to get his footing and composure realigned before she once again thrust her question into his chest like a dagger.

"Your countess? However will you know her when you meet her?"

"I haven't given it much thought." Again his tone suggested that the subject was finished.

But oh, Lucy wasn't. "That is where most men fail in these sorts of things."

"Fail?"

"Yes, fail. Utterly. You men don't give enough consideration to the sort of woman you want to spend your life with. Instead you rather just sort of pick, like one might a racehorse."

"There is more to choosing a bride than that," he said in a stuffy sort of manner.

"How so?" she asked innocently, as if such matters were well beyond her ken. Then again, he hadn't the least notion that she was leading him into a trap.

"Well, I suppose I will have to consider a lady's bloodlines," he told her, in such a pompous manner that Lucy almost wished Rusty and Sammy would arrive now and save her from this lofty lecture. "Her education should be impeccable, and I will have to examine her suitability, her countenance, the way she holds herself in public."

"Exactly as I said. Just as one chooses a racehorse," Lucy pointed out.

"Not at all the same thing."

She pulled to a stop. "By bloodlines, training and the turn of her lines. Isn't that what you said?"

His jaws worked together, his gaze fixed and narrowed on the road ahead. "Yes."

"Just like a racehorse, my lord." With that, she tugged him back into the track in the road, and they continued on in silence.

Apparently the earl didn't like being shown the shortcomings of his plans. Or the comparison of his future bride to an Arabian at Newmarket. "Miss Lucy, there is one difference you neglected to consider."

"What would that be?" she asked, confident in her ingenious and disarming banter.

He glanced down at her, dark eyes smoldering with an intensity that sent a shiver of warning down her spine. He turned that devil-may-care smile on her, the one that suggested he was looking for something — or, rather, someone — to devour.

Passionately.

Lucy tried to ignore the tremor running down her spine. It wasn't guilt, or anger, or even fear. But something else. Something she didn't even want to know.

At least not with him. For when the Earl of Clifton looked at her that way, it reminded her that she was a woman, and that he was a very handsome man.

Too handsome.

"I've never been in love with a horse," he said. "But I will love my future countess. Without a doubt, I will not marry without love."

And this time Lucy stumbled.

CHAPTER 4

"Lo-o-ve?" Lucy Ellyson stammered.

"Yes, love." Clifton glanced down at her and knew without a doubt that the tide of their conversation had changed. Or rather washed her off her lofty post. The sudden shift in their positions sent a wicked desire through him to meet her jab for jab. "Have you heard of it?"

"Of course I've heard of it," she snapped.

"Have you ever been in love?"

"My lord, that is hardly —"

"Proper?" He shrugged. "Probably not. But I might remind you, Lucy, you did start this line of questioning."

"I never meant —" She drew a breath. "That is to say, I didn't expect —"

"For the winds to change?"

A noisy little *harrumph* erupted from beneath the wide brim of her straw bonnet.

Clifton smiled. *Point the sword of marriage at me, will you?* Oh, she'd had him on the ropes for a bit, but now . . . "So, Lucy, have you ever been in love?" he repeated.

"No. Most certainly not." She glanced up at him, her lips set in a firm line.

The sort of line that either forbade a fellow from trying anything further, or one that challenged him to see if those rosy lips could be persuaded to open up . . . just a bit.

"No swain to sweep you off your feet?" He moved a little closer; to her credit, she held her ground.

"I'm not the sweepable sort, my lord," she replied, shifting her basket from one hand to the other until it hung in front of her like a flimsy barricade.

Good. She was nervous.

As she should be.

"I suppose you aren't," he said, glancing at the basket between them and then up at her. "Sweepable, that is." He edged a little closer, and this time she took a slight step back, the basket absently tumbling from her fingers.

"Try charming her," Malcolm had suggested.

And so Clifton did, smiling wolfishly down at her.

"What does that mean?" she shot back, her defiance rising in high dudgeons, her eyes wary. "I'm not sweepable?"

"It's just that you aren't the sort of lady who would encourage a man to look twice —"

"My lord, I'm most certainly not —"

"No, no, Miss Ellyson, hear me out. If you want a man to fall in love with you, he needs to look twice." And so Clifton did. He paused for a moment and took a good look at her. "Just to make sure."

She stilled, hands on her hips, brows furrowed together. For the life of him, such a bossy, unnatural, fishwife sort of stance should put him off. Utterly.

But on Miss Lucy Ellyson, it lit a fire within him.

From the challenge in her green eyes. Her frothy mess of black hair rose about her pretty face like Boadicea's heathen wreath. A warrior miss unwilling to relent an inch.

The sort of fiery misses who enflamed kings, who rose to infamy by their sheer audacity, who challenged a man to dig deep into his reserves and use all his wits to merit her affections.

But then again, she obviously didn't realize that when she stood thusly it forced her frumpish and ugly gown to actually reveal the curves and feminine lines that it hid beneath its dull calico shield.

From where he stood, there was no doubt Lucy Ellyson was a curvy bit of baggage. No willowy debutante, no iconic, statuesque Original. No, she was a lady in all the ways that made a man's head spin.

Or rather, got his blood up.

So when she declared that she'd never been in love, he found it hard to believe.

He grinned at her, seeing her in an altogether new light, because there was another way besides merely flirting with a lady to entice her to give up her secrets.

"Whatever do you think you are doing, Lord Clifton?" she demanded, edging another step back.

"Taking a second look."

Lucy knew right there and then that the Earl of Clifton was going to kiss her.

And she also knew that while she should flatten him with a facer for such presumption, she wanted him to do this . . . right down to her toes, which at this very moment were curled up inside her scuffed and worn boots.

He's an arrogant fool, Lucy Ellyson. Whatever are you thinking?

That in the last few moments, he'd gone from being a pampered gentleman to something more.

I will not marry without love.

Those words had challenged everything she thought of him. He hadn't said them in an off-handed manner, nor had he made some impassioned, romantic statement.

He'd said them as a vow, in a way which said that of all the noble considerations for matrimony, love would be his single deciding factor. Those words, that notion, whispered to her.

Ignited her own longings — for she'd always dreamt of such a love as well. Lucy Ellyson put on a brave face, was the rock of steadiness for her off-kilter family, but deep inside bubbled a hunger for so much more.

For a man to love her for all her faults and follies . . . love her despite her bloodlines, despite her parents and unconventional upbringing.

Love her because he found her the most remarkable woman he'd ever laid eyes on.

So when Lord Clifton declared he was taking a second look at her . . . well, she found she couldn't breathe.

For there was something about the way he studied her, as if she might possess that something he was seeking. That, and the dark, burning passion in his eyes held her with an uncanny power. It ignited a fire inside her, a desire for . . .

Oh, heavens, she didn't know what she wanted.

Except to be kissed.

And he was going to, for he was drawing closer, moving to catch hold of her. Draw her up against him, put his lips to hers and make her insides whirl about in a dizzy flutter like the colorful ribbons of a Maypole dancing in an unexpected breeze.

Demmit, she thought, *how has this man become so handsome, so charming, so utterly desirable?*

How had she never noticed that his dark eyes were really a deep, dark blue — or the way they glowed with a dangerous fire? How had she not seen the strong, determined line of his jaw, the commanding line of his shoulders, the resolute set of his lips, parted and ready to steal from her the one thing she'd never in a thousand years thought she'd ever give to him?

A kiss.

But much to Lucy's despair, this golden moment, this dreamt of chance — her first real kiss — was also the moment when Rusty and Sammy decided to spring their trap.

For one triumphant moment, Clifton thought he had Lucy Ellyson right where he wanted her. Her eyes, now wide with amazement, were fixed on his, and the entire world seemed to melt away as he found himself lost in the meadow green shadows of her gaze.

Distracted by her full, ripe lips, distracted by the thought of her lush —

And right then, his entire world lurched forward as a blinding pain erupted in the back of his head. Stars burst to life in front of his eyes, and they weren't the sort you felt when you had a beautiful slip of muslin in your arms and thought the rest of the afternoon would be spent . . . well, not buckling to your knees, your senses blinded and only one thought ringing through your aching head.

Never let yourself get distracted.

It was George Ellyson's first tenet of staying alive. One he had been pounding into Clifton's and Malcolm's thick skulls since the first day they'd walked into his study.

Never let yourself get distracted.

And he had. In Hampstead. On a single-lane track walking into the village. Within an hour of having heard Ellyson mutter those very words for about the hundredth time.

Yet here he was, oh, so very distracted. By a lady he had no rights to even consider for such a dalliance. For such a moment.

Clifton staggered up and turned to face his assailant.

No, make that assailants.

He blinked a couple of times until he was able to make the jumble of fellows in front of him focus into two discernable figures, the closest one being an oversized ruffian with bright red hair and a murderous light in his eyes. A man who wasted no time, no pleasantries, before burying his meaty paw into the earl's gut, knocking the wind from his lungs and sending him sprawling onto his arse in the dirt and the dust.

So it's going to be that *sort of fight,* Clifton thought as he once again staggered to his feet, shook the stars out of his eyes and balled up his fists.

Oh, he'd been distracted. For a moment.

But he wasn't now. And these two fellows had his full and complete attention.

Lucy had also landed on the hard-packed earth, down beside her long-forgotten basket. She cursed, using her father's favorite expression, one that had gotten her banished at the tender age of seven from Mrs. Fishwick's Boarding School for Young Ladies.

Instead of worrying over her indiscretion

— the curse, not the kiss — she swiped at the wayward strands of hair falling over her face so that she could see what the devil was happening.

And it wasn't a pretty picture.

Rusty and Sammy had Clifton boxed in, with the hedge at his back and no means of escape.

"Oh, dear heavens," she managed to gasp. For as much as she had wanted to see the earl tossed around a bit, that desire had been before . . .

Before he'd been about to kiss her. Before he'd teased her. Tempted her. Turned the tables on her. Had left her so distracted that she'd forgotten about Rusty and Sammy and her father's plans.

And now? Before she could manage another word, one that might put a halt to the entire proceedings, Sammy rushed in.

Lucy squeezed her eyes shut. *Oh, I can't watch. I can't watch.*

For she knew what was going to happen next. Sammy would get a bear hold on the earl, then Rusty, with his big fists and rapid reflexes, would work their devilry up and down the earl's midsection, cracking ribs as easily as one might crack a dozen eggs.

Not enough to do real harm, but enough . . .

"Oh, no, you don't, you bastards," she heard the earl say in a low, dangerous voice. The sort of warning a mastiff growls before it happily takes off a thief's leg.

Her lashes sprang open just in time to see Sammy go flying, shaken off like a flea. The big lug landed hard, the air rushing out of him in a *whoosh* and leaving him dazed and stunned on the lane not far from where she lay sprawled.

She looked over at the dumfounded expression on the experienced fellow's face — a sort of "how the devil did that happen?" shock that fled as his eyes rolled into the back of his head and he fell over, passed out cold.

Clifton shook off Sammy? No, she corrected herself, *he'd done Sammy in.*

Lucy shivered, her father's prophecy coming to fruition before her eyes.

I know you think Clifton a tiresome fool, but I think he'll surprise you, Goosie.

She glanced up at the two men still standing and swallowed.

"Oh, you've got a bit of rum luck to you, do you guv'ner?" Rusty said, cocking his head back a bit, like a rooster ready to crow his supremacy.

Unfortunately for Rusty, that moment of brash impudence cost him.

For Clifton didn't fight like a nobleman — all rules and Gentleman Jim order, with his fists held high and in plain sight.

No, he fought like a blacksmith's son.

He dove headfirst into Rusty's midsection, carrying them both to the ground, where they rolled a bit, fists flying, the brutal *thunk* of a hard paw as it found a fleshy target, curses rising like the dust, and suddenly it all cleared, the flurry of fighting coming to a momentary pause.

Lucy's mouth fell open, or rather, it was already open, she didn't know which, for Clifton had Rusty pinned to the ground, his hard, dangerous fist cocked and ready to land a punch that could stop a man cold.

"No!" she screamed, scrambling up and over, catching the earl's hand. "Don't hurt him."

He turned to her, all wild-eyed and full of fury. "Why the hell not?"

Lucy's breath caught in her throat, for she'd never seen a man so angry, so full of fire. . . . His eyes blazed with malice, and beneath her fingers she could feel his tremendous strength barely held in check, just on the edge of exploding.

She trembled but held fast, her father's warning echoing through her frantic thoughts.

. . . He'll make a good accounting of himself.

A good accounting? That was an under-statement.

He'd shocked her. He'd managed to tempt her into nearly kissing him, and now . . .

Oh, heavens! The way his hand shook with a fierce passion beneath her fingers . . . it made her . . . well, she didn't want to know how it made her feel.

Because the dangerous desires it sent through her, the want to feel those arms around her, to have his solid chest up against hers, his lips taking what they wanted, was too treacherous to consider.

Especially now that she knew exactly what he was capable of.

He pulled his hand back further, hauling her along. "Give me a good reason not to darken this bastard's lights."

"Good heavens, my lord, he was supposed to do this," she sputtered, clinging to his hand and utterly convinced he was about to consign Rusty to his just rewards.

Clifton's fist hung in the air for a moment longer, then his tense and battle-ready muscles flexed, shaking her off, breaking her hold on him.

Rusty scrambled out from beneath the earl, crawling over to his friend and rolling him over. Sammy groaned and struggled up to a sitting position.

"What the bloody hell happened?" Sammy complained, his hand going to his head, one eye already swelling shut. "Did I get hit by a coach?"

"Miss Lucy! I demand an explanation!" Clifton said, getting to his feet and leaning over to retrieve his hat, which had rolled to a stop near her basket. He dusted off his pants, then raked his fingers through his hair before he slammed the tall beaver back in place. "What is the meaning of this?"

Lucy blinked and gaped up at him, for here he was again. The same arrogant, demanding fellow she'd been ready to toss to the lions half an hour ago.

Oh, better this, Lucy, than the man you were so willing to kiss.

"I demand an explanation now!" he ordered.

Still, she didn't know which angered her more — the fact that she lacked a wagonload of lions into which to heave him or that Rusty and Sammy couldn't have delayed their arrival for just a few moments more.

But his sharp tone and the arrogant tilt of his brows were enough to spark Lucy back into the safe and comfortable world of detesting him utterly.

"Well, I would think it is quite obvious, my lord," she said, shaking off her own skirts and marching over to where Rusty and Sammy sat defeated and battered in the dust. As she knelt down to inspect the damage, she said, "These men were hired to test you."

"Test me?" Clifton towered over her, as commanding as a duke, every bit the pompous, arrogant man she'd so happily dismissed.

But now? She glanced up at his handsome, albeit furious, face. Took a glance at his lips, the ones that had been about to kiss her.

"Yes, test you." She shuddered as she took stock of the poor fellows before her. "Oh, heavens, Sammy, you're going to have a terrible shiner," she told him, reaching out and gently touching his rough cheek. Then she glanced over at Rusty's bloody nose. "And you're not much better, I fear," she told him. Rising, Lucy shook out her skirts again and turned to Clifton. "You're bleeding as well. And your eye . . ." She flinched at the sight of it.

He swiped the back of his hand across his face, wincing as he touched it, but, with all the arrogance of a gentleman, he refused to give any ground. " 'Tis of no matter," he told her in his usual standoffish manner.

Lucy wasn't fooled. "You won't say that tomorrow when your eye is shuttered and you've bruises enough to deter even old Gertie's interest." She heaved a sigh. "Well, there is nothing left to do but take the lot of you home and get you fixed up."

She went to help up the still reeling Sammy, but he was too much for her and she landed in a heap beside him. Glancing over her shoulder, she said in a voice as imperious as the earl's, "Well, you might as well help, my lord, because you seem to be the only one left standing."

"There now, Sammy," Lucy said, bustling about the kitchen and holding out a beef-steak for the poor fellow's battered face. "This ought to help."

Carefully, she avoided looking over at the earl. For right now she felt as dazed as Sammy looked.

How could she have been so wrong about the Earl of Clifton?

Against her better judgment, she stole a glance at him and found the man watching her with that unnerving gaze of his.

For the life of her, she had no idea what he was thinking, or worse, what he thought of her.

Not that I care. Not in the least.

Sammy groaned a bit, and she shook her head as she shook the steak at him. "I've never heard a man fuss so over having his eye blackened."

"Ain't had it happen in quite some time," Sammy admitted, gingerly putting the slab up against his shuttered eye.

Rusty snorted. "Hey there, guv'ner, where did you learn to fight like such a bruiser?"

Lucy stilled, for it was a question she'd been dying to ask since the earl had landed his first blow. Nor did she dare look again over her shoulder to where he sat at the table, a pint of ale before him. He'd insisted she see to Rusty and Sammy first, claiming they'd had the worst of it.

Which they had. And at his more-than-capable hands.

Gracious heavens, never in her life had she actually feared for the French.

"Oh, aye," Sammy chimed in. "Where did a bang-up bloke like you learn to fight?"

Clifton chuckled. "You could say I had a rare education at the hands of a regular brawler," he told them. "The cooper's son in the village near where I grew up was quite the goer. Used to corner me and my brother all the time. We finally had to learn how to best him or spend all our days with one of

96

our eyes shuttered. And worse, explain to our father why we kept losing."

Rusty snorted. "Spoiling it with the local lad? Thought you were some fancy fellow. Ratter told us you were nothing more than a gentleman."

Lucy flinched, for she knew what was going to come next.

"Ratter?" The earl's brow arched.

Oh, yes, he would have to ask that question.

"My father's nickname," she supplied, hoping that would be the end of it.

But not so for Rusty and Sammy.

"Aye, Ratter," Rusty said, raising his glass in a mock toast. "No finer fellow ever made good for himself out of the Dials. Not one to forget his friends, he don't. Still, not like him to steer us wrong. Never met one of you London toffs, especially no earl, I couldn't finish."

"So now you have," Lucy told them, as she was back to carving at the big roast. "Might I remind you this 'London toff' is the Earl of Clifton and most likely a magistrate —"

To which the earl nodded in concession.

"— so I would mind your tongues, both of you."

"Still, you don't fight like no earl," Rusty

said, taking a drink from the mug of ale before him.

"I suppose I don't," Clifton admitted. "But I've found life is full of surprises."

Lucy would have wagered her pink silk gown — the finest one she owned — that he was looking at her, his gaze boring into her back, full of questions and accusations.

Ones she had no intention of answering. Instead, she drove her knife back into the roast before her and carved a thick steak from it, ignoring the way her hand shook.

"And what was a fancy fellow like you doing hanging around the village lads and not up in your fine house?" Sammy asked.

"We — my brother and I — liked to go to the village to visit his mother. He's my half brother, you see, and his mother ran the local alehouse. I spent a good deal of my youth loitering about the village, much to my tutor's dismay."

"No owl-eyed fellow taught you to hit like that," Rusty said, tipping his glass toward the earl to make his point.

"No, he didn't." Clifton poured them both another serving of ale and finished by topping off his own cup. "He considered me his greatest failing."

"Ah there, don't you worry about that," Sammy told him. "No man who can topple the pair of us is a failure. If you ever want, we can always use a third. We do a bit of business, by the by."

"I might remind you, you're talking to a man who sits in the House of Lords," Lucy said. Then, without realizing what she was doing, she stole a glance at the earl. Their gazes met and she was trapped, much as she had been earlier.

His deep blue eyes seemed to have darkened, and she found herself unable to look away. Lucy swore she could hear his commanding voice, what he was thinking as he studied her.

Don't think this is going to be settled so easily, Lucy.

She wrenched her gaze away and went back to the roast, cutting at it with a dangerous vigor.

Behind her, Rusty chuckled. "Seems to me yer da was paying the wrong fellow to teach you, milord. Should have hired this lad from the village. He sounds like old Bruno back in the Dials. 'Member him, Sammy? Always spoiling for a fight? A meaner cur never walked the streets."

"Taught you that hook, I'd guess," Clifton said, catching up the steak she held out for him at the end of a meat fork. Yet when he settled it awkwardly against his swollen eye, much as Sammy had, she reached out and readjusted it, settling it into place and guiding his hand as to how to hold it.

But that was a mistake, for the moment her fingers brushed against his, that spark, that fire she'd felt in the lane when he'd taken her in his arms, when he'd been about to kiss her, flowed through her like a bit of lightning, catching her unawares and shocking her with an awareness that left her breathless.

This time, she knew better than to glance at him. She turned quickly and fled to the sink, where she could wash her hands in hopes that the cool water would quell the unwanted fires the earl provoked.

"Aye, he did," Sammy said proudly. "Didn't expect that, did you?"

"No," Clifton admitted. "But don't think it will work a second time. Never quite seen a hook like that."

"Sort of the same bit of magic you used to take down Monday Moggs, eh, Goosie? Chopped him right good, didn't you, girl?" Sammy slapped his knee. "Ain't a gel this side of the Dials with a better right hook than our girl Goosie."

Lucy cringed, her eyes scrunched shut and her back still to the earl. "Samuel Trouncer! I haven't the vaguest notion of ever —"

Sammy just waved her protests aside. "Ah, how like you, Goosie. Modest as you are sweet." He turned to the earl and winked. "Don't let that fair face and those sweet lips fool you, guv'nor. 'Iffin you know what's good for you, you'll never cross our girl here. She'll send you aloft without a second thought. Just ask 'ol Monday."

"Oh, that is quite enough out of you," she said, pointing toward the door. "One more word, Mr. Trouncer, and you'll —" Lucy's threat stopped in midsentence as out of the corner of her eye she spied Clifton watching her, one brow raised, a sly smile on his handsome lips.

The dastardly fellow. She huffed a bit and turned from him. He would find her mortification amusing.

"Your brother, does he know how to do that left cut of yours?" Rusty asked, changing the subject.

Clifton paused, pulling his gaze away from her. "No, he doesn't. But I would be quite remiss if I didn't tell you that he favors his right side," he said with a grin, and all three of them raised their glasses in a conspiratorial toast.

Lucy wiped her hands on the towel, then fisted them to her hips. "Oh, now I've seen everything. A pair of dodgers like you, looking for the advantage to take down a pigeon. You should both be ashamed of yourselves. Why, you sound like a pair of old men."

"Old men?!" Sammy protested. "Do you think I want to go back to the Dials looking worse than I already do? I've got me reputation to keep."

"And me as well, Goosie-girl," Rusty said. "Can't have it getting out we got beat. Not something a man likes to remember."

"Aye, and has a devil of a time forgetting," his partner added. "Not when the evidence is right there on his mug for all to see." He tapped his cheek, then winced in pain.

"Exactly, Lucy," Clifton chimed in. "No man likes being taken advantage of. Nor does he forget when he is."

He raised his glass to her, but she had to imagine he wasn't toasting her. He'd told her exactly how he felt about her part in all this.

And that he wasn't the type to forget either.

With the pitcher emptied, the earl excused himself, shaking hands with his former adversaries and wishing them well before returning upstairs.

As for her part in all this, Lucy noted, he didn't offer her the same courtesy.

But once he was gone, she shook her head at the pair of dodgers before her. "Should I tell my father you got beaten?"

Sammy's eyes narrowed. "Should we be tellin' your da what you and that toff were about to do afore we stopped you?"

Wretched bastard. He had her there.

"That won't be necessary," she replied, feeling her cheeks grow hot.

"Think you might owe us a bit more than our usual fees," Rusty told her. "You know, for our troubles and all."

Lucy wanted nothing more than to hold her ground, but she knew there was no bluffing these two rats. They smelled a chance to line their pockets, and this time they weren't going to lose.

Heaving a disgruntled sigh, she went over to the cupboard and got down an old blue sugar pot. Reaching in, she collected a few coins more, then made a note to move the sugar pot before they came back to visit again.

"Thought as much, Goosie-me-girl," Sammy said as she dropped the yellow coins into his open hand. "Not your type anyway, if you don't mind me saying. Yer a sensible gel. Not the sort to let a fancy bit of fine words and sweet talk tell you different. But I'll remind you here and now, he'll never love you like one of us would."

She pointed to the door and they went to leave. She didn't need any lectures from the likes of them.

"Aye, Goosie, just say the word —," Rusty said, doffing his hat and giving her a saucy wink as he picked up the earl's discarded steak and dropped it into his pocket before she pushed him the rest of the way out the door.

"You don't have to worry about me," she told them as they lumbered down the garden path. "I know the likes of him will never offer a girl like me naught but empty promises."

Oh, but for a moment there . . .

For a moment she could have forgotten such things and let herself believe that the Earl of Clifton would look twice at her.

That he'd see beyond the walls she'd built around her heart, be the sort willing and daring enough to breach them.

Still, even as the garden gate shut behind them, clanging in her ears much like Sammy's warning, her gaze rose unbidden to the window of her father's map room overhead.

But that doesn't mean I couldn't fall in love with him.

CHAPTER 5

Clifton came down from Mr. Ellyson's map room a quarter past midnight, his head pounding with all the information his taskmaster was trying to cram into the confines between his ears.

That, or it was the lingering effects of meeting up with Rusty and Sammy.

And Lucy . . .

There was no denying it now. She was Lucy to him.

He set aside that thought. At least he tried, as he had most of the afternoon, moving from anger over being tricked by that cheeky bit of muslin to regret that he hadn't taken advantage of her just a bit quicker.

At least then, in addition to a headache, he could claim to have tasted her sweet, lying lips.

"We haven't studied this much since Cambridge," Malcolm was muttering behind him. "I don't remember Temple or Jack mentioning all this work when they came calling to recruit us."

"Who are you trying to deceive? You never studied at school to begin with," Clifton said over his shoulder. "Let alone be able to recall what Temple and Jack said that night."

Malcolm grinned. "Oh, that was a fine evening. Temple has the best taste in claret. Probably would have agreed to anything he set before us, as muddled as I was." But then Malcolm's interest turned to more immediate concerns. "Bloody hell, I'm starved and parched. I don't know which I want more."

Clifton agreed but didn't say it aloud. The house was eerily silent — for much to his surprise, he found he'd gotten used to the nearly constant cacophony of the Ellysons, which made the silence all that much more unnerving.

And it was that stillness that made their stealth all that much more imperative, for one misstep could awaken Ellyson, who had finally dozed off in his chair by the fire.

If the man awoke, the earl wouldn't put it past the fellow to rise up with another long list of "must knows" and "have we gone overs."

No, this was the opportunity Clifton and Malcolm had been waiting for, and, after sharing a glance that spoke volumes, they had made their escape the first moment the man snored.

Demmit, I hope that innkeeper still has a pot of soup on the fire.

Clifton nodded. *And a good bottle of claret.*

If they were lucky, the earl thought. He was exhausted enough that more than likely half a bottle would put him into a deep, sound sleep, where worries over coming home alive wouldn't compete with visions of Lucy and her luscious, kissable lips.

For in those moments, as they'd ambled up the lane, her capable hand on his sleeve, her witty repartee challenging him to think beyond the usual limited subjects one had to draw from to converse with a lady, he'd found himself . . . well, not captivated, certainly not that, but something else . . .

Just as he didn't understand whatever had compelled him to think of kissing her. Well, the fact that she was a pretty bit of baggage might have had a hand in that.

A fiery, passionate, beautiful woman lurking beneath her fierce bravado.

So Lucy, have you ever been in love?

No. Most certainly not.

It wasn't just the denial in her voice that still resonated through him but the challenge behind her words as well.

As if she dared him to try. To try and seduce her, to uncover her secrets, unlock her lips and ignite the passions lurking beneath her unfashionable gown.

Not to just let her be his faux mistress in this deception but to actually take her to his bed and make her his mistress by deed.

With his heart and his body.

Clifton took a deep breath and did his best to shake off that notion, but when he opened his eyes and took a glance down the rest of the steps, who but Lucy herself stood there in the foyer, waiting for him.

Tray in hand, that wry, challenging look on her face, and her glorious black hair tumbling from its pins.

"Well done, gentlemen," she said. "Am I to surmise that you are practicing an escape and found the right moment when Papa finally fell asleep?" She glanced over her shoulder at the mantel clock. "Yes, and right on schedule. He usually does doze off about now. Have a care as you come down the stairs, the last one is a bit uneven," she said with that saucy air of importance of hers, "or you'll be eating your dinner from the floor."

"According to your father," Malcolm said, "that may be the best we can hope for in the days to come."

"Frightening you with tales of starvation, is he?" she asked. "*Tsk. Tsk.* He usually doesn't start scaring recruits with stories from Egypt until the end of the second week."

"We are not easily frightened," Clifton told her.

"You would be if you had any sense," she shot back. Her gaze flitted up and just as quickly glanced back down at the tray in her hands. "Besides, you have no worries of an empty stomach tonight. I've seen to that."

"Is that what I think it is?" Malcolm asked, elbowing past Clifton and reaching out to take the tray from her, relieving Lucy of her burden.

For which he was rewarded with one of her rare, bright smiles.

Clifton cursed himself for not thinking of it first.

But then again, good manners didn't seem to come right to mind when she was in front of him — for a thousand different reasons.

"We were just leaving," he told her. "You needn't have gone to any trouble on our account." For suddenly he wanted to be gone from this house, from her.

"Oh, do shut up, Gilby," Malcolm said, apparently immune to Lucy's charms. "If

109

you're thinking I am taking potluck over at that scanty inn, when I can smell" — he inhaled deeply again — "stew?"

"Beef stew?" Clifton blurted out. He had visions of the thick steak up against Sammy's pocked face.

She must have seen the horror on his expression, for she blew out a loud breath, her gaze rolling upward. "I didn't use the steaks from this afternoon," she told him. "Those went home with the boys . . . extra compensation for their troubles."

"Yes, of course. I never would suggest —"

But then again, he had, hadn't he? Oh, good God! What had happened to his manners?

Turning her back to him, she returned her attentions to the more appreciative audience of his unwitting brother. Moving aside so Malcolm could go on into the parlor, she ticked off the contents of the tray. "It isn't much, just some fresh bread. A pudding Mrs. Kewin made up, and some cheese. And in a moment I believe Mariana will be around with a bottle of claret. You do like claret, don't you, my lord?"

While Malcolm happily carried her offering into the parlor, Clifton took a step back, wary of her sudden thoughtfulness.

Just as he should be wary of her lips.

"His favorite," Malcolm said as he set the tray down on the table. "When he isn't being a pompous ass."

Lucy smiled again. "He won't be so stuffy when he tries it — for it is an excellent vintage, or so Mad Jack claimed when he sent it over."

Stuffy? There it was again. He didn't know why he cared — for he certainly didn't — but each time she made her pert opinion known either through her words, deeds or that dismissive glance of hers, he had the overwhelming urge to prove her wrong.

Very wrong.

"And the delay with the claret?" Malcolm was asking. "Perhaps I can be of assistance."

She waved his question off. "I doubt it. That is unless you have a passing knowledge of locks. For Mariana is having a devil of a time picking the one on the wine cabinet."

That statement was enough to clear Clifton's distracted thoughts. "Your sister is picking the lock?"

Her bright eyes sparkled. "Yes, Papa likes to change the locks from time to time so she keeps her skills up. He recently put in a rather ingenuous Swiss design that has eluded her so far, but perhaps you shall get lucky."

No Bath school with dancing masters and

lessons on menus in this house. The man actually wanted his daughters proficient in larceny?

Meanwhile, Lucy swept into the parlor and shot him a glance over her shoulder. "What will it be, my lord? Your pride or your stomach?"

"Never pass up a meal, for you don't know when you shall get another," Malcolm called out from the table inside, quoting the bit of advice Ellyson had given them this very afternoon. Advice Malcolm was taking to heart, for he had a napkin tucked under his chin and a spoon at the ready.

The cozy-looking chamber boasted a table set for two, and the empty seat across from Malcolm begged to be filled. Another table sat in the corner near the Franklin stove, the faded and well-used boards of a card game sat atop the green baize waiting for the players to return and finish the hand. Candles burned low, as if they had, like Miss Ellyson and Lucy, waited for him and Malcolm to come down.

"It wouldn't be proper," he managed over the protests of his stomach, which was growling in impatience as the aroma of the stew curled into his senses, as beguiling as the woman offering it.

"Proper? Not to eat a meal set before

you?" she asked.

"No," he said, shaking his head. "This —"
He shook his hand at the softly lit room. It
was the sort of late-night setting that would
have a London matron in horrors. "We
couldn't dine without some sort of —"

"Without some sort of what?" she asked,
her hands going to her hips.

Clifton drew a deep breath and glanced
over at his brother. No help there, for
Malcolm was already buttering a thick slice
of bread. "It isn't proper for young ladies to
dine alone with gentlemen. It might impugn
your reputation."

She stared at him. No, rather she gaped at
him as if he'd grown a second head. "Are
you suggesting I go wake up Thomas-
William or my father so you can eat your
supper?"

Well, when she put it that way it did sound
rather ridiculous. But couldn't she see that
he had her best interests at heart?

Behind Lucy, Malcolm sat back negli-
gently in his chair, arms folded over his
chest and a devil-may-care smile on his face.
*Oh, you've fallen into deep waters there,
Gilby. Good luck with that.*

But before he could formulate a response,
a slender hand tucked into the curve of his
arm and towed him forward, leaving him no

choice but to enter their comfortable den.

Miss Mariana Ellyson. With the grasp of a stevedore.

Hard to believe of the willowy form beside him, but she carried him along with the same stubborn determination that her sister exhibited more vocally.

"Oh, don't be so reserved, my lord," she told him merrily, hauling him into the room. Mariana settled him into the chair opposite Malcolm's and then proceeded to dish him up a bowl of stew.

Only then did she turn and look at his face. "Goodness! Lord Clifton! Lucy didn't mention that you'd been set upon. No wonder you are so put out this evening."

Malcolm glanced up at him. "Who would have thought that ruffians could be found here in Hampstead. And all this while, I've found it quite dull, Miss Ellyson."

"Oh, Mr. Grey, I thought we were past such formalities. Mariana, if you please."

"Only if you call me Malcolm," he said.

"Delighted! As for Hampstead, it is dull no longer, sir," Mariana told him. "For I have successfully broken into father's cabinet and liberated a very fine bottle of claret. We must celebrate, for Papa will be quite vexed in the morning that I've outwitted his new lock and that his claret has been drunk." The pretty little minx handed the bottle over to Malcolm, who uncorked it quickly and filled the four glasses on the table.

Mariana took up hers and, after a taste, grinned.

Malcolm did the same, and his eyes lit up after the first sampling. "I would like to have my turn with those fellows who dared jump you, Gilby," he said. "Give them another trouncing, eh?"

"Oh, I'm sure you will . . . see them, that is," Mariana told him in her own flighty fashion. Then she paused to take a drink, and, as if realizing her faux pas, quickly diverted the conversation. "That is, if you stay long enough. Oh, how dull it would be here in Hampstead if it weren't for the occasional incident. Like last spring when Monday Moggs tried to marry Lucy."

"Ah, the illustrious Monday Moggs!" Clifton said, perking up at this bit of news.

"You've heard of him?" Mariana asked.

"Just in passing — but not that he was in love with your sister." Clifton turned his gaze on the lady who had declared herself immune to love. "You've been holding out on me, Lucy. I thought you said you'd never been in love."

Her face turned a bright pink.

Mariana failed to notice — or ignored outright — her sister's embarrassment. "Gracious heavens, my lord, Lucy wasn't in love with that rumpot. He just got it in his head to marry her." She paused and said in a not-so-quiet aside, "He was, as Mrs. Kewin likes to say, 'corned, pickled and salted.' "

Clifton laughed. "The man was drunk?"

"Completely tossed!" Mariana said. "Threw Lucy over his shoulder and carried her from one side of the Mayday fair to the other where there was a pater-cove — one of those traveling curates — marrying couples."

"Mariana!" her sister finally managed to protest. "No one wants to hear this story!"

"I disagree," Clifton said, refilling Mariana's glass and handing it back to her. "Miss Ellyson, pray continue. I am riveted. How did your sister escape this unscrupulous Mr. Moggs?"

"Oh, yes, do tell," Malcolm encouraged.

Thus cheered, the girl continued. "Well, eventually Monday Moggs had to put Lucy down. The curate insisted —"

Lucy threw up her hands and fled to the other side of the room, albeit to add more coal to the stove, though the set of her jaw suggested she wouldn't mind consigning her

116

sister to the flames.

Mariana continued unabashed, "Then the fellow asked Lucy if she wanted to be married to Mr. Moggs and she said no."

"But that wasn't good enough?" Clifton asked.

"No, for Monday Moggs had given the man extra coins to ignore her protests. So Lucy had no choice," Mariana said. "She hit him right in the nose and knocked him over."

"You floored this Mr. Moggs, Lucy?" Malcolm asked.

Mariana laughed. "Not to begin with. She flattened the curate first."

"The curate?" Clifton gasped, twisting around in his chair to look at her. Why he'd never heard the likes of such a thing. At least not involving a lady.

From her spot at the stove, Lucy rose to her own defense. "He was about to pronounce me married! I had no choice but to stop him."

Malcolm and Clifton exchanged a glance, then both began to laugh.

"Very resourceful, madam," Malcolm managed to say. "But I thought Mr. Moggs was the victim in all this?"

"Oh, he is," Mariana added. "Once she was convinced the curate wasn't going to get up, she made sure Mr. Moggs wasn't going to come calling ever again."

"So then you hit Mr. Moggs?" Clifton asked.

"I only —"

"Oh, it was a muffler, my lord!" Mariana exclaimed, cutting off her sister's response. "A stunning blow."

Lucy let out a loud sigh, as if her accomplishment hardly warranted the retelling. "He was very drunk, so it wasn't all that hard," she said, crossing the room and shaking out her skirts as she went. "It was that or end up Mrs. Monday Moggs." She shuddered from head to toe.

"Poor Mr. Moggs! He's had to endure the shame ever since," Mariana told them. "Of being bested by Lucy."

"And what of me?" her sister demanded. "Everyone is in such a flutter over poor Mr. Moggs."

Malcolm leaned forward. "But Lucy, no man likes being bested by a mere slip of a girl. I dare-say Mr. Moggs has had to endure much."

"I believe my brother makes a good point," Clifton hastened to add. "No man likes being bested."

"Then they shouldn't arrogantly assume to know what is best for a lady. There is such a thing as *asking*."

Her hands went to her hips. This, he should have realized by now, was the first warning, but when she stood thusly, she challenged him. He'd never met a lady who just out and out defied him, and it left him unsettled and determined to put the world back to rights.

Besides, she wasn't talking about Monday Moggs any longer. But about him. And the kiss he'd nearly stolen this afternoon.

No, Clifton wasn't about to be bowled over like this Moggs fellow. "And if this gentleman had asked, would you have granted him the favor?"

Her brow furrowed. "Certainly not!"

"Ah, but love will make a man do things he would never have considered. Even take without asking."

"Then he is no gentleman," she declared as if she had him cornered. "Besides, a lady knows when a man is truly in love with her and when he is just toying with her."

Touché. Point to Miss Lucy.

But Clifton wasn't about to yield the field to her just yet. "And you think Mr. Moggs was just toying with you?"

Her brows drew into a stern line. "Monday Moggs was not in love with me. He was merely pot valiant and full of his own worth, which, I might note, is a leaky cottage, a wobbly wagon that he uses for his carting business — when he is sober enough to know the difference between north and south — and an old nag of a horse who has the good sense to nip at him regularly to remind him who is the smarter of the two."

Clifton smiled. "So if he'd had a title, estates, an income and a stable full of well-mannered horses, you wouldn't have floored him? You'd have let him carry out his nefarious plans?"

She pressed her lips together, for now she could see he had her right where he wanted.

Because they both knew that while he'd been about to steal a kiss from her this afternoon, knocking out his daylights had been the last thing on Lucy Ellyson's agenda.

"Come now, Lord Clifton," Mariana declared. "That is hardly a fair comparison. What woman wouldn't marry such a fellow? Even Lucy would be hard-pressed to refuse."

"I would," she said, but she hardly sounded convincing. Certainly not to his ears.

"Well, it isn't like it is apt to happen," Mariana said, turning to the table and filling the bowls and plates. "There aren't many men who will dare come around here as it is, for fear Lucy will darken their daylights as she did Monday Moggs."

As laughter filled the little parlor, Clifton realized the only person who didn't find that notion amusing was the lady herself. Lucy wasn't laughing.

And in that unguarded moment, he saw the same wary light he had beheld just before he'd been about to kiss her.

Cutting off the others, Clifton raised his glass to her. "Madame, my brother and I have forgotten our manners. I must thank you for this generous and delicious meal. You have been too kind to us."

"Hear, hear," Malcolm added. "My brother is right. We should not be amusing ourselves at your expense when you have given us such a good supper — this stew is most excellent, and I am thankful for your kindness."

Mariana raised her glass as well for another, different sort of tribute. "What you should be thankful for is that it isn't at all like the stew Lucy made for Lord Roche."

"Sister!" Lucy protested. "Be still."

A bit of the conversation from earlier trickled back through the earl's memory.

. . . and no dosing his stew . . . He is no Lord Roche . . .

Clifton took another glance at the pot on the table, and down at the half-eaten bowl before him.

"Whatever did your sister do to Roche?" Malcolm asked.

Mariana laughed. "He was ever so haughty and full of himself —"

"Rather like my brother?" Malcolm suggested.

Mariana shook her head. "Oh, your brother is far higher in the instep than Lord Roche, but he isn't as much of an . . ."

"An ass?" Malcolm supplied.

"Oh, yes, that's it exactly. Thank you, sir," she said, as if he'd supplied her a cup of tea rather than an obscenity. "Well, Roche was such a, well, as you said, an ass, so Lucy dosed his stew and he spent the next day and a half in the necessary." Mariana bit her lips together for a moment, her eyes sparkling. "He left soon after and returned to London a much more humble fellow. He never did join the rest of Mr. Pymm's associates in Portugal."

"Nor should he have," Lucy pointed out. "He would have been a terrible disgrace. A risk to all."

Now it was Clifton's turn to gape, first at Lucy and then at the stew set before them. Even Malcolm had edged back from the table a bit, his enthusiasm for this unexpected supper having cooled.

"Oh, good heavens," Lucy declared, tearing off a piece of bread from the loaf and dunking it deeply into the pot. Then, as they watched, she ate it. "Will that do?" she asked before using one of the napkins to wipe her lips.

Then she refilled their bowls, setting them down on the table with an impatient *thump*. Catching up her glass of claret, she retreated to the card table in the corner.

Mariana had already settled into her chair. She leaned over to ask, "Whose card was it?"

"Mine," Lucy declared, nodding to the discarded ones in between them. The two girls reconvened their game, and the two men were all but forgotten as the play began anew.

Clifton sat there, a bit in shock over Roche's fate. That Lucy Ellyson had weeded him out, sent him packing because he'd been . . . well, an ass.

And so are you if you fail at this . . .

A rare sense of disquiet ran down his spine, followed by the hint of a suggestion, whispered in his ear. *So leave.*

It was a voice not unlike hers.

Startled, he glanced over to find her

watching him. With those sharp, intelligent eyes of hers. With an air of superiority that would make a duke weep with envy.

The same look that had challenged him to kiss her this afternoon.

In that moment, in the blink of an eye, Clifton's heart constricted. Not out of some waffling emotion, but a stab of determination to show this meddlesome bit of muslin that he was no Roche.

Clifton tipped his head toward her with all the noble grace of his ancestors, if only to get on her nerves. But what he really wanted to do was discover more about her.

Then he glanced over at her sister and asked, "So, aside from Mr. Moggs, have you any other admirers, Lucy?" Just as he suspected, Mariana — already on her second glass of wine — filled in nicely, all too eager to spill the family secrets.

"Naught but Archie, the clerk at Mr. Strout's office," she jumped in to say.

"Mariana!"

"Archie at Mr. Strout's office?" Clifton asked as innocently as the worst sort of gossip.

Mariana followed his lead quite happily. "Mr. Strout is Papa's solicitor in London. When he has business matters for Papa, Mr. Strout sends it over with Archie. He's taken a fancy to Lucy."

"He has not!"

Mariana ignored her sister's protest. "Then why did he bring you flowers Sunday before last when he had no business being here?"

"Yes, and I sneezed for three days straight." Lucy shifted in her chair. "And what Archie fancies is a position with the Foreign Office and thinks if he charms me, Papa will help him."

"Hasn't he the connections to gain his own place?" Malcolm asked. "Or is he another Mr. Moggs?"

Mariana shook her head. "Oh, heavens no. Archie is very well connected, but his grandfather thinks him a great fool."

"His grandfather thinks everyone is a great fool," Lucy amended.

"True enough," Mariana sighed. "But you should be thankful he is foolish enough to fall in love with you."

"*Harrumph!* Do you want to play cards or gossip?"

"Well, both." Mariana laughed.

Malcolm chuckled. "Are you two planning on attending the assembly Wednesday night? The innkeeper's wife, Mrs. Turkel —"

"Turnpenny," Mariana corrected.

"Oh, yes, Mrs. Turnpenny told us that all

the ladies and gentlemen from around the Heath would be there."

Clifton glanced up and saw Lucy stiffen, her cards trembling in her hand for just a moment. "I prefer not to dance, Mr. Grey."

"My sister is being too polite, sir," Mariana said, her gaze fixed attentively on her cards. "We cannot attend because we are not received."

This fell like a cannonball onto the carpet.

"Not received?" his brother said. "Why ever not? Is it because of that Moggs business, because that hardly seems —"

"Malcolm!" Clifton chastened. "Perhaps it is none of our business."

"Oh, in Hampstead it is everyone's business, so it is of no matter," Mariana said. "We are not received because our mother is the Contessa di Marzo." She paused for a moment. "Yes, I can see from your expression you know who she is. And since Father never married her, not that he could —" There was a pause, and the girl let out a loud "ouch." She reached down to rub her shin. "There is no reason to kick me, Goosie. They will discover the truth soon enough. I'm surprised Mrs. Turnpenny hasn't warned them off yet."

"She has not," Clifton supplied.

Mariana shrugged. "Oh, she usually takes

great delight in scandalizing all with our presence." She paused again and made a mulish face not unlike their landlady's, then spoke in perfect imitation of her country tones, "The daughters of that woman! In our neighborhood! Be warned, my good gentlemen. Be warned!"

"You are in excellent company, then," Malcolm told them. "For my mother was not married to my father either." He paused and winked at Clifton. "Which makes my noble brother the oddball of our lot, eh, Gilby?" He grinned at Mariana. "We must stick together, our sort. And never fear, Miss Ellyson, I would dance with you at any assembly and be the envy of all."

"You wouldn't like to go to an assembly?" Clifton asked Lucy.

"It doesn't matter what I would like to do, my lord. We are not received, so I give the idea little thought. Rather like wishing to fly to the moon." She glanced up at him. "I try to concentrate my efforts on what is before me." Then she turned her attention back to her sister. "How do you ever expect to win if you do not pay attention?"

At this, Mariana smiled triumphantly at her sister, then laid her cards down. "Ha! I've beat you, Goosie. I have to wonder where your attention is this night."

"Distracted by your nattering, I imagine. Besides, this is only a temporary setback," Lucy told her as she gathered the discarded cards together and began to shuffle with the skill of a sharpster.

"Where did you learn to deal like that?" Malcolm asked, as mesmerized by her deft handling of the cards as Clifton was.

"Thomas-William," she said, referring to her father's servant. "When he and father traveled together on the Continent, Thomas-William would play cards with the other servants —"

"— because servants usually know more of their master's business than he knows himself," Clifton and Malcolm said together, quoting another of Ellyson's maxims.

The ladies laughed.

"Don't be so dazzled by my sister's dealing," Mariana offered. Then she winked at Malcolm and Clifton. "For it is how she cheats."

Does she now? Clifton glanced up at Lucy, who had her gaze fixed on her cards, but that telltale pink hue had returned to her cheeks.

"What a terrible thing to say, Mariana," she said. "What need have I of cheating, when you are such a poor player?"

"I just beat you," her sister shot back.

"Mere luck," Lucy replied with that smug sort of arrogance Clifton liked about her.

"Do you truly believe in luck?" he asked Lucy.

She shook her head almost immediately. Too quickly, actually. "No. I think we make, or take, our own luck."

He paused, for he knew that statement was naught but another of Ellyson's proverbs. Everything about Lucy Ellyson — the way she ran the house, held her secrets, even disavowed love — rang with that same practicality that was her father's hallmark, but Clifton suspected that they were all parts of the same carefully constructed façade, just like her faded fashions and ugly bonnets.

Parts of a great conspiracy to hide her true feelings, her heart.

He glanced down at the tray before him, the supper offered with a nonchalant air on the sole purpose that "they were most likely hungry," but he knew what it truly was.

An apology and a peace offering.

And for just those reasons alone, Lucy fascinated him.

He reached for the bottle of claret and was about to pour himself another glass, when out of the corner of his eye he watched her finishing the deal. And spied something he doubted he would have noticed a week ago, before he'd come to this madhouse and listened to Ellyson's lessons on being observant.

While her fingers moved skillfully as she dealt, making the cards fly across the green baize of the table, he realized that their whirling flight distracted nearly everyone from discerning that she could pluck a card from anywhere in the deck.

He looked from her hands to the cards on the table and shook his head slightly. And when he looked up at her, her eyes widened in recognition.

Just then, her sister said exactly what he was thinking, for she had picked up her cards and frowned heavily at the hand she'd been dealt. "You're cheating, Goosie. I declare I won't play if you continue to cheat."

Lucy straightened, rearranging her cards. "Mariana, what a terrible thing to say. *And in front of company.* You know I never cheat."

Then she did something she shouldn't have. She took a furtive glance in his direction and their eyes met.

"Well, I don't," she insisted, looking away, her hands no longer as skilled. She dropped one of the cards and nearly overturned the rest in her trembling fingers.

No one other than Clifton seemed to notice her distracted movements.

"I'll catch you one of these days," Mariana muttered for all to hear. "I'll catch you, Goosie. See that I don't!"

"You can try," her sister shot back. "You can try."

Then Lucy looked up at him again, and he couldn't help himself; he grinned back at her.

For he already had.

Caught her, that was.

Lucy's breath froze in her throat. *He couldn't have. No, he must be bluffing . . . teasing me. He couldn't have caught me.*

But the truth was right there in the arrogant tilt of his brow, the grin that cut across his square jaw.

The Earl of Clifton had caught her plucking a card from the middle of the deck.

Had the world as she knew it been tipped upside down? First he flattened Rusty and Sammy, and now this? Who was this man before her, this mystery of a nobleman?

Wasn't that the reason you made this intimate little supper? Invited him here for this very improper encounter, so you could ply him with claret and discover more of his secrets?

Yet here he was chiseling out hers as easily as she could deal herself an ace.

Oh, gracious heavens, she'd always considered herself a matchless judge of men, of their characters, of their ability to fulfill the tasks Pymm selected them for, and now this!

The Earl of Clifton. A man she'd dismissed at first glance as completely unworthy, an arrogant mistake. And he'd fooled her. Pulled the wool over her eyes and deceived her utterly.

For he hadn't cared a whit for her good opinion. Or for currying her favor. Or anything beyond stealing a kiss from her lips to prove that he had . . .

Had what?

A better notion of love than she did?

What if he does? a wry little voice whispered in her ear. *What if he does know more?*

"Picking locks and cheating at cards," Malcolm said. He wiped his lips with his napkin and placed it beside his empty bowl. "You two are an illustrious pair."

Much to Lucy's horror, Mariana dashed right into that opening and, without the least bit of shame, said, "Thank you, sir. We have our father to thank, for he insisted we have much the same education as he had, just in case we ever discovered ourselves . . . in need, shall we say." She pulled a hairpin slightly out of her hair and then tucked it back in. "Then again, if we hadn't had those lessons, I'd have never liberated that wonderful bottle of claret."

"And what education was it that your father had?" the earl asked.

Lucy opened her mouth to stop this line of questioning, but Mariana went on blithely, "Why, growing up in Seven Dials, of course. He was the finest fork who ever worked the streets of London." Mariana preened before she glanced down at her hand and played her next card, as if she'd just commented about the pudding, or the weather, or the state of the coals in the grate.

Not telling their guests that their father had grown up pursuing criminal endeavors.

Lucy tried her best to concentrate on her cards and tell herself it didn't matter as to their good opinion. It mattered naught.

And no, she wasn't going to look at him and see if Mariana's revelation had left him gaping in shock. No, she just couldn't.

"Your father was a . . ." Mr. Grey struggled for a polite way to say it.

"A fork. A foyst. A buzman. A diver," Mariana supplied, her delighted gaze fixed on Lucy's absentminded discard. "In essence, gentleman, a pickpocket." She plucked up the card before her, then glanced over at their guests. "Well, he was until His Grace caught him."

"His Grace?" the earl sputtered over his glass of claret, nearly spilling it.

"Why, yes, the Duke of Parkerton. The old one, not the one who has the title now. Mad Jack's father."

"The Duke of Parkerton?" Clifton set his glass down, as if he didn't trust himself to hold it. "He caught your father picking a pocket and didn't have him hung for it?"

Lucy hadn't a care that Mariana was her dearest sister or best companion.

She kicked her under the table.

Hard.

"Lucy!" Mariana protested. "Whatever is wrong with you? That hurt! And if you think such a distraction is going to help you, I'll have you know I win." She laid down her cards to show her perfect hand. "No, not at all," she said, answering the earl's question. "Why ever would the duke want to have Papa hung? He was only a ten-year-old lad." She made a *tsk, tsk* noise as if she thought perhaps Clifton had quite possibly had too much claret.

Malcolm laughed. "Because, Mariana, stealing is a crime. And child or not, picking pockets is a hanging offense."

She laughed, as if she had never heard

such nonsense. "Not when it can be put to good use."

The earl, still struggling to recover some semblance of his usual composure, asked, "You want us to believe that the Duke of Parkerton caught your father stealing and instead of handing him over to the watch, put those 'talents' to good use?" He said this not to Mariana but to Lucy, looking at her directly with that piercing gaze of his.

She felt rather like a butterfly pinned to a mat, but still she managed to reply. "Parkerton was Papa's mentor, and our benefactor all these years."

"Parkerton?" Clifton asked as if he hadn't heard her correctly.

"Yes," Lucy told him, sitting up straight. For something about the earl's doubt nudged her. Really, she had nothing to be ashamed of. Her father had served his King and country with all the loyalty of a good Englishman. While at times her father's actions had been both morally and legally questionable, he'd done what had been necessary to keep Britain's enemies at bay.

And there was no shame in that.

Mariana began gathering up the discarded cards, tallying the points and adding them to the sheet of paper at her elbow. "After His Grace plucked Papa from the streets,

135

he hired him tutors, sent him to Oxford and then on a Grand Tour. That was the beginning of Papa's career for the Foreign Office." She glanced over at her sister. "Oh, Goosie, remember the stories he used to tell us as children? Wonderful tales about his time in Egypt, in Russia, of how he met the contessa . . ." She paused for a moment. "Oh, yes, and when he saved Thomas-William from a slaver in France. Remember how he used to tell us all those glorious tales before we went to bed?"

Lucy considered kicking her sister again, for the claret had her prattling on like Mrs. Kewin and her spinster sister discussing the neighbors. "Yes, nothing like a story of murder and high treason to give one nightmares. I believe you spent most nights with bad dreams," she replied. "But it is hardly a proper subject —"

"Proper, Lucy?" the earl asked, reaching for the bottle and coming over to the table to refill Mariana's now empty glass.

As if her sister needed another glass of claret. She was already tippled enough to spill all their family secrets like an old ewe bleating in the field.

The earl paused, the bottle poised over Lucy's half-filled glass. "Pray tell, what is this sudden concern for propriety?"

Lucy shifted uneasily, blocking him from pouring by placing her hand over her glass. "It is just that Papa isn't always easy discussing his past with others." When he withdrew the bottle, she reached for the cards Mariana had dealt, gathering the boards in her hands. But she didn't look up at him. For she didn't want him to see the racing tumult within her.

My lord, I'm not easy with the subject. Not with you. Not yet . . .

Not before I can trust you.

Still he stood before their card table, and Lucy felt his presence like an immovable mountain.

"Malcolm," he said over his shoulder. "I fear we've overstayed our welcome. Ladies, my sincere appreciation for the excellent supper."

"Thank you, my lord," she replied, still not willing to look up, not wanting to stand up.

"It is well past time that we sought our beds. Morning will be upon us far too soon, I fear," he said.

"And more of those demmed codes of Ellyson's," Malcolm muttered in reply as he rose, drained his claret and set the empty glass back down.

"Actually, the codes are Lucy's," Mariana

137

corrected as she rearranged the cards in her hands. "She's quite brilliant at them, though Papa gets all the credit. Why, it was Lucy who came up with the idea of putting the codes in love letters."

Lucy's gaze sprang up; she couldn't stop herself. And there she found the earl studying her.

"You?" he asked. "I thought you disavowed love."

But before she could reply, Mariana laughed and said, "Lucy?! Oh, my lord, wherever did you get such an idea? I'll have you know my sister is the most romantic soul you'll ever meet."

Oh, good God, could this evening get any more mortifying? Lucy wished her sister in Egypt . . . or Portugal . . . or whatever front that would put her in the line of fire and prevent her from prattling on ever again.

Well, there was one other way to ensure that she didn't.

"I daresay you've had too much claret, Mariana," Lucy told her sister as she got up from the table. "And it is best that we call it an evening." She marched out of the parlor and was back in thrice with the gentlemen's hats and greatcoats, thrusting them toward Malcolm and Clifton without the least bit of subtlety.

138

Malcolm, cheeky devil that he was, grinned and wished them both a good night as he took his belongings and headed out the door.

But of course, the earl had to linger.

He bowed slightly after retrieving his coat and hat. "Lucy, you are a constant surprise," he said. Then he shocked her by reaching out and taking her hand, bringing it to his lips and placing a chaste and well-mannered kiss on the back. With his voice low, yet filled with a smoky hint of passion, he said, "It seems I have much to learn from you." Then he departed into the night, following his brother into the inky darkness.

And Lucy Ellyson had the distinct impression that he wasn't talking about just her codes.

CHAPTER 6

Lucy closed the door and listened to the receding thud of Clifton's boots as he followed his brother into the night. And the moment she gauged he was well out of earshot, she turned on her sister.

"You prattling nit! Whatever were you thinking?"

Mariana, who had been gathering up the plates and glasses and putting them on the tray, glanced over her shoulder. "What do you mean? I thought this evening was quite enjoyable." She paused. "Except for you and Lord Clifton sparring with each other."

"I was not sparring," Lucy shot back.

Mariana's response was one arched brow, but she didn't say anything further.

That didn't let her off the hook. Lucy pressed on. "Telling them about Monday Moggs. And Archie. And our lives." She drew in a deep breath and lowered her voice. "About Mother."

"Lucy, I don't see what —" Then Mariana stopped, her gaze narrowing. Most everyone thought Mariana was just as Lucy had said — a prattling nit — for she was her mother's daughter, but she was also an Ellyson, through and through. While perhaps not as talented as Lucy with letters and languages, she was a master at the subtleties of social codes. The sort of skill that had made their mother infamously successful at finding protectors amongst England's richest gentlemen. "Gracious goodness! You've fallen in love with Lord Clifton!"

Lucy about swallowed her teeth. "I have not!"

The tray and dishes forgotten, Mariana swept forward and circled her sister, eyeing her carefully. "Oh, no, I think you have. Something has changed about you."

Shaking out her skirt in hopes of shooing her sister away, Lucy crossed the room and began wiping down the sideboard. "Mariana, you've had too much wine. There is nothing changed about me. I find Lord Clifton as arrogant and loathsome as I have since the day he arrived."

Her sister stood her ground, her finger tapping her chin. "No, something has changed about you, Goosie. Whatever happened today when you took him up to the village?"

"Nothing unusual," she said, glancing away. "Rusty and Sammy came upon us just past the old oak."

Mariana waved this reply off. "Yes, yes, I could see that much. But I have to say the earl didn't look all that much worse for wear. One black eye? Do you remember poor Mad Jack? He looked as if he'd been run over by a freight wagon. I think you should tell Papa that Rusty and Sammy are holding back."

"Oh, they weren't holding back," Lucy said without thinking, images of the afternoon flitting through her thoughts. Clifton raised up to his full height, his features full of indignant fury, his fists squared and ready for battle.

A shiver ran down her spine. Lucy shook it off, for she didn't want to think about how he'd made her feel — trembling and full of desires she'd never suspected she could harbor. How had he done it? How had he set her knees knocking and her heart hammering?

Because this afternoon he showed you what a hero could look like . . .

"Not holding back? Truly?" Mariana shrugged. "I wouldn't have thought the earl capable —"

Capable? More than one could imagine . . .

Which Lucy tried her best not to do. Imagine, that is . . . the earl stripped to his waist, his muscles knotted across his chest . . . no, she couldn't think of him that way . . . not at all.

She glanced up and found Mariana eyeing her curiously. "If you must know," Lucy said, hoping to give her sister some tidbit so she'd toddle off happy with her nugget, "since it is obvious you want naught to do this evening but gossip, I had to stop him from dispatching Rusty to his reward."

The moment came back to her in a heated flash.

The way his hand shook with fierce passion beneath her fingers . . . it made her . . . oh, heavens . . .

The desires he'd sent through her — the need to have his arms around her, to have his solid chest up against hers, his lips taking what they wanted — were too dangerous to consider.

Especially now that she knew exactly what he was capable of . . .

Mariana whistled under her breath, as if she had read her sister's thoughts. "That must have been quite a sight. The earl turning the tables on the boys." Then she paused, and Lucy could practically see her thoughts awhirl as she stood before the tray of dishes she was absently rearranging. "Oh, heavens! You don't suppose he became so virile in order to protect you? That must be it! How terribly romantic!"

Lucy cringed, for her sister was getting far too close to the truth. "Good gracious heavens, Mariana, that is utter nonsense. Obviously we have misjudged the earl and he is far more competent than we had previously assumed."

"You mean to say, *you* misjudged him and that Lord Clifton is a far sight better man than *you* assumed," Mariana corrected. "I suppose if he'd rescued me, I would have the self-same change of heart. Especially if he had battled to save my honor."

Lucy closed her eyes. Why couldn't her sister have inherited a little more of their father's practical Ellyson side, rather than so much of their mother's Italian passion?

"My opinion has hardly —" Lucy said in her defense, but Mariana quickly cut her off.

"— hardly? You cooked *him* supper."

"I cooked *them* both supper," Lucy corrected. "For I knew they would be working late —"

Her argument hardly even dented Mariana's theory. Her sister now wore a sly smile and said in quick retort, "Papa works all the gentlemen who come through here late into the evening. And I don't recall you ever cooking a special supper for any of them . . . with the exception of Lord Roche. And that was only because he dared to corner you and try to —" Mariana came to a stop, a cup rattling in its saucer. "The earl tried to kiss you?"

Lucy wanted to protest, wanted to lie, but this was her sister, her dearest friend, and there was no getting past Mariana when she was snooping about. Still she tried. "No-no-no," she stammered. "He would never —"

Her sister's gaze narrowed. "He did! He tried to kiss you." She set down the cup and began circling Lucy once again. "And you wanted him to!"

If Mr. Pymm and Papa had had any sense, they would have sent Mariana abroad — for she could have unearthed a kingdom's secrets in a single outing.

Then again, she would have had to learn how to hold her prattling tongue. Like Lucy wished her sister would do right now. But it was too late.

"Lucy Louisa Ellyson! You fell in love with that man today, didn't you?"

■ ■ ■ ■

"Well, well, well," Malcolm mused as Clifton caught up with him. "You must have discovered your charm today."

"Pardon?"

Malcolm chuckled a bit. "That, or Lucy Ellyson assumed you'd been humiliated enough for one day and decided to declare a cease-fire."

Clifton shook his head. "I haven't the vaguest notion what you are talking about."

"The lady's obvious change of heart," Malcolm said. "But whatever you did, keep doing it, for that supper was the finest we've had since we left London. Even if it means you've got to go find another pair of thugs to shutter your other eye."

"You are mad — that, or just plain drunk," Clifton told him. "That meal was nothing more than a meal. She did it because . . ."

Well, demmit, he couldn't think of a good reason other than the obvious one.

That she'd had a change of heart today.

Or the other startling realization.

So had he.

From the moment he'd decided to take her into his arms and steal a kiss from her. The most rakish thing he'd ever done, but something about Lucy Ellyson emboldened him, provoked him into stepping out of his comfortable station in life and taking risks.

From the challenge and doubts in her bright green eyes, to the aching desire that had filled his very veins as he'd pulled her delectable curves up against him.

"She did it because . . . ?" Malcolm prodded. "I would venture to say you did more today than just attempt to charm her."

"I would leave off if I were you," Clifton warned.

But his brother wasn't so easily diverted. "What did happen on the way to the village? Besides you getting knocked about a bit."

"Nothing of note," Clifton told him. "I did take your advice and reached an accord with the chit. Perhaps her offer of dinner was her way of agreeing to my terms."

"You offered the lady terms?" Malcolm asked, a wry smile turning his lips. "Are you sure it wasn't Lucy Ellyson who gave you that shiner? Perhaps you and the illustrious Mr. Moggs could share a pint and the sad remembrances of your association with Miss Lucy Ellyson —"

"What drunken nonsense," Clifton said. "I believe you are as jug bit as Miss Ellyson."

"Quite contentedly so," his brother said. "Ah, the delightful Mariana. Wasn't she a fountain of knowledge this evening? Amazing that their mother is the Contessa di Marzo, isn't it?"

Shocking, really, Clifton would have said. But for his own reasons, he held his tongue. For how could he tell his brother that he had discovered that Lucy was as passionate as her mother was reputed to be?

Malcolm didn't seem to notice his silence and continued on, "Didn't old Latchford and Seawright fight a duel over the contessa last spring? Up in Buxton, wasn't it?"

"Yes, quite so. Old fools! Why, Latchford is nigh on eighty," Clifton remarked. "And Seawright had to steady himself with his cane to shoot. Dueling at their ages, indeed."

Malcolm snapped his fingers. "Yes, yes, now I recall it. Latchford insisted on settling her debts, and Seawright claimed it was his obligation. The Contessa di Marzo must be quite the Incognita to still inspire such passion. Then again, having seen her daughters, I can understand what would drive a man to such distraction — have you ever seen such eyes, such hair?"

Clifton felt a moment of possessive jealousy, until Malcolm continued by saying,

"Can you imagine Mariana in town?" He shook his head and let out a low whistle. "No wonder Ellyson keeps her hidden away here in Hampstead. But how the devil did an Italian contessa ever come into Ellyson's company? Let alone bear the man two daughters."

"Ply Miss Ellyson with more claret and I dare-say you will find out."

"I just may do that," Malcolm said. "Perhaps I can discover if she has inherited her mother's passionate nature."

"You had better hope she hasn't inherited her father's ruthless disposition," Clifton pointed out, thinking of Lucy's sharp gaze and challenging glances. "Or that Ellyson doesn't discover you plying his daughter with spirits."

Malcolm laughed, for he'd never been one for caution. "Are you warning me off or just giving yourself a bit of advice?"

Clifton glanced at his brother and realized that perhaps he wasn't as drunk as he'd assumed.

For in truth, perhaps he was. Warning himself off.

If only he hadn't discovered the truth about Lucy Ellyson this afternoon.

That she was an intriguing, irresistible handful. And that he wouldn't leave Hampstead without one kiss from her pert, tart lips.

Even if it meant he'd be sent packing from the Ellyson household with both of his eyes shuttered.

The next night and the night after that, once the clock tolled midnight and Mr. Ellyson fell asleep in his great chair in the corner of his map room, Clifton and his brother retreated down the stairs to find supper waiting for them courtesy of the Misses Ellyson.

The earl suspected that the elder Miss Ellyson, the affable and feather-headed Mariana, was more the instigator than her sister, for since their first impromptu supper, Lucy had said little, save to cut off her prattling sister when she'd begun to reveal too much information about their father or their lives in Hampstead.

Or as Lucy had muttered under her breath the previous evening, "Marry you off to Monday Moggs, I will."

Then again, Mariana Ellyson was a born storyteller and loved to have an audience to regale.

This evening, Clifton had stayed upstairs to finish translating a pouch of coded dispatches. He'd been stopped by the last lines, which were beyond his skill, but his distraction might have come from the previous letter, which had left him chilled to the bone.

I fear there is no good news to report on the fate of Bricknell. According to a local man I trust, he was caught just north of the Sierra de la Peña and shot the next morning. Assign a new agent to travel to this district and . . .

Clifton set his pen down, then pushed away the papers before him. He closed his eyes to the lines that summarily finished a man's life.

No ceremony, no hero's fanfare for poor Darby Bricknell. Just a notation in a report.

Shot by a French firing squad and his body tossed aside.

Assign a new agent . . .

Suddenly everything in Clifton's life became more precious than he'd ever imagined.

It was one thing to imagine the valor of serving the King, but quite another to face the reality of that commitment.

He bowed his head into his hands and tried to blot out the image of Bricknell's body.

Of his own tenuous fate.

What if he never came home? There was his uncle to inherit, yes, but something inside him tightened at the thought of Clifton House, the lands and the people left to his feckless relation's care.

What had he said to Lucy the other afternoon? Oh, yes, he remembered.

"I will love my future countess. Without a doubt, I will not marry without love."

His future had seemed so certain at that moment. He'd been so very confident. So smugly arrogant. He'd serve his country, come home, fall in love, marry and live out his days on his estate surrounded by his wife and children and all the comforts of his place in society.

But suddenly . . . he couldn't find the indisputability of such a future.

There was no time now to find that bride, obviously not one to love, let alone ensure that there was an heir before he rushed headlong into the madness that was Spain and Portugal and France. . . .

His eyes wide open, he sat back in his chair and raked his fingers through his hair, heaving a sigh.

And what of Malcolm? What if he was leading him into a fool's bargain . . .

Clifton shook that thought aside. He

didn't even want to consider a life without his brother by his side.

The documents before him argued that this was a likelihood he might well have to consider. For they contained lists of troop movements, skirmishes fought, men lost, requests for aid.

And there was more to the last dispatch to discover, but he needed help if he was to unlock the code.

Glancing over at his sleeping mentor, he knew he could wake the man and he'd easily show Clifton the pattern to deciphering the letter, but then again . . .

Go ask her to help you . . .

Going to a lady to ask for help went against everything he'd ever been raised to think. This business was no affair for a woman. Wars and espionage were the province of men, not to be inflicted on the delicate nature of ladies.

And then there was Lucy Ellyson, who defied every convention, working tirelessly beside her father to serve England with the same diligence as any loyal, upright Englishman might.

It was the sort of tenacity of spirit, the sharp intelligence, that made her more akin to a great queen of old than a mere lady.

She will save your life, Clifton. One day, she

will rescue you from a depth you will never have imagined.

The odd whisper of words tread over his soul like the hand of fate, sending a shiver down his spine.

He rose abruptly, nearly overturning his chair. In the corner where Ellyson slept in his great chair, the man stirred at the noise, but only for a moment before he let out another snore and was once again lost in his dreams.

What haunts you, George Ellyson? the earl wondered as he glanced at the old man. Here was a spy who'd served his country for fifty years, thirty of it in the field across the Continent. His adventures and narrow escapes were legend, as were the rumors of the dangerous, dirty deeds he'd done or overseen.

And yet here he'd come to rest in the quiet of Hampstead, beside his own fireplace surrounded by his daughters and loyal servants.

Let me come home, Clifton prayed as he gathered up the yet-to-be deciphered document and left the map room, making his way down the stairs. It wasn't fear that made him say those words but a deep desire to return to the green shores of England, to his estate beside the Thames, and continue his family line as so many of his forebears had done before him.

And to find a woman to share that life with . . .

That thought gave him pause and he stopped on the stairs, the light from the parlor down below gleaming like a tempting beacon.

She's right there, if only you dare. . . .

Clifton shook his head, as if trying to dislodge such a notion.

Lucy Ellyson indeed! His countess. What a ridiculous thought that.

And yet here he was continuing down the steps, his heart waking up and beating a little bit quicker. It wasn't just the thought of what she would have prepared for their dinner — for she was a devilish good cook — but what might the evening bring?

Last night the four of them, he and Malcolm, Lucy and Mariana, had played cards until the wee hours. Oh, it had been like playing with a pair of sharps, but so much more entertaining.

Mariana had flirted outrageously, giving every bit of evidence that she was indeed the daughter of the notorious Contessa di Marzo. She'd even offered to loan them the books their mother had sent them recently — French treatises on the arts of *l'amore* —

and from the blush that had risen on Lucy's face, he'd imagined they weren't the usual romantic drivel that young ladies devoured.

Still, Mariana's outrageous antics aside, he couldn't remember a night when he'd laughed more, or had been more reluctant to lay down the last card.

That is until he'd revealed it.

A queen of hearts.

And he'd glanced up to find Lucy shyly smiling at him. At him, and him alone.

Had she dealt it to him deliberately, or had it been by chance? Not that it mattered, for in that moment, Justin Grey, the fourteenth Earl of Clifton, had found himself mesmerized. Lost in her eyes, his mouth dry, his heart stilled.

Lucy Ellyson had gone from being George Ellyson's headstrong, wily daughter to the most enchanting miss he'd ever met. He would have told her as much right there and then, but knowing her, she would have laughed him right out of her parlor.

Or worse, sent him packing, as she had Monday Moggs. And since Clifton currently had only one good eye, it was risk he wasn't willing to take.

Not until he'd gotten that kiss.

He heaved a sigh at that folly, but then realized that perhaps Lucy Ellyson was why he'd decided to take up Jack and Temple's offer to join the Foreign Office.

Not Lucy per se, but he'd looked at the available misses in London and found them a dull lot. The prospect of marriage to one of those manageable, proper ladies had been a worse sentence than being caught by the French.

But here was Lucy, like the gatekeeper to a rare and dangerous world, and all he needed to do was dare to steal the key from her.

Steal that kiss.

As he got to the bottom of the stairs, he paused on the last step. From this vantage point, he could see the table set for four, though only Mariana and Malcolm were in there, already eating and chatting away as if they had known each other for years.

Lucy was nowhere to be seen, which was probably why her sister was in the middle of an outlandish tale about how her father had escaped Paris with the help of Thomas-William.

He stood in the doorway and listened, as rapt as Malcolm appeared to be.

"The French agent who shot Father had left him to die in the alley, not knowing that Thomas-William was close at hand," Mariana was saying. "Thomas-William could have fled, for he would have had his freedom if he'd done so."

Malcolm laughed. "Yet he stayed and helped your father."

"He saved Papa's life," she said. "Got him out of Paris and to the coast where they could gain a ship home. Papa remembers none of it, but as I've heard it told, they barely escaped with their lives. In one village, Thomas-William lied to the authorities, hinting that Papa was a Russian nobleman who had dallied with *le duc*'s wife and been shot trying to escape the lady's bedchamber."

"A Russian nobleman? And the authorities believed that?"

Mariana leaned forward and smiled like a conspirator. "It helped that Father was feverish and all he would speak was Russian."

Malcolm laughed. "He's lucky the French authorities didn't turn him in."

"Oh, no! Bless the good people of that village. They thought Thomas-William's story and Papa's perilous situation quite romantic!"

They both laughed, and Clifton was struck by the pure sound of his brother's high spirits. Malcolm fit into this household so easily; Clifton envied his brother.

For as much as he tried, something still held him back.

Too many centuries of Grey blood in his veins. The weight of his forebears keeping him in place, reminding him of his obligation to dutifully and properly safeguard the family's inheritance, their perfect lineage, their place in Society.

By not falling in love with the daughter of a thief and an Italian Incognita.

"Whatever is she going on about now?" Lucy whispered from behind him.

He nearly jumped out of his jacket, for she'd come upon him with that catlike skill of hers. "The time when your father and Thomas-William escaped Paris," he whispered back.

She rolled her gaze upward. "Which version?"

Clifton glanced over at Mariana's animated features and smiled. "Something about *le duc* and your father being Russian."

Lucy nodded. "That's her favorite one."

"Is it true?"

She shrugged. "I don't know. Father doesn't remember how he got from Paris to England, and Thomas-William, well, he's never very forthcoming about the past. So Mariana" — she flexed her shoulders — "gives the story her own embellishments."

"Malcolm is entertained."

"Then Mariana will be pleased," she said in a wistful little voice. "It isn't often she has such an attentive audience."

"But surely —"

She stopped him right there. "No, my lord. As Mariana said the other night, we are not received. You and your brother are the most company we've had — well, ever."

"Because of your mother?" he asked softly.

She glanced toward her sister, her gaze more far away, and then she nodded. "That, and of course, Father's reputation."

"How did your father . . ." he began. Oh, bother, how did one ask such a question? "What I mean to say is . . ."

She crossed her arms over her chest. "What you want to know is how did a man like my father end up in the company of a married Italian contessa?"

"Yes, I suppose that is it," he said.

Lucy smiled and told the story in a soft tone that he'd never heard her use. It was like a child reciting a favorite bedtime tale, and this one had all the requisite pieces.

"Our mother was married at a very early age to the Count di Marzo, who was nearly thirty years her senior and a disreputable brute. Parkerton had gone to meet with the count in hopes of forming a trade alliance with the man, for he was one of Venice's leaders."

"And that is how they met," Clifton said.

She nodded. "There was a masked party and the English contingent was all there, including my father. He spied my mother from across the room and was immediately smitten." She paused. "Do you believe in love at first sight, my lord?"

He shook his head. "Not really."

"Nor do I," she agreed. "But Papa claims he knew right then she would be his. And at midnight, at the unmasking, he searched for her but couldn't find her. So, being who he was, he made a more thorough search of the count's palace."

"He stole through the house," Clifton said.

"Yes, like the thief he was. And he found the contessa — for he had no idea who she was — on a high balcony with her back to him. It was evident she'd been crying. She begged him not to come closer, but he insisted on knowing the reason for her distress." Lucy glanced away.

"Whatever was wrong?" the earl asked.

"She'd been beaten by her husband and couldn't stay for the unmasking because everyone would have seen her disgrace — the bruises on her face and throat."

"Dear God! Her husband had done this?"

"Yes, because she had yet to bear the count a child. Never mind that his previous four wives had all been childless, the count was convinced the problem could not lie with him, and so . . ."

"He punished her."

Lucy nodded. "Papa asked her why she didn't leave, but she explained the count kept her a virtual prisoner, didn't trust her out of his sight, and even this — her leaving the party — would most likely have her punished further."

"So he saved her," Clifton supplied.

"Yes. Snuck her out and onto the Duke of Parkerton's ship in the harbor. Parkerton had no idea what Papa had done and they sailed with the early tide, taking the contessa with them. When he discovered the count's wife aboard, he was furious, until he met her — and was charmed. Utterly and completely, as Papa was."

"I've heard your mother could sway an entire legion to lay down their arms."

"She has a way about her," Lucy conceded. "Mariana is very much like her."

"Yet there is more to the story," Clifton said.

"Oh, certainly, though most people know it," she said with a shrug.

"I don't," he said.

She laughed. "Then you haven't been out in Society enough, for there isn't a Season that passes without some new scandal and the contessa embroiled right in the middle of it. She loves to be in the eye of the storm."

"Like you?"

Then, as she always did when the topic got too close, too personal, she changed the subject, nodding at the papers in his hands. "Papa doesn't approve of dispatches leaving the map room."

He glanced down at the forgotten missives. "My apologies. I didn't know. But I needed some help with these last passages, and thought . . . well, hoped . . ." He faltered to a halt and looked at her. Dared to gaze into her intelligent eyes.

"You want my assistance?" she asked, as if amazed that he'd even made such a suggestion.

He stilled and glanced down at the woman before him, her gaze alight at the prospect of a challenge. "Why, yes. I've come to realize in the last few days that you are quite extraordinary . . ."

She took a wary sort of step back, as if she knew what he truly meant. But there was a spark to her eyes, a shiver to her arms.

". . . at these sorts of things," he added hastily. "These codes and alike."

"Yes, of course, with the codes," she replied, glancing away.

He couldn't tell if she looked relieved or vexed.

"And your father was unavailable . . ." he said, nattering on like Mariana after her second glass of claret.

"Yes, I suppose Papa is asleep —"

"He is, and I didn't want to —"

"No, no, it is best not to disturb him."

They both glanced at the parlor, where Mariana and Malcolm were laughing over some bit of gossip Mariana had gleaned from Mrs. Kewin. Their laughter filled the room.

"Perhaps we could go in the kitchen," she offered. "It is quieter in there." Then she turned and headed — some might even have said fled — for the kitchen at the back of the house.

Not that he was about to let her get away.

He followed her down the hall, smiling to himself at the purposeful click of her heels, like a regiment going into battle.

The kitchen was cast in shadows, the single light of a candle burning on the large table in the corner and the glow of the coals in the hearth the only light.

Lucy moved through the room as if she could have done so blindfolded, fetching another candle down from the hearth and adding its glow to the table, giving them enough light to read by.

But instead of settling down, she went to the stove and pulled a plate from the warming chamber.

"Malcolm said you might be delayed, so I set your supper in there to keep it warm." She smiled and settled down beside him. "I hate cold meals, don't you?"

"Very much so," he said. "You really do an excellent job of managing your father's house."

"Thank you. I've been doing so since the contessa left."

"When was that?"

"About ten years ago. She never fit into Hampstead, and Hampstead was just too small for her. One day she was here, and the next . . ." Lucy shrugged. "As for my skill as a housekeeper, be grateful you weren't here in the early days. I had much to learn. Thank goodness I have become good at it, for once Papa is gone, it may end up being my livelihood."

"When your father is gone?"

"Yes, of course. He's not a young man."

"No, I suppose not." George Ellyson was well into his seventies. "But why wouldn't you stay here?"

Why wouldn't you marry?

She shook her head as she uncorked the wine and poured him a glass. "The house isn't ours. It belongs to Parkerton. The old duke granted Papa the use of the house during his lifetime, but when he dies, the house goes back to the estate."

"But Parkerton would never —"

"The old duke perhaps. But his son hasn't a notion of what his father did —"

"You mean the spying?"

"Yes." Then she laughed. "Jack swears it would give his brother apoplexy to think of their sainted father as 'mucking about with the lower classes.' Can you imagine the fit the current duke would have if he knew what his brother was doing with Thistleton Park? The smuggling he might not mind, but the spying?" She shuddered.

"Well, the current duke has never been a fan of Mad Jack's antics — heroic or otherwise." Clifton smiled, for the current Duke of Parkerton was renowned for his fastidious and lofty notions.

"Exactly," Lucy said as she returned to the stove and set it to rights. "No, I am resigned that when Papa dies, Mariana and I will have to make our own way in the world."

"But certainly if you were to ask Jack or

Templeton to —"

She turned sharply toward him. "No. Mariana and I would never use our connections thusly. An Ellyson never takes charity. We earn our keep." She shuddered, as if asking such a favor would be too close to . . .

Too close to being like their mother. Taking favors and money from men to pay her rent and alike.

And in the bargain, gaining the scorn of proper Society.

Expertly, she moved the conversation in a different direction. "If all else fails, I will make an excellent housekeeper. Though I still hold out hopes that Mariana's fair face will grant her good marriage despite our lack of decent breeding. That way, if I cannot find a placement, I can make myself useful in her household."

"I have to imagine your forthright, managing ways will serve you well," he said, knowing that most ladies would deplore being described in such a manner.

"Thank you," she replied, taking his words not as censure but the praise that they were.

Without asking, she traded the papers before him for a plate of bread and butter and settled in to start deciphering.

It didn't take her long to find the problem.

"Bloody hell," she muttered under her breath.

"Pardon me?" he asked, glancing up from his supper and his musings about the contessa and her remarkable daughters.

"Oh, my apologies, my lord," she said.

Was it his imagination, or was Lucy Ellyson blushing?

"It is just that this is completely muddled. It is almost as if it was written in a very great hurry and he hasn't remembered which code to use." She heaved a sigh and continued to scan the lines.

"Do you recognize the hand?"

"Yes, 'tis Darby's." She shook her head. "Dear man. Though a bit high-strung — Baron Risby's third son. I wonder what has him in such a fettle?"

"Darby?" Clifton managed. "Darby Bricknell?"

"Yes. He's engaged to the Earl of Wyton's daughter. Patient creature to put up with Darby's hijinks. Do you know him?"

"No," was all he could manage, his mouth dry, his appetite having fled.

Rising, she went to a sideboard and brought over a pen and ink. Taking up a blank page, she began to move the words around, changing letters in an order that was boggling. But finally she had the passage written out.

"However do you know this is correct?"

"Because I wrote the code," she said. "Though Darby got overly hurried here and substituted the wrong numerical sequence. 'Tis what makes it confusing. Though I can see why. He writes that the French are closing in on his position and that he fears there is a traitor in Marseilles. He wants Larken sent to stop who might be betraying us."

Clifton's blood chilled. "*Is* betraying us."

"Is? No, Darby writes *might*. He isn't certain of the matter. Papa says to never jump to —"

He didn't know why he did it, why the words burst out of him. "Darby is dead, Lucy. He was betrayed. There is no 'might' about it."

She stilled beside him. "No, that isn't so. You see he's written this. I know his hand."

"But that wasn't the only missive in the packet," he said, shuffling the papers and pulling out the one that told the entire story.

She took it from him, scanning the lines quickly. By the time she got to the end of the page, her hands trembled. "Darby lost?" she said, her voice a strangled whisper. "No, I won't believe it. You've translated this wrong. You must have."

She rose abruptly and backed away from

the table. "It happens often. Bad news turns out to be naught but a rumor, and in a month or so, the truth . . . the truth is . . ."

Clifton rose as well, for the tremble in her voice wrenched at his heart.

"I won't have it," she declared. "Not Darby. Not any of them. Not . . . not . . ."

She looked up at him, her features stricken, her eyes filled with tears that had yet to fall.

Not you . . . her words seemed to cry out.

"I won't allow it," she continued. "I won't."

And then she proved his earlier worries wrong.

For there was someone to grieve Darby's loss.

With her hands pressed to her face, Lucy Ellyson wept for the man lost to England.

And he knew without a doubt this wasn't the first time she'd shed tears for one of her father's students.

Nor would it be the last. Not until there was an end put to this bloody war.

Lucy tried her best to stop crying, but Clifton's revelation had tipped her world upside down.

If an agent as good as Darby could end up dead, then they were all at risk.

Of course, she knew that. Knew it like one knew not to show Rusty and Sammy where you kept the silver. But it wasn't something she spent too much time considering as the men came and went from her father's house. Some gentlemen, like Darby, stuck in her memory because he'd been such an apt pupil and an engaging personality.

Or men like Jack or Templeton or Larken, who served for their own reasons, whose skills were honed by the very devils that drove them into the Foreign Office's elite service.

She helped her father train them, read their dispatches home, followed their travels on the collection of maps upstairs, worried when no word came from them for months at a time, and drank a glass of wine in quiet celebration when a note finally made its way to Hampstead via a long string of alliances . . . and small miracles.

But Darby? Not Darby! His parents, his betrothed. He'd had a future planned as a solicitor. And now all that was gone.

Lost to a French firing squad.

Damn the French, she wanted to cry out. *To hell with Bonaparte and his unholy ambitions.*

She beat her fists against something hard and unforgiving and at that moment realized that the wall before her was Clifton's chest.

When he'd pulled her into his arms, into the safety of his embrace, she didn't know. Though it had been long enough to make a wet mess of his cravat and a good portion of his shirt.

And as much as she wanted to stay there, in the warm confines of Clifton's arms, with the steady, confident rhythm of his heart beating beneath her hands, she pulled back and pushed away from him, embarrassed to have turned into such a watering pot in front of him.

How he must think her a foolish nit.

But he wasn't about to let her go just yet. Clifton caught her easily and tugged her back into his arms, his hands smoothing back the wayward strands of her hair, gently banishing the tears from her cheeks with soft, tender strokes.

With each touch of his hand, she felt her fears brush away, replaced by a need she couldn't understand. A need that welled up inside her with the same fierce passion, the same hunger that had left her railing against the French.

A burning desire for something that would last. Something no one could destroy.

Lucy dared a glance up at the man who

held her, and in an instant she tumbled headlong into the dark tempest of his gaze.

Knew exactly what she wanted . . . needed . . . this terrible night.

She needed to feel something other than this aching emptiness that seemed capable of consuming her.

"Please," she whispered, reaching up and touching his lips with a single finger. "Please, my lord."

For what seemed like an eternity, he just gazed down at her, as if he was memorizing every line of her face, every nuance, every curve.

As if he was taking that second look, the one he claimed every man had to seek before he knew.

What he was thinking, what he thought of her, she couldn't fathom; she only hoped he held the same desire for her, the same need that clamored inside her.

Then something flashed in those dark eyes of his, an acquiescence of sorts. Dare she even think it, a resolve? And without saying a word, he lowered his mouth to hers and kissed her with a rare hunger that matched her own.

Oh, the other afternoon had been but a hint of what was to come, and now Lucy discovered what it meant for a man to claim a woman.

There was nothing tentative about his hold on her; he tugged her close and kissed her thoroughly, as if he understood her ragged need to *feel* and not be treated with gentle compassion.

His tongue swiped over her lips and she opened up for him, her heart hammering. His lips tasted of the wine she'd just poured, but it was this kiss, this deepening kiss, that was leaving her intoxicated, trembling.

Then again, Clifton wasn't just kissing her, he was ravishing her, his hands roaming over her, leaving a trail of desire that rang with a dangerous chord.

She even heard the *plink* of a hairpin as it fell victim to his assault, her hair tumbling loose in his fiery wake.

Not that she was about to protest, for his touch was bringing her to life. Sending a very symphony of pleasure down her limbs.

Touch me again, my lord. Oh, yes, again. Never stop . . . never.

And when she thought she couldn't take it anymore, when her insides began to twist with an ache that would have begged him to do so much more, she moaned.

At first softly, then louder when his hand came to her breast and cupped it, held it, caressed it. She couldn't help herself, for his touch was unleashing all the pent-up dreams she'd hidden away for so long.

But it was that earthy, passionate moan that was her undoing, for it seemed to reach inside the earl and awaken some sort of devilishly noble sensibility.

He broke away, his chest heaving, as if he'd just battled Rusty and Sammy. And his face held the same sort of fierce passion that she'd witnessed then as well.

Was he furious with her? Was he taking a second look now and regretting his actions?

Damn this man, if only she could decipher those unreadable eyes of his.

Oh, how she must look! Struggling to catch her breath, her lips swollen from his bruising kiss, her hair all a-tumble.

"I'm so sorry," she gasped. "I don't know what I was thinking. It was just that as I considered what happened to Darby, I feared what could . . ." Her voice began to tremble again and she pressed her lips shut, afraid of what would tumble out if she dared to say more.

If she said the words that pounded with the same hammering beat as her heart. *I feared what could happen to you . . .*

Oh, heavens, Lucy, pull yourself together. But every time she tried to banish the image of Darby's bullet-ridden body from her lurid imagination, it was Clifton's handsome face she saw lying there. His eyes blank, staring heavenward.

"Was Darby a good agent?" he asked quietly.

She blinked and stared at him. "Pardon?"

"Darby. Was he a good agent?"

Lucy drew a breath to steady herself and nodded. "Yes. One of the best, or so I always thought."

He straightened a bit, his shoulders going taut. "And now?"

"Well, he failed," she said, hating herself to have to say such a thing about the man.

"And what would have made him the best?"

"Coming home," she said, sitting back and looking up into Clifton's eyes, so darkly serious.

She could see it now. See it so clearly. He knew. He knew now the cost.

But there was no fear in his eyes. Just that resolute determination to do the task ahead.

No matter what the Fates had in store for him.

In the face of his stalwart resolve, something inside Lucy cracked. It wasn't just the lingering passion of his kiss, or the fond memories of the evenings past. No, something had grown between them in the last few days, so quickly, so stealthily, that she couldn't quite believe it.

But there was one thing for certain. The very idea of reading some dusty, wrinkled dispatch, a note, a line in a report that held the words that would break her heart, wasn't one she intended to face.

She wouldn't even consider.

Lucy tossed her hair back out of her face and drew up her shoulders, much as he had. She gazed into those dark eyes of his and silently made her vow.

Demmit, she was going to make this man the finest agent the Foreign Office had ever seen.

So that no matter what, he would come home.

CHAPTER 7

The next week turned into a whirl of activity for Clifton. Instead of cozy suppers, cards and Mariana's lively conversation, or *ahem,* gossip, their evenings were now spent — once a hasty supper was concluded — with added lessons, ones that encompassed all the skills that made the Ellyson sisters unique.

Mariana spent hours showing them the intricacies and vagaries of opening locks. Before the dawn, Malcolm had picked George Ellyson's safe open, as well as the locks to his wine cabinet and the lockbox he kept hidden under the floorboards in his map room.

Under his great chair.

That one had been tricky, for they'd had to go into the room and pry the floorboard up without waking him, but Lucy had shown them how to move quietly through the room, and what to look for.

Clifton hadn't Malcolm's touch with the picks, but the next night, Lucy dragged a reluctant Thomas-William up and coerced him into teaching the Greys everything about cards — how to deal from anywhere in the deck, counting cards, how to read the faces of less-skilled players and, of course, how to spot other cheats and the best means to outwit them.

By the end of the evening, Clifton sat at the end of the table with a pile of markers before him, having trounced Lucy soundly in round after round of *vingt-et-un* until she had cried off and declared him the worst cheat she had ever met.

The next night, unsure of what they would find upon entering the parlor, Clifton was shocked to discover a grinning Rusty and Sammy waiting for them. All dressed in black, they'd also brought dark coats for Malcolm and Clifton, whom they then took out to "teach the fine art of being a cracksman."

" 'Tis a privilege for you to be learning from the best, I tell you, milord," Sammy said, before showing Clifton how to use a "bess," a small pry bar that opened a door quickly and quietly to gain entrance to a house.

They then proceeded to rob four houses

in Hampstead. The next day, the entire citizenry was in an uproar over the ring of criminals who had targeted their quiet corner.

As the debate raged around them in the public room of their inn the next morning, Malcolm glanced across the table at Clifton and said quietly, "What do you think they would make of the bess in my coat pocket?"

Clifton laughed, for none of the descriptions of the craven criminals the locals suspected fit the earl and his half brother.

The next day the hullabaloo died out when all the households that had been broken into found rich purses sitting innocently on their front steps and the mystery became a local legend.

The real challenge, Clifton discovered, was trying to ignore his desire for Lucy. To keep his thoughts off that unforgettable moment when she'd sought his arms, his lips, and he'd discovered what a passionate fire burned beneath her determined façade.

The moment when he'd kissed her and discovered that a woman could fit into your arms like no other, that she could move from your arms into your heart in the blink of an eye.

But there was no obvious sign from Lucy that their passionate encounter had ever happened.

She'd gone back to her brusque, no-nonsense manners, consumed by the lessons she laid out each evening. And Clifton let her, for he knew she shared the conflict raging inside him — for he'd caught her on more than one occasion slanting a glance at him with a finger on her lips, as if she were recalling that wayward moment.

So you find this as vexing and utterly impossible as I do, Goosie, do you? Whatever are we to do? he thought as he stood in the parlor after a delicious supper of roasted chicken and listened as his unorthodox teacher explained the rudimentary arts of picking a pocket.

For it was a skill, she declared, that was indispensable to a good agent.

"Come now, Lord Clifton, try again," she coached, gesturing him to move toward her, not that he needed any encouragement to draw closer, for tonight she'd donned an enchanting pink silk gown and looked, in his humble estimation, like a vision.

But when he came across the room, she shook her head vehemently.

"No! No! No!" she protested. "You are much too stiff." She stood with her hands on her hips, elbows thrust out and her face set with determination. "You walk and move like an earl."

"But I am an earl," he reminded her with an equal measure of lofty mettle.

"A pity that," she said, shaking her head as if he had the pox, not an estate, fortune and a name that went back fourteen generations.

Clifton threw up his hands. "A wha-a-at?"

"A pity, Gilby," Malcolm said, laughing from where he stood leaning against the doorjamb. "She thinks your illustrious breeding and enviable title are a damned pity."

And much to his dismay, Lucy held out her hands to Malcolm in agreement. "Exactly. You must stop thinking so nobly. So honorably."

"Good luck there," Malcolm teased before he started to laugh again. "My brother is Clifton through and through. But I daresay I haven't such hindrances, Lucy." He pushed off from the door and nearly collided with Mariana, who was coming in from the kitchen.

"Whatever has everyone laughing?" she asked, joining the party by sitting down on the bench in front of the pianoforte.

"I am trying," her sister told her, "to get his lordship to loosen up his approach so he seems more nonchalant."

"Yes, and he's bungling it," Malcolm teased. "For he hasn't got our common touch."

Mariana laughed. "I wouldn't be so smug, Mr. Grey, or tease your brother so mercilessly."

"And whyever not?"

"For you will never realize that your watch and fob have gone missing."

Clifton glanced first at Malcolm, who began to pat his coat, and then to Mariana, who pulled from her pocket the watch and chain their father had given him.

"Dear me," she said quite innocently, glancing at the treasure dangling from her fingers, "however did I come by this?"

"What the devil?!" Malcolm exclaimed. "You blasted minx! How did you —"

Mariana laughed and preened, while her sister and Clifton joined in.

"Mind the lesson a little closer, will you, Malcolm?" he advised.

His brother glared at Mariana and then sent the girl a rakish wink. "I'll get that back."

"You'll try," she said just as flirtatiously.

There was the stomp of a heel from their taskmaster in the corner. "Come now, if you are going to learn this properly, you need to attend me," Lucy ordered.

Clifton bowed slightly to her, precisely and elegantly so, if only to irritate her.

And it did. "*Harrumph.* Blast it all, my lord, you will never be able to pick a pocket if you persist on being so . . . so . . ."

"Stiff-rumped?" Malcolm suggested.

Mariana was polite enough to cover her mouth and cough slightly to hide her amusement.

Clifton threw up his hands. "I ask you, how the devil am I supposed to retrieve the key in your pocket when you know I am coming for it?"

"You need to focus, and concentrate on what needs to be done," Lucy told him.

"Oh, Lucy, now you sound as top-lofty as he does." Mariana got up and sauntered toward Malcolm, offering her own advice over her shoulder. "My lord, picking a pocket is nothing more than a seduction." She turned and flashed a dazzling smile at Malcolm, who stepped back warily.

Apparently he wasn't about to give up his wallet as well as his watch.

Mariana continued to talk as she stalked Malcolm like a lioness. "Pinching a purse is about seeming to be about one thing when your intention is quite different. You can appear to be choosing items from a buffet supper, distracted by a letter you might be reading, or approaching a lady with a light in your eye that suggests you would like to divest her of something altogether different."

And with that, Mariana had Malcolm cornered, and simply offered him back his watch.

Malcolm took a deep breath. "Are you asking *my* brother to flirt?"

Mariana glanced over her shoulder at Clifton. "Of course."

Malcolm laughed, and this time he doubled over until tears ran down his cheeks.

"What?" Clifton protested. "I am damn well capable of flirting with a woman!"

Much to his chagrin, they all began to laugh.

"I'll have you know I had Lady Galloway on tenterhooks when we were last in town," he declared.

"Oh, yes, I had quite forgotten," Malcolm said, then, in an aside to the ladies, revealed, "quite the conquest there. What he neglects to say is that the marchioness is a grandmother of seven."

Clifton straightened. "She is?"

This time, they all laughed, and in that moment, he realized why he'd done this — let himself get talked into something as ignoble as spying: he'd always envied Malcolm his freedom, and for the first time in his life, the Earl of Clifton was no longer encumbered by his name, his rank, his title, the expectations that clung to him like a Weston jacket.

He was Justin Grey. A man with desires and dreams and a willingness to dare to defy Society's expectations. The freedom was a heady brew, and it opened up his eyes to a world that had always been out of his reach, out of his realm.

But now that he'd stepped out of his privileged existence, he'd discovered a life worth living. What it meant to feel, to fight, to live. Just as he had the other afternoon when he'd found himself brawling in the lane like a common bruiser, relishing every punch . . .

Just as he had when he'd kissed Lucy Ellyson. She'd opened a door to a passion he'd pledged to find. One he'd certainly never thought to discover in a kitchen in Hampstead.

That, and this new life gave him a license to commit all sorts of felonies and crimes, real and imagined, that no honorable man would ever consider.

And he rather liked that notion.

Clifton shook off their amusement at his

expense and turned his attention to Lucy, who was right now wiping tears from her eyes.

"Are you sure you wouldn't like to practice on Mrs. Kewin?" she said, that wry, teasing, daring smile on her lips.

"No, I can manage you," he said back, drawing a deep breath.

"Oh, can you now?" She swaggered a bit toward him. "So try again, just as I taught you."

He shook his head. "No. I prefer your sister's suggestion."

Her eyes widened just a bit as Mariana's words rang through both their thoughts.

My lord, picking a pocket is nothing more than a seduction.

And when she glanced up at him, her eyes betrayed her. *You wouldn't dare.*

"I don't think —" she began, her swagger now replaced with a retreat as she edged backward.

And in her sudden change of demeanor, Clifton saw it all so clearly, as if the room stilled and his mission came into sharp focus.

He fixed his gaze on her and began to move forward.

From her place by the pianoforte, Mariana offered encouragement. "Yes, yes, milord. That is it, exactly. Envision Madrid. A ballroom." She sat down and began to play notes both soft and seductive. "Ask her to dance."

"Madame," he said, bowing slightly, his gaze never leaving hers, keeping her trapped in his unmoving scrutiny. "May I have this dance?"

"No!" Lucy told him. Because they both knew it wasn't merely a dance he sought.

Malcolm had moved beside Mariana and was turning the pages for her as she continued to play. "Convince her."

"Yes, you must," Mariana added. "She has the information that will bring you home, my lord."

Bring you home.

Those words spurred him forward. And as he looked into Lucy's green eyes, so very much like the color of an English spring, he found his heart. He found the steadfast resolve to face the trials ahead of him. Because demmit, he would come home. He would. He'd come home to her.

It was a startling notion. He wanted her. Her alone. And to get her, he needed to convince her he was worthy.

Worthy of stealing the keys tucked in her pocket. Worthy of unlocking the padlock she kept over her heart.

"Come now, Gilby. Don't give up. Convince her to dance with you," Malcolm called out.

Clifton bowed again, lower this time, then caught her hand as he rose and brought it to his lips. "Madame, may I have this dance?" he murmured over her fingertips.

"No!" she said, trembling and snatching back her hand.

No? So she was going to make this difficult. He liked that about her. No fawning miss, no anxious debutante looking to win his favor.

Just Lucy Ellyson, and her stubborn, obstinate defiance. But he could also see that he had her on the ropes.

"But I insist," he said, moving closer.

This time she stood her ground. "And I must insist as well. I do not dance with gentlemen whom I haven't been properly introduced to."

"Not introduced?" He shook his head and reached out to recapture her hand. "Such an oversight." He raised her fingers to his lips and kissed them, tasted them. It was like being given the merest drop of an intoxicating, tantalizing liquor, for just the feel of her fingers on his lips sent a thunderbolt of desire through him, urging him to pull her into his arms and kiss her again.

189

But this was a seduction, and he let go of her hand, watching with some satisfaction as she brought it to her lips, to cover her gaping mouth.

Was it him, or was she shivering?

Leaning closer, Clifton paused, his lips not far from her ear, and there he let his words whisper over her. "For you, my dear lady, will one day be my countess."

"I beg your pardon?" she managed as she tried to move away. But with him in front of her and the fireplace behind her, there was little room for escape. "I don't think —"

"My countess," he repeated. He vowed. His other hand planted itself on the mantel behind her; now he had her completely cornered. "My only desire."

He reached out and cupped her chin, forced her to look up into his eyes so she could see that he meant it. That he wasn't going to forget her.

"I-I-I . . . that is, I don't think —"

Clifton grinned, for he hadn't seen her this undone since he'd told her he'd marry only for love. And now with her off balance, he let his hand drop, curling it around her waist and pulling her close.

And in that moment, with her wonderfully curved charms tucked up against him, with her mouth parted, ready and willing, he began his larcenous career, stealing from her the one thing he wanted to take. . . .

However could she object? These were her lessons, after all.

His lips crashed down on hers. At first there was nothing but a *mew* of protest from her, her hands balled up against his chest as if ready to beat out her refusal.

But that refusal never came.

It was as if the last week had left Lucy as filled up with pent-up need as it had him, and she kissed him back, her fingers twining into his lapels, tugging him closer.

Her tongue slid against his, enticing him to explore her, to give her the pleasure she hungered for.

As her hips brushed over his growing need for her, Clifton nearly forgot himself. Forgot where he was.

Forgot that they were kissing before an audience.

"Bravo! Bravo!" Malcolm called out. "Well done, Gilby! I didn't know my proper brother had it in him."

Lucy pushed away from him, her eyes bright and her face flushed.

He didn't know whether he was about to suffer Monday Moggs's fate or she was about to send Malcolm and her sister packing.

"Yes, yes, quite improper, my lord," Mariana added, clapping her hands like a delighted audience. "I think you have rattled Lucy right out of her slippers. But the real question is, did you gain your reward?"

He glanced back at Mariana and grinned, then turned to Lucy and held up his real prize.

The keys she had tucked in her apron pocket.

Her mouth fell open in a wide O. "You wretched devil!" she exclaimed as she snatched them back. "You cheated."

"All is fair in love and war, Goosie," he whispered to her, chucking her lightly under the chin. "And you are the fairest of them all."

She moved past him, her steps as determined as ever. "I can see you are going to be entirely insufferable from here on out. You great, conceited —"

Before she could finish, Mariana's laughter filled the room. "He's bested you, Lucy. What does it feel like to have finally met your match?"

And Lucy Ellyson's answer was telling.

She let out a disagreeable *"Harrumph."*

Clifton took it as evidence that he had indeed stolen more than her keys — not that she was going to let on.

Not yet, anyway.

The rest of the evening was a blur for Lucy. Even after Clifton and his brother left, she found no peace in the silence of the house, so she went upstairs to her father's map room to file away the dispatches that had come in earlier.

But when she got up there, she found her father awake, sitting in his chair and staring at the flames in the fireplace.

"Papa, you're awake," she said, surprised to find him so.

"That I am, Goosie," he said, taking a long look at her. "I've been considering a difficult matter."

His scrutiny left her unsettled, but she crossed the room and began to sort the maps on the table as if there was nothing unusual about her arrival in his study.

"And that is?" she asked as nonchalantly as she could muster.

"You've taken a keen interest in the earl and his brother," he said, eyeing the pink gown she wore — her finest dress, in fact.

She stilled and waited, for she knew him well enough to know this was no mere observation but merely the beginning of his inquiry.

The fire crackled, and after a few moments, her father cleared his throat and asked, "Do you think that is wise?"

Lucy glanced up at him, for that was the last thing she'd expected him to say. "I only meant . . . that is to say, Mariana and I thought to help them."

"You and Mariana?" One bushy brow cocked with skepticism.

"I did," Lucy replied, taking full responsibility.

"I thought as much," he said. "Be wary, daughter."

"I don't know what you —"

"You know exactly what I mean. Guard your heart. You can try as hard as you may to give someone everything they need, but that won't guarantee they will come back to you."

She wondered if he was speaking of Clifton or her mother. For she knew her father had tried every way possible to give the contessa the life she'd desired, but it had never been enough.

He had never been enough.

"You have no cause to be concerned, Papa," she told him. "Naught but lessons in a bit of thievery and cards."

"And?" he pressed.

"No more," she told him, feeling the press of his questions, the weight of his scrutiny.

194

But this was George Ellyson, and there were few who could escape his examination.

Even his daughter.

"Goosie, I won't bandy this about, any more than I will see your heart broken. As much as you fancy this man, he will never have you. Not in a way that is honest and noble. He cannot."

But he could, she wanted to tell her father. Clifton had said as much himself.

"I will not marry without love." The earl's words echoed inside her, sparking her defiance.

She was, after all, George Ellyson's daughter.

But her father wasn't finished yet. "He's an earl, my girl."

"I'm well aware of his —"

"And when he returns —"

"If he returns," she pointed out.

"Oh, he'll return," her father said, sounding none-too-pleased over the fact. "You've seen to that. You've done more than teach that man 'thievery and a few lessons in cards.' Oh, don't look so surprised. As if I wouldn't notice what is going on under my own roof. You and your sister have been quite busy." He shook his head. "Now, if this were Mr. Grey we were discussing, that would be one thing —"

The natural brother. The illegitimate one.

She straightened, hands fisted to her hips. "I'm not good enough for the likes of Clifton? Your own daughter, and you say I'm not worthy of the man's love?"

"Goosie, you are worthy of a prince, but that doesn't mean I'd let you run off with one. Can't you see that Clifton could never have you for anything more than his mistress? He can't."

Something in her father's desperate tone cut through her anger, and she knelt beside his chair and laid her hand on his sleeve. "Papa, he is different from the others."

"Aye, I'll grant you that. But that is because he is here, in our society, in this house, with you guiding him into a realm he's never imagined. But what of his world, Goosie? Of the *ton* and London? You aren't prepared for such a life. You have no idea what it takes to navigate those streets. I'd sooner see you dropped in the middle of the Dials than into Mayfair."

Up until this moment, Lucy would have denied with her every breath that she'd even considered such a future, of Clifton returning, declaring his love and sweeping her off her feet, but something about the dire lilt to her father's words upended that secret part of her heart.

For there was too much truth to his words.

She knew nothing of Society and, as her father had said, would most likely fare better on the mean streets of London than on the elegantly appointed ones.

How she wanted to tell her father that if two people loved each other, truly and deeply loved each other, such odds could be surmounted.

But when she looked into his misty green eyes, so very like her own, she knew he'd walked this rocky path once before. When he'd fallen in love with her mother and whisked her away from Italy.

And as much as the two of them had tried to merge their two worlds, to live a life that would have made them both happy, her father's origins and shadowy past had always barred the contessa from living in the lofty circles in which she'd been raised, to which she'd been accustomed.

Hampstead had not been enough for her, and London held too many reminders for George Ellyson of where he'd come from and where, as many liked to point out, he still belonged.

"Guard your heart, Goosie," her father said. "Guard it well, before it is lost."

"I assure you, Papa, my heart is not

engaged. You needn't fear for me," she told him as she slipped out of the room.

And after she left him, he glanced back down the hall to where she'd disappeared and wondered when she'd learned to lie so convincingly.

Just like her mother.

The next night, Lucy met Clifton and Malcolm at the bottom of the steps with their supper packed away in tin buckets.

"I've a bit of an adventure planned for you this evening," she said, handing over their meals.

"Are you coming with us?" Clifton asked.

"Heavens no. Even I have lines of propriety I don't dare cross."

Clifton and his brother exchanged a glance.

Do you think she means to get us both killed?

You should never have kissed her, Malcolm's upraised brow seemed to say.

"Dare I ask where we are going?" Clifton said, sending a grin at her, hoping to see a flash of mischief in her eyes.

But there was none forthcoming. "Sometimes it is better not to know," she told him as she handed him a dark, patched coat. She had another similarly shabby one for

Malcolm.

"More larceny?" he asked.

"Not unless you are of a mind for it," she told him. "No, tonight I think it is time you made some new friends." Just then there was a soft scratching at the door. "Ah, right on time." She opened the door to reveal Rusty and Sammy, shuffling nervously about the front steps, the larger of the pair holding an unlit lamp. "They are ready for you. Please don't get them killed." She turned to Clifton and his brother. "Enjoy your adventure," she said, then paused for a second. "Oh, and you have new names — you are the Drayton brothers. From York. And don't get caught, for I have it on good authority that you are wanted for smuggling, robbery and at least three counts of murder."

With that, she handed them both pistols, prodded them out the door and closed it on them. The sound of the latch and lock were hardly the "good luck" one might want to hear before being sent off to what appeared to be certain death.

"Come along now," Rusty said, eyeing the pails in their hands. "Is that roast beef?"

Clifton raised his to his nose and sniffed. "I believe so." He glanced up at Rusty. "Would you like it?"

"Oh, that would be awful nice of you, guv'ner."

Clifton surrendered his supper and hoped that was the least of what he was about to lose this night.

The nefarious pair led them out of the humble and quiet streets of Hampstead, and they set off across the countryside until they came to a track, which they followed to an inn, situated a few miles off the main road, well hidden by the rolling hills.

Glancing around, Clifton realized that if one didn't know of the inn's whereabouts, one would never find it. But to that end, Rusty and Sammy showed the brothers the signs and marks their brethren used to show the way to a "flash ken," as Rusty called it.

A safe house. It was naught but an old alehouse, a disreputable, run-down shambles filled with shifty souls and a few women, who, having gone well past plying their trade at respectable inns, had come to this poor end.

The moment the four of them stepped inside, a deep hush fell over the crowded room. Never in Clifton's life had he seen such a dark collection of souls.

And here he'd given his last supper to Rusty, of all people.

Malcolm looked over at him. *Oh, yes.*

She's sent us to our death.

Sammy stepped forward. "Brought me new friends for a bit of business. The Drayton brothers. Heard tell of them, I'd imagine."

There was a murmured response to this, and every rummy eye was on them now.

"Oh, aye, a rare pair of rushers they are," Rusty told them, elbowing his way closer to the fire and daring anyone who didn't step out of his way to challenge him.

Clifton followed suit, doing his best to mimic the rogue's swagger and manners. Malcolm followed, bringing up the rear and offering a glare worthy of the foulest, most ruthless criminal.

"We're looking to put together a gang for working in London next month," Rusty said, waving to the slattern behind the bar to bring a round of pints. "Thought we might find some likely lads here."

Rushing, Clifton had learned on their walk to this dark hole, was done by sending a decent-looking fellow to knock on the door of an empty house of some rich family who spent their summers anywhere but London. When the poor, unsuspecting housekeeper answered the door, the crew overcame her, as well as anyone else in the house. They then entered and looted everything they could carry.

A big fellow moved forward, and from the way the others moved out of his way, he was likely the most dangerous man in the room. "How do we know they are who they say they are?" He stood nose to nose with Rusty. "You pair of scurvy stupid rats wouldn't know a Bristol man from a sneakin' budge."

Clifton rose to his full height and ignored the way the stench of the man sent his stomach rolling. Elbowing Rusty and Sammy out of the way, he spat on the ground between him and the fellow before him. "And you are?"

"Black Britch. Who's askin'?"

"Drayton. I've never heard of you. Should I?"

The man ruffled, glaring at Clifton over such an insult.

As much as Clifton was generally afforded every consideration because of his title, this wasn't the turf of a Mayfair drawing room. Here, Black Britch was the ruler of the land, and he, Clifton, was naught but a mushroom, an interloper.

Yes, he had much to learn about living a different life, for he'd never been anything but the noble gentleman, with all the rights and comforts that position afforded. Lucy had sent him here so he could learn to adapt.

Quickly, as it were, for while in Mayfair an unwanted guest was escorted out the door, Clifton suspected that here, before he and Malcolm were tossed out of this coven, their pockets would be rifled and their throats slit.

And not necessarily in that order.

So what would this Drayton fellow do?

Clifton immediately narrowed his gaze and stared Black Britch down, using every bit of swagger and haughty disdain he could muster without giving himself away. He reached over and took up the pint the girl had brought over, tipping it back and emptying the contents down his throat.

It blazed a trail of fire all the way down to his gut, and it was all he could to do to keep his eyes from watering.

Never in his life had he tasted such deadly swill, but he drank it down and slammed the pint to the table, then nodded to the barmaid to bring another round.

Black Britch eyed him closely, then reached out and clapped him on the back, nearly knocking him out of his boots. "Oh, now, I like you, Drayton. Got the manners of a toff, you do. But if you can stomach a pint of Notton's worst, you must be a rare dodger indeed."

Everyone laughed as if they'd never heard anything so funny, and from there the night continued in jovial, if not eye-opening, congeniality.

For Clifton knew exactly why Lucy had sent them out with Rusty and Sammy. And it wasn't just to see that he never found himself sharing Darby Bricknell's fate.

She was giving him a look inside her life, as well as a good examination of her father's upbringing. And when he got over to the Continent and needed to run to ground, he would be able to find his way through the rough currents of the underworld and mix among them, hidden from the grand workings of Society.

Even if she got him killed in the process. Or the very least, hung for this Drayton fellow's crimes, which apparently were legendary.

Clifton spent the next four hours "interviewing" his new crew, listening to inflated tales of criminal prowess, including Black Britch's detailed explanation of how to silence a fellow "good and well" and leave "no trace of the deed."

Hours later, as they walked home through the quiet meadows, a bit dazed and knocked up from more pints of Notton's "worst" than he cared to count, Malcolm leaned over to Rusty and asked, "What will happen when we don't return for our crew? Won't they be suspicious?"

The man shrugged, a drunken sort of careless waver, both in his shoulder and his step. "Not to worry, guv'ner. We plan on telling them you got snapped by a China street pig and danced the Paddington day frisk."

Clifton staggered to a halt. "You mean to say that we got caught by the runners and hanged?"

"Exactly," Sammy said, snapping his fingers. "Sad day, that. They'll raise a pint to you both, they will, 'cause they're decent lads at heart."

"Yes, quite," Clifton agreed, amused at the idea of such honor among thieves and at his own untimely demise.

"There you go now," Rusty said, swinging his lamp to the road that led up the hill to Hampstead. "This is where we leave you be."

Clifton held out his hand. At first the man seemed taken aback, but then he latched on and gave it a hearty shake.

"You're a fine one, guv'ner," he said. "Do well against the Frogs. Cut a throat or two for me."

"I will," Clifton replied most solemnly.

"Aye, milord," Sammy said, muscling in for a shake as well. He took Clifton's hand and pumped it heartily. "Remember all Black Britch said about that sort of business — he'd never steer a fellow wrong."

"Yes, I will take his example to heart," Clifton promised.

They shook hands with Malcolm, slapped him on the back a few times, then sauntered down the road toward London. When their light was but a twinkle in the distance, Clifton leaned over and said to his brother, "Do you still have your watch on you?"

Malcolm patted his vest. "Aye. And yours?"

Clifton nodded. "Wouldn't put it past either of them."

"No, I fear not. Such fine company your Lucy keeps."

Clifton stumbled a bit, then caught himself. "She's not 'my' Lucy."

"Could have fooled me with that performance last night."

By chance or fate, they'd come to the Ellysons' house at that moment and found the entire place shuttered in darkness. They both stood there, lost in their own thoughts as they looked up at the rooms where their lives had changed so much over the course of the last few weeks.

Malcolm broke the silence with a softly cast-out question. "Do you think we are in over our heads?"

"Decidedly so," Clifton told him. There was no point in not being honest. "But this is what we must do. What we've agreed to do."

His brother nodded. "Most decidedly. Though it seemed a fair sight easier when listening to Templeton espouse the virtues of the Foreign Office over a decent bottle of claret at White's, eh?"

Clifton smiled. "I believe he choused us."

Malcolm grinned. "You think?"

"Entirely!" he laughed. "But he's caught us well and good now."

"He and others," Malcolm persisted, shooting another glance at the house. "Do you think we'll come home?"

This question sent a raft of shivers down Clifton's spine. "I want nothing more."

"So do I," Malcolm echoed, conviction ringing in his words. "Will you come back here?"

Clifton didn't even hesitate. "Yes."

"For her?"

He nodded. "If she'll have me. If I don't fail at this."

Malcolm stared at him. "Not have you?

You're the Earl of Clifton. She'd be mad not to —"

He cut him off. "She'd be mad to take me. And if I fail — I could never face her."

"Then don't fail," Malcolm advised him, staggering a bit, then grinning drunkedly. "Demmit if that Notton fellow doesn't brew a wicked pint. I fear when I wake up . . ." He shook his head ruefully.

"Oh, aye," Clifton agreed. "We'll both be casting up our accounts before morning."

"No wonder those fellows are so ruthless," Malcolm said, wagging his finger. "If I had to drink that swill seven days a week, I'd be the meanest cur in England."

"That or dead," Clifton told him, steering to the right and opening the gate to the Ellysons' yard without even thinking.

As if guided to her by an invisible, unbreakable thread.

Malcolm pulled him to a stop. "What the devil do you think you are going to do? At this time of night? She'll as likely shoot you as welcome you." He wagged his finger at him. "Remember the tale of —"

"Of Monday Moggs. Yes, yes, but —"

Malcolm tugged at Clifton's arm. "You're well into your cups. Now come away, Gilby. Sleep this off and go seek your lady love in the morning." He tugged him away from the gate and back into the dust of the road, where they stumbled on toward their gate.

"I wonder what her hair looks like when it's completely undone . . ." Clifton mused aloud, feeling the effects of too much of Notton's worst freeing his usual reserve.

Malcolm shook his head. "Enough to tempt a man to risk his neck? I wager that's the least part of what you'll have to worry about losing if Ellyson discovers you nosing about his daughter."

Clifton glanced over his shoulder as his brother tugged him past the gate. "Ah, but some risks . . ."

And from the side of the Ellyson house, a shadowed figure stepped out.

Letting the shawl that covered her head drop away, Lucy watched Clifton and his brother disappear around the curve in the lane. She'd been waiting out here for some time, worried out of her mind that she had sent them to a certain death.

But her fears were nothing compared to her shock at the conversation she'd overheard.

"Will you come back here?" Malcolm had asked.

"Yes. If she'll have me."

There hadn't been a moment of hesitation in Clifton's determined voice.

But discovering that the earl wanted her wasn't the triumph she'd thought it might be, for her ears still rang with her father's warning.

"*. . . he will never have you. Not in a way that is honest and noble. He cannot.*"

"No," she whispered. "It isn't like that."

"What do you want it to be?" came a deep whispered voice from behind her.

Chapter 8

Lucy whirled around and found herself caught in a man's arms. He pulled her close, and she immediately knew it wasn't her old adversary Monday Moggs but a man who meant to steal more than just her hand in marriage.

He wanted her heart.

And how she longed to give it to him. Or perhaps she already had.

"Oh, Goosie, my love, you are a sight for me eyes," Clifton whispered in her ear.

His words, loosened by copious amounts of Notton's infamous ale, drifted over her in a hazy, delicious fashion.

No longer the formal, tight-laced earl, the man holding her — yes, holding her — had lost all his veneer this evening. She glanced up at him, and he was staring at her haphazard tumble of curls.

"I wonder what her hair looks like when it's completely undone . . ."

And by the set of his jaw and the glint in his eyes, he looked about ready to discover exactly that.

Oh, good heavens! She'd accomplished far more than she'd thought possible when she'd sent him out with Rusty and Sammy.

He snuggled her closer. "Goosie, what are you doing out here?"

"I was . . . I was . . ."

"Waiting up for me?" He nuzzled her neck, inhaling deeply, which only enticed her to move toward him.

Then his words registered. *Waiting up for me.* Like some blowsy milkmaid. She ruffled a bit at the implication.

Even though she had been.

"Of course not," she told him, struggling to get out of his grasp.

He chuckled and held her fast, for he believed her protest no more than he did her halfhearted struggles. His hands roamed beneath her cloak, exploring her every line, her every curve, as if he was memorizing her, drinking her in.

And like Notton's wicked brew might, Clifton's touch left her intoxicated and trembling.

Suddenly she went from being the teacher to the student, longing for the lessons his hands offered, the desires his touch brought out in her with an insatiable curiosity.

Especially when his fingers curled around one of her breasts and cradled it, the tip puckering with a delicious languor and her knees threatening to buckle at the sheer wonder of it all.

Her lips parted and her hips rocked forward, for suddenly her body needed no lessons and knew exactly what she wanted.

Clifton's kiss. His body to claim hers.

Lucy looked up at him and saw the desire in his eyes, the smoldering fire that burned for her and her alone.

"You aren't going to darken my lights, are you?" he whispered, teasing her. "You won't send me packing if I dare to kiss you again?"

Kiss her? Oh, if only he would.

She licked her lips and drew closer. "That depends on the kiss."

"Minx," he growled in a deep, hungry voice as he lowered his head and claimed her lips.

Fool, her better senses railed against her, for the moment his hard lips touched hers, she was lost. Oh, she was drowning in a heavenly, wild passion.

His tongue teased over her, taunting her to open up to him. Daring her to match him.

Kiss for kiss.

And she did, for suddenly he was all she craved. All that she'd been missing.

She opened up to him and reveled in the feel of his lips, his tongue caressing hers, their bodies twining together.

Where she'd shown him how to pick a pocket, he now stole away her senses. Where she'd taught him to decode a missive, he effortlessly unraveled all her secrets.

And when she'd instructed him in finding the safest routes over the Pyrenees, he carried her to a different sort of heights — dizzy, breathless heights nonetheless — a place she never wanted to leave.

His hands began to explore her again, cupping her breasts, teasing her nipples to tender points, and when one hand began pulling up her skirt, the cool night air whispered up her bare legs beneath.

Lucy shivered, and he pressed her backward into the garden wall so he covered her, his coat concealing them in the shadows, leaving them in a world of their own making.

He eased the shoulder of her gown down and freed one of her breasts. She gasped at the feeling of his bare skin on hers, but that wasn't enough for the earl, for his head dipped down and he took her nipple into his mouth and sucked deeply on it.

"O-o-oh," she gasped at the sweet sensations he pulled from her very core — the part of her that was growing more sensitive by the moment, tight and anxious.

He continued to tug up her gown, his fingers sliding up her leg. As much as she wanted to clamp her legs together — for she was enough of a lady to consider that was what she was supposed to do — his touch undid any such thought of modesty.

How could she refuse him when his every touch, every stroke urged her upward, called her to explore this wild, starry world he was carrying her into?

"I don't want to leave you," he said, his lips nibbling at her neck, at her earlobe. "Not yet. Not ever."

But he must, and they both knew it.

Not that she wanted to let him go. Either right this moment, or in the days ahead.

"Then stay with me for now," she whispered back.

When his fingers brushed over the curls between her legs, she gasped, for it sent a rocket of desire through her. And when he found the hidden nub beneath, her entire body stretched like a cat's, urging him to continue, to both ease her longings and stoke her desires.

She swayed with the music of it, unheard

by any but the two of them, her body rocking until she brushed against the hard lines of his manhood straining beneath his breeches.

He wants you, he desires you, a siren voice whispered to her. *Feel him. Touch him.*

There was no way to resist such a clarion call, so she let one of her hands fall from his lapels, let it explore the muscled lines of his stomach, follow the band of his breeches to where they buttoned.

She hesitated for only a moment before she slid her fingers over him, from the top of his manhood all the way to the base. She cupped him, as he had done to her earlier, and listened with a feline pride as he groaned, his mouth leaving her breast and coming crashing down on her lips, kissing her, devouring her with a hunger that drove her to unbutton his breeches, enough so she could slip him free and stroke him.

The head was slick, and she let her fingers slide over it, marveling at the thick hardness, the masculine length.

He pulled back and stared down at her, as if he was seeing her for the first time, seeing something he'd never imagined.

As much as her father's warnings waged a noble war on her desires, the passionate fire burning inside her easily swept them aside.

She saw how her days would be without him, without ever having known the secrets that her body clamored for Clifton — and only him — to reveal.

And what if he didn't return? Her entire life might hold only memories of this night.

She blinked and her gaze focused again on him. He was still studying her.

"Demmit, Lucy, what are you doing to me?" he said in a voice hoarse with need.

"I don't know," she said quite honestly. "But I want you. I want you to take me. I want you to love me."

There was a long moment of silence between them. The entire world stilled, and for Lucy it seemed she had said far too much.

Asked too much, and she regretted her hasty words.

He reached out and brushed her tangled hair back from her face. Then he smiled at her. Grinned, really.

And her heart hammered in her chest at the sight of his almost boyish glee.

"But Goosie, my love, I already do."

With her hand clasped with his, they raced like wayward children through the darkened lanes and byways of Hampstead, Lucy leading Clifton along.

Every once in awhile, he couldn't help himself. He pulled her to a stop, hauled her up against his chest and kissed her. Once, he leaned over and plucked a stray blossom from the grasses and wild flowers, which he tucked in her hair.

"I'll press it and keep it always," she teased, and then he kissed her anew.

The scent of her filled his nose, drove him as mad as the way her body fit to his. With every kiss, she grew more bold, her hands and lips pushing him beyond any sense of control.

God, he'd never wanted a woman as badly as he wanted Lucy. She had filled his very soul with want, a craving to have her, completely and utterly.

This was sheer madness, that he knew. But it wasn't the copious amounts of Notton's ale that he'd consumed or this time in Hampstead, or even the fears of what he faced in the coming months that was driving him onto this reckless course — no, it was having finally discovered what it was to find one's match, one's heart.

Lucy Ellyson made him feel.

And Clifton found himself a man starved, hungry for the love she offered, delirious to discover her every secret.

They snuck up the back stairs and into

his room, and when the door closed behind them, he paused and looked down at the starry-eyed woman before him.

Her dark hair fell down well past her shoulders, a tumbled mess of curls that enticed a man to run his fingers through them, to discover what they hid. . . .

But it was how she made him come alive that left him dumbstruck. The fire she lit inside him, not just with her kiss but also when she'd tried to cheat him at cards and he'd outwitted her, when she'd stolen glances at him when she thought he wasn't looking, the times their hands had touched, and that unlikely spark ignited them both.

While he hadn't noticed it before, he now saw that she was wearing the same gown she'd had on the night before, a pink silk, trimmed in black velvet. On any other woman it would have bespoken innocence. On Lucy Ellyson, the silk revealed in so many enticing ways her two sides — sensible and passionate, intelligent and fiery. And as he reached out and slid the sleeves down over her shoulders, bared them to his touch, to his kiss, she moaned, a hungry, earthy purr that said which side had prevailed this evening.

It was an invitation no man could refuse.

He continued to slide the gown down,

slowly, letting his lips, his fingers explore every inch.

The taste of her skin was like some ethereal brew, something no man could ever bottle, and it filled him with a freedom from every constraint that had ever confined his heart.

She was his, his glorious, wondrous beauty.

And in his arms, she writhed with impatience, reaching for him, opening his shirt, pulling it and his jacket off at once. Her hands smoothed over his chest, over his belly, down to his trousers, her fingers tracing a line over his rock-hard manhood.

"Demmit, Gilby, please," she whispered.

He obliged her by tugging her gown down the rest of the way, until it pooled at her feet. She arched toward him, her bared breasts rising up.

He took one, then the other nipple in his mouth, sucking hard on them, bringing them to hard peaks. She moaned again, this time louder, and he grinned, pulling her close and kissing her, pressing his tongue into her mouth and letting it slide over hers in an erotic dance. All the while, her hips rose and fell against him.

He swung her around and pressed her up against the door. One of her legs twined seductively with his, rubbing against him like a cat.

Letting go of the tangle of hair he'd been toying with, he reached between her legs, slowly parting the curls there to explore that very private part of her.

Her eyes fluttered open wide as he began, ever so slowly, to stroke her, explore her. Sliding first over the nub, and then around the wet, slick opening.

Her mouth fell open, but no sound came out as, in wordless amazement, she tried to catch her breath. Her body trembled and she clung to him. "I want . . . I want . . ."

He knew exactly what she wanted. Sweeping her into his arms, he carried her to the bed, tumbling into the deep, soft mattress in a tangle of limbs . . . and desires . . . needs about to be answered.

She was his.

His tonight. His always.

As they fell into the bed, Lucy reveled in the passion that enveloped her, much as the thick, soft mattress folded in around them, pressing them close.

She should have been completely mortified — her without a stitch, the earl utterly naked — but instead she basked in the sheer heat of Clifton's glance, his unrepentant desire to explore every inch of her. His need for her only that much more apparent now that he'd shed his breeches and his manhood thrust out, erect and hard, pressing into her thighs.

As innocent as her experience with men might be, she hadn't just set her mother's birthday books aside; she had read them, memorized each print and wondered how such positions could bring the rapture the books described.

Hardly a proper gift from one's mother, but right now Lucy was ever-so-thankful for her unconventional upbringing.

Now her body — awakened to this state of wild abandon by Clifton's skilled touch — trembled with desire, craved for him to drive deeper between her legs, to fill her until she found the rapture, the release that was his to give.

He caught her lips with his and kissed her again, deeply, thoroughly, and Lucy grew more bold, meeting the sally of his tongue with her own, thrilled to find that she could leave him as breathless as he left her.

He touched her again, his fingers slowly stroking her, and the fire, that irresistible yearning, began to take over her senses.

She writhed and stretched, aching to feel more, to feel him.

Her fingers ran down his back, caught hold of his hard ass and pulled it closer to her, even as she ran her foot down his leg, winding hers around his, opening herself up.

Over her, Clifton stilled, and Lucy's lashes flew open.

He gazed down at her, his eyes so very dark, but it was evident he was hesitating.

No, no, no, she wanted to cry out. *This will never do.*

Not with her body racked with longing, in a frenzy for release.

She knew she wasn't thinking straight, hadn't been since he'd taken her in his arms in the garden, but this was hardly the time for him to shake off the effects of Notton's brew and discover his honorable side.

No, that would never do.

"What is it?" she whispered, her fingers stroking his back again, urging him closer.

"Lucy, I —"

She pressed a finger to his lips to stop his words. At worst he was about to cry off or, even more frightening, he was about to declare himself.

And she knew she'd probably kill him over the former and give him her heart over the latter.

Both disastrous considerations.

"Sssh," she whispered, kissing his lips, nuzzling at his neck. "I know, I know." Then she paused, looked directly into his eyes and smiled, a wicked, enticing tilt to her lips that was about the only useful thing her mother had ever given her.

Besides those French instructional manuals.

"Please, Gilby," she said, her voice throaty and full of passion. She rocked her hips up against him, let his manhood slide between her legs. "Love me. Please, I beg of you, take me now."

His answer was a kiss, deep and hard, while his arm slid beneath her, hauling her close, raising her hips so she was completely open to him.

"You are mine, Lucy Ellyson. Mine," he said, in a dark, dangerous voice. "Mine always. Never forget it."

Lucy opened her mouth to promise, but it was then that he entered her, taking her innocence in one quick stroke, fulfilling his vow.

She gasped at the brief flash of pain, but it faded quickly, for he seemed to have known what was to happen and began again to kiss her, his thumb rolling over the hard nub of her nipple, his mouth moving down to suckle the other one. All the while his body moved inside her, at first with slow, even strokes, then, when she moaned softly, her hips rising up to meet him, he began to move faster.

He filled her, inflamed her, made her insides molten as she eagerly matched him stroke for stroke.

She arched back, let him drive into her as she clung to him and found herself getting closer and closer to her release.

The room, the moonlight, everything whirled around her dizzy vision as she found herself pulled and tormented.

Clifton's thrusts grew harder, more frenzied, and Lucy welcomed them, for they only drove her higher until suddenly she was there — one moment she was on the precipice, and the next she was tossed over the edge, her body exploding with pleasure.

"Oh, yes! Oh, yes," she called out, arching upward to get every last inch of him inside her, to be filled completely.

And as she rose up, he thrust hard into her and groaned deeply, his body shuddering as he found his completion.

His mouth opened as if he was going to say something, but he hadn't the breath to form the words, so lost was he in his pleasure.

But Lucy knew exactly what he was going to say.

Mine. Never forget it. You are mine.

And she knew it now that she would always be his. Marked this night by his love-making, her heart etched now and always.

Some time later, Lucy found herself awakening from an all-too-short doze. Beside her, Clifton slept.

Between Notton's brew and the last few hours spent in vigorous lovemaking, the man was lost in a deep, contented slumber.

Glancing at the window, she saw the slight hint of light starting to illuminate the sky, the moon having gone to find its rest some time ago.

It was nearly dawn, and there was little time for her to get home before she was missed.

Lucy slipped from the bed and began to gather up her clothes, dressing quickly and slanting smile-filled glances at the man in the bed.

She loved him. That much she knew.

And he loved her. He'd proposed to her. Promised to come back to her.

"It cannot be, Goosie," she could hear her father saying. *"He is from another world."*

"Who is to say we can't find our own

place?" she whispered. As she went to slip out of the room, she spied the flower he'd picked for her the night before. A token of this glorious night.

Retrieving the wilted blossom, Lucy left, making her way quietly down the back stairs. Somewhere in the inn Mrs. Turnpenny was rousing the maids to answer some pounding at the front door, and Lucy escaped as only an Ellyson could, without being caught.

Navigating the still streets and keeping out of sight, she was all the way home, feeling quite smug, when she carefully opened the door to the kitchen, plotting the rest of her course . . . *up the back stairs and into her room and no one would be the wiser.*

At least so she thought.

That is, until she closed the kitchen door and turned around and found her father sitting at the table with a pot of tea in front of him and a look that could have sent an entire brigade scrambling for cover.

"Lucy Louisa, what the devil have you done?"

"I-I-I-," she stammered and stopped when he held up his hand to stave her off.

"Don't tell me. I know demmed well what you've gone and done."

She stood her ground. "He loves me,

227

Papa. He wants to marry me. You'll see when he comes this morning. He'll ask for your permission, and I beg of you to give it."

"He won't come," her father declared.

"Of course he will, why wouldn't he?"

A shiver of gooseflesh ran down her arms. There was something about the set of her father's brows, the line of his jaw that said he knew more to this business than she did.

"He will," she insisted, though she didn't feel as sure as she had a few moments ago.

Her father raised his hands and revealed a packet of papers, bound in blue paper and tied with a gold ribbon.

The air rushed out of her lungs, out of the room. She didn't need to see the seal to know what her father had before him.

Orders.

"No," she whispered, shaking her head. "It is too soon. He isn't ready."

"Actually, he is quite ready. You've seen to that. And if all is going according to plan, the earl and Mr. Grey are being roused as we speak."

The knocking on the door. Mrs. Turnpenny's strident cries demanding to know who was calling so early.

That had been for Clifton. Even as she'd gone tripping out the back, he'd been awakened and his orders relayed.

She turned to the door and began to open it, her hand trembling so badly that she could barely hold the latch, yet she had to catch him, to follow him.

But her father crossed the room and closed the door before she could escape.

"It is too late, Goosie. He's gone. By now he will be in a carriage going to the coast. You cannot hope to catch him." He paused and looked at her. "His orders are to get to Dover without a moment's delay, for they must catch the evening tide."

She shook her head, even as she sank into the chair beside the door. "No, this cannot be. Whatever have you done?"

"What is best for you, Goosie."

"And if he doesn't come back? Have you thought of that?"

Her father's brow furrowed deeper. "That is exactly why he is leaving. I won't have you left a widow. Where would you be then?" He rose from the table and shook his head. "You'd be at the mercy of his world, and that is a fate I will not allow."

But as Fate was ever a fickle, wily creature, it was exactly the state Lucy Ellyson Sterling found herself in years later.

Lost and lonely in a world she didn't belong to.

CHAPTER 9

London, seven years later

Not one to stand on ceremony, Lucy Ellyson Sterling, the Marchioness of Standon, shook off the recollections of her past and pulled the bell at the door before her. She hoped, nay prayed, that whatever matter this summons to meet with the Duchess of Hollindrake was for, it would be less unsettling than running into the Earl of Clifton.

He's changed, Mariana, she would have told her sister.

But Mariana was gone now, as was her father. Lost to a fever that had swept through their quiet village, taking so many with it.

Taking everything Lucy had known. Upending her life.

As much as Clifton had. For he hadn't come back to her. Hadn't written. Not even when Malcolm had been killed.

Lucy pressed her lips together and willed

the moisture in her eyes not to give way to tears.

Oh, Mariana, how he looked at me! As if we were barely friends, as if he'd never loved me. As if I was the last person he ever wanted to see.

What had he said? He'd come to Hampstead to thank her father for all he'd done?

And not one word for all she'd done to ensure that he came home? No thanks to her?

Arrogant, ungrateful bastard.

To give herself something to do other than ordering her carriage after the earl and running the man down in broad daylight, she reached for the bell again and would have given it another good yank if, to her surprise, Mr. Mudgett, the duke's former batman, hadn't opened the door just then.

"There you are, my lady," he said in that familiar curmudgeony voice of his. Then the man glanced over her shoulder, his thick brows furrowing together. "Brought the child along, have you?"

Lucy flinched. For unfortunately, as dear as Mickey was to her, he was not all that beloved throughout the Sterling households.

But when she'd agreed to marry Archie Sterling, she'd wrenched a promise from him that she would not have to give up

231

Mickey — that he would never be taken from her. Ever. And so the boy had remained with her, no matter how deplorable the Sterlings found the scandalous situation.

Lucy Ellyson Sterling and *that child.*

"Ever consider leaving him at the wayside, would you now?" the man asked, looking past her like a watchman instructed to guard against the barbarian horde. Or small, rambunctious lads.

"Of course not, Mr. Mudgett," she answered, trying to sound not the least bit put out by his less than charitable greeting.

"Well there, you might as well come in and join the lot of them."

"The lot of —" she began to ask until she saw what he meant.

The marble floor was carpeted in luggage — hatboxes, trunks, traveling bags and cases. And standing on either side of the entry were the other two dowager Lady Standons, Minerva and Elinor.

She didn't know why she was surprised to see Minerva, for hadn't Clifton said as much . . .

"The lady just sent me packing with a flea in my ear."

Yet here was Elinor as well, and from their corners across the way, neither of the ladies

232

looked none-too-pleased at her arrival.

Lucy glanced back at Mr. Mudgett to see if he had any explanation for this. *All three of them? Summoned here? But to what end?*

Oh, this didn't bode well at all. She should have known that running into Clifton had been just a harbinger of the disaster yet to come.

Before she could map a plan on how to meet the coming apocalypse, her entire party came trooping up the steps like the loyal companions and servants they were.

Mickey arrived first, tumbling into the foyer and immediately setting off Elinor's collection of dogs, who yapped and barked with excitement.

"Dear God, not the child," Lucy heard Minerva mutter under her breath.

True to form, Mickey couldn't just enter the house and take his proper place. No, he looked around until he found the quickest route to trouble.

"Aunt 'Nirva!" he called out, making a beeline for the lady, wrapping his arms around her waist and giving her a big hug. He glanced over his shoulder and winked at Lucy.

Little devil, he knew how much Minerva hated having children underfoot, let alone one attached to her.

But before Lucy could pluck him to safety, for Minerva looked to be in a mood — not that she wasn't most days — Mickey was off.

"Tia!" he cried out as he spied Elinor's young sister across the way. Pushing off Minerva and leaving the lady teetering to find her footing, he bolted over the trunks like a little monkey to gain a spot next to his old friend.

Once again Elinor's terriers set up a deafening cacophony of yips and barks.

Not so much that Lucy couldn't hear Minerva's muttered complaint. "At least the dogs can be put on a leash and sent to the stables."

"Mickey!" Tia exclaimed, her pretty, fresh face brightening with a wide smile, until a nudge from her sister brought a renewal of her previous composed stance. The girl drew a steady breath, then said in even tones, "How nice to see you again, Michael," holding out her hand to him, instead of the hug and kiss he expected.

He stared first at the outstretched hand, then glanced over at Lucy, puzzled by the change in his old friend. Sadly, it appeared that Tia had grown beyond joining Mickey in his exuberant rambles of going fishing in the pond and merrily chasing Elinor's dogs about the meadow.

But before Lucy could explain things to him — that girls become young ladies — she had to negotiate with the rest of her party.

"Come now, Mr. Otter," she said to the tall, thin fellow as he poked his head through the door, blinking as he surveyed the cluttered foyer, a place filled with ladies and their belongings. Lucy took him by the arm and pulled him inside as one might when one ran out of patience with a timid maiden aunt.

Then came Clapp. Dear old Clapp. "Oh, goodness!" she exclaimed in that wheezy sort of way of hers that burst out like the notes from a hand organ. "Lucy, this cannot be correct, for here is Lady Standon —" There was a pause as Clapp, too, took in the entire foyer. "Oh, and Elinor as well. All three of you? Heavens, this cannot be right, Lucy, I just know it."

"This is the right place," Lucy told her, guiding Mickey's beleaguered nanny into the fold.

A woman of a good number of years, Clapp, like so many of her elderly lot, held a resigned expression of being perpetually put upon. "Oh, my! Did I muddle the invitation? For it hardly seems like the duchess meant for all of us . . ." The lady paused and took in the strained expression on Elinor's face, but before she could comment further, she finally took notice of her charge. "Mickey," Clapp scolded, "do not bedevil Tia another moment. I doubt she has any sweets in her reticule — she's grown to be a proper lady now. Why, she's quite filled out."

Lucy cringed at this indelicate remark, while Tia blushed at having everyone notice that she was no longer a child.

Elinor, for her part, looked ready to clobber Clapp with the nearest valise.

Lucy closed her eyes and prayed that mayhem wouldn't ensue before the duchess arrived and she would be blamed for it.

Yet again.

Quickly she went to work, taking stock to ensure that everyone had come inside. "Mr. Otter, Clapp, and yes, there you are, Thomas-William." Her father's loyal manservant had to duck his head to enter, for he towered over everyone, an imposing, implacable statue of a man.

His entrance gave Lucy a measure of comfort — for besides Mickey, Thomas-William was her only remaining link to her former life. How she would manage without Thomas-William's steady presence, she knew not.

Even now, he stood silently surveying his surroundings with an expression that needed no explanation.

"Yes, yes, it isn't what we expected," Lucy told him. "But there is no reason to frown. Come along and close the door before Minerva gives us all one of her infamous looks."

Minerva, from the furrow on her brow, had been about to send the entire lot of them one of her most scathing glances, but Lucy's statement had brought all eyes upon her and she forced a smile to her lips to appear the gracious lady, the product of proper breeding.

"So I wasn't the only one summoned," Lucy commented as she adjusted the shawl wrapped around her shoulders.

"How very apt you are," Minerva said in return. She took a long, measured examination of Lucy's ensemble, then sighed heavily, as if Lucy's lack of fashion sense was just another trial yet to be borne. Minerva would never be called an Original or one of Society's great beauties, what with her nutbrown hair and eyes that didn't lend her the kind of starry blonde splendor that was Elinor's claim. But Minerva knew how to dress and hold herself like a queen, giving herself a regal appearance that overshad-

owed many of the more reputable Dia-
monds. "Yes, we've all been summoned. But
to what end, I cannot imagine."

"No, indeed, it seems very odd," Lucy
said, winding her way through all the trunks
and watching with a wary glance as her
ward made his gamboling way up the stairs
with Elinor's dogs in hot pursuit. "I went to
the duke's residence first — that is why I
am late."

She glanced around the crowded foyer
and realized that it and the sitting room
beyond sported only a few meager pieces of
furniture — a rose-colored settee and a
couple of high-backed chairs. No pictures
or decorations brightened the entryway, and
the paper on the walls curled in several
places — and not inconspicuous ones.
"Rather a dismal place, don't you agree?"

Neither of the other ladies replied, for
once again, the answer was all too obvious.

The strained detente that enveloped the
foyer continued, while up a few flights there
was Mickey's echoing laughter, accompa-
nied by a chorus of barks sifting down the
stairs.

And then there was a long silence above
as well, one all too unnerving to ignore.

A quiet Mickey was a portent to calamity.

Everyone looked in that direction. Then

all eyes turned toward Lucy.

Mickey, she had no doubts, was already in trouble. "Clapp, Mr. Otter, will you see what amusement Mickey has discovered?" She shot a baleful glance at Thomas-William as well. "You might be needed."

The man snorted, as if that was the most obvious statement that had been uttered so far. He followed Clapp and Mr. Otter up the stairs.

Elinor nodded at her sister. "Tia, be a dear and go see that Lucy's little devil hasn't brought on Isidore's litter prematurely."

Tia looked to be about to open her mouth and protest such a thing, but then she heaved a sigh and went up the stairs, reluctantly following Lucy's servants like one condemned.

And just as the last of Tia's white muslin hem disappeared up the stairs, the bell jangled, and in unison they turned toward the door wondering what was to come next.

Mudgett, who huffed in dismay at having to pick his way through the overflowing foyer for a fourth time, muttered as he went, "This ought to be herself, 'iffin I'm not mistaken."

And it was, for once the door opened, the Duchess of Hollindrake swept inside.

Lucy watched the duchess warily, for she

239

found the former Miss Felicity Langley a formidable lady — a bustling, calculating, bundle of nerve and determination who could have marched single-handedly across the Continent and contained Napoleon in a fortnight, with time to spare for shopping in Paris.

Hadn't her father, Lord Langley, been infamous in the Foreign Office circles for his daring?

The duchess came by her audacity naturally.

Instead of waiting for proper greetings, she launched right in with her usual military fashion. "Excellent! You've found your way to your new home without any problems, I see."

Even from across the room, Lucy swore she could feel Minerva stiffen. For she was having much the same reaction as Lucy.

What the devil had the duchess just said?

"Our new what?" Minerva managed, for she of all three of them seemed the least bowled over by the woman who wore the title that each of them had once thought would be hers.

The duchess turned sharply and eyed her for a second. "You heard me. Your. New. Home."

"Ah, Minerva, you seem to have found

yourself a fine establishment," Elinor said smugly, picking up her skirts and moving toward the door. "Now, if you don't mind, Your Grace, I would like to remove myself and my sister to Grosvenor Square. My rooms are still in order, are they not?" This last question she asked with the same manner and tone one might use with a housekeeper or any other hapless servant.

The duchess studied Elinor with a gaze that sent a shiver of dread down Lucy's spine.

Again, as the daughter of a man who was neither a nobleman nor, even, a gentleman, Lucy knew her place and had enough sense not to aggravate the woman before them.

This lady, she would like to remind Minerva and Elinor, held their future well-being in her tan kid-glove-clad hands.

The duchess, for her part, wasn't about to suffer any sort of rebellion, and she stepped into Elinor's path even as she shot the lady a withering glance. "Lady Standon, this is your new home as well."

"This?" Elinor sputtered as she regarded her surroundings like one might a dirty stable yard. "That cannot be. For you have just told Minerva this is *her* house."

The duchess nodded. "It is. Her house. Your house. And Lady Standon's house," she said, tipping her head toward Lucy. "You three are to share it."

Lucy shot a glance up toward the stairs, hoping to find Thomas-William standing there.

What had he said earlier?

"I don't put it past her high and mighty to be up to something."

Oh, yes, she was . . . she was, indeed!

And while Lucy could see the writing on the wall as if it were one of her father's old codes, Elinor and Minerva were having a bit more trouble deciphering the situation.

"Yes, that is all well and good," the second Lady Standon continued with a dismissive wave of her hand, "but while Minerva is living here, where shall I live? Or for that matter, Lucy and her mob? You cannot mean to suggest that we . . ." She studied the duchess with an unblinking expression, one of pure stubborn triumph, and took a step back. "Dear heavens, you aren't suggesting that all of us . . . that we are to . . ."

The duchess's features never changed — the stern set of her jaw and the determined light in her eyes — and that was answer enough.

She did mean it. Their house. All three of them. Together.

Then came a wary exchange of glances

between Minerva, Elinor and Lucy, like a trio of alley cats squaring off over a scrap of dropped mutton.

And that was what this house was, Lucy knew without a doubt, a scrap of week-old mutton in the middle of Mayfair, with its bare rooms and peeling paper. And so she joined into the chorus of yowling protests that erupted through the foyer without any thought of propriety.

"Your Grace, there cannot be room here for all of us to live —"

"You cannot mean to take away my dowry rights! If you think I will stand for this —"

"This is banishment! I will write the duke, for I doubt he would cousin such outrageous, nay, scandalous treatment of his —"

The duchess whirled around and shook her finger at Minerva. "That is exactly why you are being 'banished' here. The duke and I are tired of your petty squabbling, fighting and ridiculous demands —"

"We have rights," Elinor interjected. "Our marriage contracts specifically give us —"

Wheeling around, the duchess was ready, sounding like the most pernicious, stubborn solicitor that ever graced the Inns of Court. "Have you read your marriage contract?"

This took Elinor aback. "Read it? Why would I have read it, I know exactly what I am due —"

"Apparently you don't," the duchess interjected. "For your marriage contracts do not give you the right to beggar the duke with your outrageous requests, scandalous outbursts, constant orders and high-handed ultimatums."

"But you cannot —" Minerva began, but then, just as quickly, she stopped, for apparently she hadn't read hers either.

Still, Lucy couldn't fathom Minerva's father, the previous Earl of Gilston, ever signing a contract that could possibly leave his only daughter to the capricious whims of the Sterling family.

Then again . . .

Felicity tugged at her gloves, then patted at her bonnet, the plumes bowing in perfect unison. "From this date forward, this is the Sterling dowager house and your only address." She paused and glanced at Minerva and Elinor as if challenging them to contradict her.

But for all her good sense, that didn't stop Lucy from wading in. For while Minerva and Elinor had family connections and solicitors at the ready to join their howls of protest over this unconscionable situation, Lucy had no one to carry her banner into this fight.

Save herself.

Save him, a voice whispered. *What of him?*

Hadn't he just said, not half an hour earlier, *"If you ever have need of anything, you or Thomas-William, please do not hesitate to contact me."*

Lucy straightened. She'd rather live with Minerva for the remainder of her days than go crawling to Clifton.

"Your Grace, I beg of you, what of my household? Of Mickey?" Lucy asked, using every bit of manners she possessed. "You cannot mean to say that we must share this residence with Minerva and Elinor and their servants?"

Without even batting an eye, the duchess nodded.

And before there was a new explosion of protests, there was an explosion of another sort. From upstairs came a terrified chorus of yelps from the dogs, followed by a cloud of black, sooty smoke. After a few moments of shocked silence, a coal-stained Tia came down the steps, a dog under each arm and another following on her heels with its tail between its legs.

"It all happened so fast," she stammered, awkwardly pointing up the stairs.

Lucy cringed. It always did where Mickey was concerned.

"Mickey decided to see if Ivo would fit up the chimney, since he himself could not." Tia tried to hand one of the filthy dogs to her sister, but Elinor backed away in horror at the soot-covered terrier, which would surely ruin her new gown as it had Tia's more modest one.

Thomas-William appeared at the top of the steps, Mickey under one arm, being carried in much the same fashion as Tia carried the dogs.

And like the dogs, Mickey was howling for all to hear. "I thought he could climb. Weren't my fault that darn thing got stuck. Tommy Saunders has a dog that climbs the chimney, and it's just an old mutt."

There was a low groan from Lucy, while Elinor whirled about to face the duchess.

"You cannot expect me to live like this, with that —" Her finger shook at Mickey with a trembling fury. "That —"

"Rather dirty child," the duchess said, glancing at the boy. "Thomas-William, would you please take Master Ellyson downstairs and acquaint him with Mrs. Hutchinson, the cook. She'll be able to provide you with enough hot water to wash both the child and Lady Standon's dogs."

"A bath!" Mickey howled. "I don't want a bath."

Felicity laughed. "Then don't climb about the chimneys like some lad off the streets. Be a good boy now, and I am sure Mrs. Hutchinson will reward you with a ginger biscuit."

"Two biscuits," Mickey told her, as Thomas-William followed Mr. Mudgett to the kitchens. "Or I'll make enough noise to bring the watch."

"I believe you've already accomplished that," the duchess called after him. She turned to Lucy. "You've a solicitor in the making there. Negotiating his punishment, indeed!"

She wiped her hands over her skirt, as if washing herself of this errand, then turned to leave, but this time, Minerva stepped into her path.

"You cannot mean to do this to me. To abandon me here in this wretched house? Leave me here with . . . with these . . . these . . ."

Lucy almost pitied her, for she'd never heard Minerva sound so, well, unnerved.

"Members of your family?" Felicity supplied. "Why yes, indeed I do. I happened to have lived in this very house with my sister and cousin before I married the duke, and if it was quite acceptable for us then, I see no impediment to you residing here now."

"I won't," Minerva said, shaking from head to toe. "I won't stand for this. There must be some other way."

"You are welcome to leave," Felicity told her. "But realize that you leave this house with the understanding that you forfeit your allowance for good. Not a single ha-penny more will you ever receive from the duke."

Elinor gasped, for apparently she'd already been making her plans for a hasty escape.

Minerva wavered. "You'd have us cut off?"

"Completely," Felicity said with the same hard manner as a Seven Dials landlady.

"But why? However can you do such a thing to me? To us? Whatever have we done to deserve such high-handed treatment?"

"High-handed?" the duchess said, her voice deathly calm.

It sent a shiver down Lucy's spine. Oh, she'd always known that one day she'd have to face a reckoning, but at the duchess's hand?

No, she would rather have been hit by a mail coach this morning and be well on her way to another sort of reckoning than face this.

"You should have thought of what high-handed means, Lady Standon," the duchess continued, "before you fired off your last letter to the duke. And you as well," she added, looking at the second Lady Standon. "Your letter arrived the very same day. Complaining about your portions and needs, as if you lived in squalor. Hardly the behavior of ladies, let alone members of the Sterling family. That, and the mounting gossip regarding your ridiculous squabbles and feuds have made you three — and His Grace in turn — the laughingstocks of London, and I will not have it."

Lucy looked down at her boots. Try as she might to tell herself she certainly hadn't had a hand in any of this, an all-too-familiar twinge of guilt ran down her spine.

Keeping Mickey. Not adhering to perfect social conventions. Traveling from house to house and leaving outraged relations and wreckage in her wake.

"Yes, yes, some of us have behaved with a lack of decorum," Elinor said, once again placing all the blame at Lucy's doorstep, "but there must be some way to resolve this."

Lucy guessed Elinor's solution involved some remote Scottish island where Lucy and her companions would be abandoned like castaways.

The duchess stepped around Minerva, who found herself unable to move, the shock of her situation sinking in.

"There is, Lady Standon," the duchess assured her, opening the door and stepping outside into the crisp sunshine of a cold February day. "Get married."

"Married?" they all three exclaimed in unison.

"Yes, married," the duchess said. "Oh, heavens, I nearly forgot." She reached inside her reticule and pulled out a leather-bound journal. Placing it on the pedestal that sat beside the door, the one usually reserved for the receiving salver, her hand lay atop it for a few moments, as if she wasn't all too sure she wanted to leave it behind. But eventually she did, and she offered her stunned audience a smile. "That is my *Bachelor Chronicles.* Use it with my blessings. It contains the names, particulars and penchants of all the eligible noblemen in England. Find a husband and you will no longer have any need to reside here on Brook Street."

"What if I have no desire to wed?" Minerva asked in tones that said all too clearly she was outraged beyond comprehension.

The duchess shrugged. "Then I would make myself at home — for it shall be just that for some duration."

"My dear boy, there is nothing left to do

but propose to the chit and be done with the matter," the Marquess of Penwortham said, loudly enough for half of White's to hear.

Luckily for the Earl of Clifton, there was quite a stir going on around the betting book, so his uncle's booming voice drew little attention from the raucous crowd across the way.

"The wars are over," Penwortham continued, adding hastily, "thanks be to God. And now that they are, you must get on with your most sacred of duties — begetting an heir, which begins with getting married to Lady Annella. You just need to draw upon that infamous courage Wellington was boasting about the other day and get the deed done."

Yes, yes, he knew all that. But that was the rub; Clifton hadn't the bottom to take that next step and propose. If you had asked him yesterday, he wouldn't have been able to put a name on his reluctance, why he couldn't force that final question past his lips.

Reaching for his glass, he took a long swallow of the amber whisky. It ran down his throat like a raw fire, echoing the one name that was at the heart of his trouble.

Lucy.

He glanced toward the shuttered window and took a deep breath. Dear God, he'd found her. His Goosie.

Perhaps it was why he was here at White's and not at the Nesfield musicale this evening paying homage to Lady Annella's talents at the pianoforte.

The sight of Lucy standing there on the steps of Lady Standon's house had bowled him over. Thrown him better than his horse could have.

Lucy Ellyson. He reached for his glass again.

He'd lied to her today. Told her he owed a debt to her father — well, that wasn't entirely untrue; he did owe a good measure of his survival on the Continent to George Ellyson — but it was Lucy who had been the bright light who had carried him through the darkest days.

And there had been any number of those.

The memory of her smile. The sharp light of her eyes.

Her kiss . . . her sighs . . . her touch . . .

"Well, there is naught to do but finalize the settlements with her father and propose, eh, Clifton?" Penwortham was saying, oblivious to his nephew's inattentiveness. The large man settled even more deeply into his chair — not a good sign in Clifton's estimation. "My boy, the girl is a veritable angel. Sweet, even-tempered. Rather like her mother — who I knew when I was just a strapping young man — thought to marry her myself. But no matter, her daughter will be the perfect Lady Clifton — just as my sister was to your father — and very like your mother, she comes with everything a man of your position needs: impeccable bloodlines, the right connections and a dowry that your estates could use, if you don't mind me saying."

Clifton did mind, but there was no use pointing out the obvious. Lady Annella had those qualities and more.

Everything Lucy Ellyson had never possessed.

Except her hold on his heart.

Which, up until tonight, he thought he could ignore.

What he couldn't forget was that his estates were in terrible straits. The uncle who'd had charge of them had died shortly after Clifton had gone overseas. Penwortham, his mother's brother, had been assured by the steward that all was well in hand, while the rapscallion fellow had neglected all and pocketed what he could.

Clifton was duty-bound to see his tenants and lands brought to rights.

Just as it had been his duty to serve his King and country.

That was his lot in life, duty and honor. To serve. To keep his place in Society.

And to marry.

It all seemed so nice and orderly. So easily done.

Yet what had serving his country done for him? It had cost him his brother's life. Malcolm was gone. The estate, the fields and tracts he loved were fallow and rotting.

So all that was left to do was marry and marry well, and everyone — from his uncle to his solicitor to even his housekeeper, Mrs. Calliwick — seemed to think that was the balm to quell his unrest.

And while they all thought his disquiet had to do with his years at war, it had everything to do with the trip he'd made to Hampstead just after Malcolm had died.

His heart broken, his body exhausted from two years of hiding and working undercover on the Continent, he'd come back to Hampstead seeking the one balm he'd known would restore his soul.

Lucy's love. Her smile. Her rare temper. Her fire.

He'd needed her like a starving man needed sustenance.

Instead, he'd found strangers in the old

Ellyson house, a couple who'd known nothing of the former tenants. But he had been able to locate Mrs. Kewin's sister, an aged lady in her dotage and not completely within her wits.

Still, she'd invited him into her small cottage and begged him to sit in her best chair, as she'd settled into a smaller one by the fire.

"You've come seeking the Ellysons, have you?"

"Yes, ma'am. I am an old friend of the family."

She'd regarded him warily, for the residents of Hampstead had always been a bit scandalized by the Ellysons' less-than-reputable connections.

"Well, then it is sorry I am to tell you they were all lost in the fever a while back," she'd said, her rheumy eyes filled with tears. "My sister, the master, his daughter, all of them lost."

His lungs had drained of air, his heart had stilled, but even so he'd managed to ask, "Lost? All of them?"

No, it couldn't be. The darkness threatened to overcome him. The same black spirit that had been haunting him since Malcolm's death.

"*. . . the master, his daughter . . .*"

255

But wait, she'd said "daughter," not "daughters."

"Which daughter? Which one died?" His hands had clenched the arms of his chair as he'd waited.

The lady hadn't seemed to notice his distress, for she'd tapped her chin and taken her time to pull the memory from her befuddled senses. "Oh, the pretty one. The elder. Mariana, wasn't it? But she'd been poorly for some time, so her passing was no surprise."

Clifton's heart had begun to hammer, a light of hope piercing his armor. Lucy had been spared. But that hadn't meant he hadn't ached for the loss of Mariana, who'd always been so full of life. The thought of her bright light extinguished had made the room a little darker.

"And the other daughter?" he'd prompted. "Miss Lucy?"

At this, Mrs. Kewin's sister had frowned. "Well, married of course. In haste, I might add. Don't approve of such things, but there it is, what else would you have expected from such a girl? Scandalous bit she was and good riddance. Poor fellow, though. He got a rare bargain there, he did. Such a hasty choice. But men, what can I say? When they decide to marry, no thought to the matter, just pick a lady and off they go . . ."

He hadn't listened any further. There had been no need. For Lucy might as well have died of that fever, for she was just as lost to him.

Married. She'd married another. Forgotten his promise to come back for her and married another.

He couldn't recall much else of the interview, other than thanking the lady, declining her offer of cakes and tea, and leaving.

As fast as he'd been able.

Clifton had fled England like a man possessed, his grief turned to rage. Returning to his work, he'd spent the next five years like a man consumed.

But still it hadn't banished the bitter rage of Lucy's betrayal from his heart, and seeing her today had served to crack that aching wound wide open.

Oh, the sight of her. Her dark hair slipping loose from beneath her bonnet, her face set with the same determination and her eyes as bright as he remembered. She was the same unconventional Lucy Ellyson he'd fallen in love with.

Why, Lucy? Why didn't you wait?

"Clifton, I do say! Are you listening to me?" Penwortham sputtered.

"I'd rather not," the earl said quite honestly.

"Whatever has you woolgathering this evening?" his uncle pressed.

"Nothing."

Her . . .

"What you should be thinking about is the blunt that gel will bring to your coffers. Her pin money could have Clifton House reroofed twice over."

And Lord knew, Clifton needed the money. And a new roof.

But there was an alternative to Lady Annella and her plump dowry, one that Clifton hadn't shared with his uncle, and the sole reason for his trip to Town; it was not, as Penwortham imagined, to finalize a betrothal.

Malcolm's lost fortune. The money their father had set aside for his natural son. By rights, it was Clifton's, that is if Malcolm hadn't actually willed it to another, as Strout claimed.

He glanced down at the glass in his hand. There was something not quite right about all this. A fortune to a complete stranger? What had Malcolm been thinking? Besides, when had Malcolm ever met this woman?

One of George Ellyson's old sayings came to mind. *Trust your hackles.*

And Clifton's were definitely up.

First of all, Strout hadn't been able to produce his brother's will or the name of this unknown heir. But the wily solicitor had underestimated Clifton's determination — honed by years abroad — as well as his connections. Clifton had simply followed the money to the bank where the account was held, and then pulled strings to determine the name on the account.

Lady Standon.

But when he'd gone to see her this afternoon, she'd denied ever knowing Malcolm. So he was back to the beginning of the puzzle.

What he needed was to get his hands on that will. For if Clifton could lay claim to those accounts, they would stave off the worst of his estate's creditors, put the fields back to the plow and get his lands producing again.

Without having to leap into a marriage of necessity.

"Come now, my boy," his uncle was saying, "Lady Annella is a lovely creature and an heiress, to boot. For the life of me, you'd think she had spots and was missing half her teeth. So be done with it, and propose. You'll have new roofs a plenty by the time you get home from your honeymoon."

Clifton had chosen that moment to take another desperate swig from his drink, and he now found himself sputtering it all over. "My wh-a-a-t?"

"Honeymoon! Egads, man, whatever is wrong with you? That gel is stunning. I'm starting to wonder if perhaps you got knocked in the head while you were mucking about the Continent if you can't see a woman like Lady Annella and not want to bed her."

"Uncle, I concede that the girl is very lovely, but I would like a little more time to get to know her."

Not that it had taken long to fall in love with Lucy. What had it been? A fortnight? A sennight? But a few days in her company and he'd been caught by something he couldn't explain.

That was what he wanted still. Something he couldn't explain.

Across the table his uncle laughed. "What's to get to know? That's what marriage is for. Dance with her a few more times. Make an afternoon call. Better yet, Agnes says that Lady Asterby and Lady Annella are going shopping tomorrow afternoon. I shall arrange for us to meet them, and you can invite the chit for ices or whatever it is young girls fancy these days.

Then get down on bended knee and beg the chit to take you before some other lucky devil gets his hands on her fortune." His uncle waved for one of the servants to bring another bottle.

Make that two, Clifton wanted to tell the fellow, but he suspected he was falling into deep waters and needed to keep his wits about him or he'd wake up married to this paragon.

Or worse, combing the streets of Mayfair looking for Lucy.

His body tightened, as it always did when he thought of her. Remembered her. Her lush curves, her passionate nature.

What had she called the lady with her? Clump? Clack? No, it was Clapp. But who was this Clapp? Her mother-in-law, perhaps?

Perhaps Lady Standon could direct him to Lucy, since it appeared they knew each other. Then again, he mused, remembering Lady Standon's dark scowl and ringing scold, perhaps that wasn't the most prudent course.

"Oh, you're as cautious as your father was," Penwortham declared, waxing along without any notice of his audience's disinterest. "It's that Grey blood of yours." Again, his uncle, mindful only of his own grand plans, continued blithely on, "Agnes said I shouldn't press you, but demmit, boy, the Season is almost upon us and I would hate for some young buck to come along and steal Lady Annella away from you."

Clifton glanced about the room hoping to find one who would do just that.

"Besides, you can't go much longer without some proper blunt. And Asterby has plenty of it . . . maintains a membership here and at Brooks, and a penchant for going to Tattersall's," his uncle was saying, selling his plan with all the determination of a fishwife. "Horse-mad Asterby is, always has been, but the man's got good bloodlines."

"His horses or daughter?" Clifton couldn't help asking.

The joke went right over his uncle's head. "Why both, my boy. Both!"

A round of cheers and rich masculine laughter resounded through the room as yet another bet was laid down in the infamous book.

Thankfully, it diverted his uncle's attention. "Wonder what the devil is going on? Must be some rich action to be making such furor." Penwortham leaned back in his chair and waved over a passing young cub. "You there, Harmond, isn't it?"

"Oh, good evening, my lord," the young man said, bowing low. "How may I be of service?"

"Whatever has everyone in such a state? Has that rapscallion Demple gone and chased after another married woman? How he manages to get himself in and out of so many bedrooms without being shot in his —"

"No, no," Harmond supplied, stopping the marquess's speculations. "All that ruckus is over some trio of dowagers."

"Dowagers?" Clifton said, glancing yet again at the fervor, which was now filling the room and had fellows arriving in a steady stream to add their bets. "What could three old ladies do to create such a fuss?"

"Apparently they are to be married. Or at least that is what Stewie Hodges claims, for all three have been dowered by the Duke of Hollindrake to get them off his hands."

"Not the Standon widows?" Penwortham gasped, then shuddered, his thick jowls waggling like a hog's before Michaelmas. "Those three harpies?"

"Standon?" Clifton said. "As in Lady Standon?"

"Why, yes," his uncle said, then he stilled, a feat in itself. "Just a moment! You know

263

one of them? Now, that is a surprise."

"I sought an audience with Lady Standon this very afternoon." Clifton shuddered at the memory.

"From that grimace, I would have to imagine you met Minerva," his uncle said. "She's a regular stickler. Probably sent you off with a flea in your ear."

Clifton snapped his fingers. "Yes, yes. Rang a peal over my head when I asked her how she knew Malcolm."

Penwortham choked and sputtered. "You asked Minerva Sterling how she knew your bastard brother?" His great jowls shook — with laughter or dismay, it was hard to tell. "My boy, you are lucky to still have your head attached. Whatever gave you the notion that she would have had anything to do with Malcolm?"

"Something my solicitor mentioned. Some old business."

"Not with Minerva," his uncle said. "Top-lofty, that one."

"Perhaps it is one of the other Lady Standons," Harmond suggested.

Now it was Clifton's turn to pause. "You mean there is more than one Lady Standon?"

The young man nodded to Clifton. "Yes, of course. Three of them, actually. Hollindrake finally grew tired of their bickering and has ordered them all to live in a house on Brook Street until they can find husbands. Or rather the duchess has done the dirty deed, at least that is what Stewie claims." He nodded toward the crowd. "They are betting on who is in dire enough straits to marry one. I'm off to order up flowers and get ahead of the line, so to say. Pockets to let and all," the man said, bowing and making his hasty departure.

Clifton closed his eyes and took a deep breath. So if it wasn't Minerva, then which Lady Standon had Malcolm known? Known well enough to leave his estate in her hands?

But before he could investigate further, the scrape of his uncle's chair drew his attention.

"Now don't say a word to your aunt," Lord Penwortham admonished, for he'd gotten to his feet and was tugging his waistcoat down over his belly. "I won't put down a single monkey, but I have got to see what that nincompoop Hodges thinks he knows about this business."

"Yes, worth inspecting," Clifton urged, knowing his uncle's penchant for wagers.

"Oh, don't think you'll cast me off so easily. We've got this business of your marriage to finish," Penwortham said, raising a toast.

"Marriage?" said a familiar voice.

Clifton glanced over to see his old friend Lord John Tremont coming to a halt. "Jack!" he called out, rising to his feet and taking the man's outstretched hand with warm enthusiasm.

It had been years since they'd seen each other.

"You're to be married?" Jack asked, taking the seat Clifton waved toward. "Who is the lucky chit?"

"Lady Annella Corby. Asterby's only child," his uncle interjected before Clifton could correct the matter. "Fine girl, good match. Tell him, Tremont! Tell him how marriage agrees with a man. You've turned out extraordinarily well since you married Lady John. Unusual lady, but a delight, I must say. A delight." The man looked longingly over his shoulder as another cheer rose from the crowd.

"Careful there, Penwortham," Jack offered. "Stewie's a bit of a sharpster."

This made the marquess laugh and the man continued to watch the circus across the room.

Clifton thought he was about to escape his uncle's marriage machinations completely, the man having been diverted by the betting, but such was not his luck.

The large man turned and wagged a fat finger at his nephew. "Don't forget, Clifton. Tomorrow. I expect you to be at the corner near Bond Street at precisely three. Take another look at the lady, and then I defy you to tell me how she isn't the perfect bride." He winked, then toddled off toward the action, calling out to the man in the orange jacket, bright red waistcoat and puce trousers, "How terribly rude of you, Stewie, my good man, not to invite me over."

There was an echo of laughter and much made of the marquess's arrival, and Clifton knew that was because his uncle was considered an easy mark.

"So what is this about a marriage?" Jack asked, helping himself to a drink from the bottle on the table.

"It isn't quite settled yet," Clifton said.

Jack eyed him carefully. "Do you love this chit?"

Clifton shook his head. "Love her? Good God, man, I barely know her."

Jack leaned forward. "Then take it from a man who slipped out of more near betrothal snares than one dares count: get out of Town now."

CHAPTER 10

There was a soft scratch on the door, and Lucy sat straight up in bed.

"Lucy?" came a whispered plea from the hall. "Are you there?"

She got up immediately, tossing her wrapper over her shoulders and tying it tight as she went to the door. When she opened it, Mickey came through like a shot, throwing himself into her arms.

"There is more arguing," he whispered, burying his face into her belly and his arms winding around her in a tight circle. "Downstairs. It sounds like a regular rough and tumble."

Lucy sighed at his use of cant, but now that he'd roused her, she heard the raised voices as well.

Gracious heavens, were Minerva and Elinor back at it yet again? For after the duchess had left, the two had launched into a lengthy catfight of who-was-to-blame.

Mostly, they'd leveled their charges at Lucy.

"This is all your fault!" Elinor had huffed. "I'll not be tarred with your sins when I know you impersonated me in Brighton!"

"Dash it all, bother Brighton," Lucy had shot back. "That was nothing but a horrible misunderstanding, not that I expect you to stand and listen to reason!"

How was it Lucy's fault that the innkeeper had thought her to be Elinor? He had just assumed that since she was Lady Standon, she was Elinor. It happened all the time.

As for the damage to the inn . . . well, Lucy hadn't known that the bills had been directed to the Duke of Hollindrake as Elinor's expenses and come out of her quarterly allowance, not Lucy's.

Well, not entirely my doing, she thought with a tinge of guilt, having not quite forgiven Elinor for insisting that Lucy and her entourage move out of the duke's summer house in Kent to make way for some spontaneous house party of hers.

Oh, they'd dredged up all sorts of accusations and incidents until Clapp had wandered absently into the fray and innocently asked which rooms they were to take, which had set off another round of arguments as to who was to have which chambers, such as they were.

Eventually they'd all retreated to their claimed corners of the house to lick their wounds and, Lucy had to imagine, determine a strategy for extracting themselves from this debacle.

Lucy had spent a better part of the evening trying to come up with some plan on how to escape London.

Escape *him.*

Not that she thought he wanted her. Or even cared a whit for her.

No, it was what he'd said. *"I was looking for Lady Standon . . ."* Unwittingly, he'd come to call on her.

And she knew enough of him to realize it was only a matter of time before he'd discover the truth and return.

For her. The Lady Standon he *was* seeking.

Oh, bother! *Whatever does he want with me?* she mused as she did her best to piece together the crumbs of clues he'd offered.

"Some old business" . . . "Must be all a mistake anyway" . . . "I can't see Malcolm having any association with that harridan" . . .

No, this didn't bode well in the least. She hugged Mickey closer, her lips pressed together.

Up the stairwell, the voices echoed, growing louder. "I'm going to knock their heads together," she muttered. Then she said to Mickey, "Come along, you need to get your sleep."

We all do, she mused as she got the boy tucked back into his own bed.

Then she marched downstairs, forgetting every Mayfair manner her mother-in-law, Lady Charles, had ever tried to instill upon her.

Pushing up her sleeves, she set her jaw. If they were going to act like Seven Dials slatterns, then she was going to treat them as such.

But halfway down the stairs, she spied Minerva standing in the shadows. When she turned and looked at Lucy, Lucy could see that Minerva's face was ashen with shock.

And so it would be, considering the ugly snippets of accusations coming out from behind the closed doors to the receiving room.

"— why, the gossip is all over Town as to your situation. Mine as well, not that a selfish creature like you would care." This was punctuated by the *thump* of a boot heel.

"Who?" Lucy mouthed to Minerva.

"Elinor's stepfather. Lord Lewis," Minerva whispered. She cringed as the man began to rant again.

"— a wretched disgrace, that is what you are. You've made a fool of me again." There was more stomping as the man paced about the room.

"— I'll not let you marry without my cut. I'll not be left without what I am due, since you made a mess of the last one. You couldn't even manage to get an heir. An heir, Elinor, then you wouldn't be in these straits. As worthless as your mother was to me —"

This was punctuated by a loud, hard slap.

Lucy straightened. "Did he just strike her?" For while her father had always been a man who had not minced words, he had never hit his daughters — or any other woman, for that matter.

Minerva nodded. "I feared it would come to this." She shook her head. "There is little we can do."

"Little you can do, perhaps," Lucy declared, "but I am not going to stand for this."

"You cannot interfere," Minerva said, catching her by the arm. "You'll mortify Elinor."

Lucy shook her off. "I won't let that man beat her. This is *my* house too."

She crossed the foyer and threw open the doors.

Inside, Elinor was slumped to the floor and her stepfather stood over her, about to land another blow. A pinch-nosed lady sat on the couch, watching the proceedings with a cruel gleam in her eyes.

"Hit her again, and it will be the last breath you draw," Lucy told Lord Lewis.

Brandy fumes filled the room, and from Lord Lewis's bleary eyes and ruddy cheeks, Lucy knew him for exactly what he was. A drunken bully.

The man paused; in fact, everyone in the room stilled. He looked up at Lucy and sneered. "Who the hell are you?"

"Lucy, please leave," Elinor begged. "Just leave."

At this, Lord Lewis's gaze narrowed. "Lucy? You're Lucy Ellyson? You dare to tell me what to do? Get out of here, you worthless slut. Go back to the Dials or whatever hole it was your father crawled out of. This is none of your affair." Then he eyed her from head to toe. "Or stay if you want. That is, if you put out like your fancy whore of a mother does."

Apparently Lord Lewis had never heard the tale of Monday Moggs.

Be a lady, she could hear Lady Charles plead. *Don't let your temper get out of hand.*

"Please leave," Elinor whispered again.

But it was a different sort of advice that stuck in Lucy's resolve. A bit of wisdom from the erudite pockets of Rusty and Sammy.

Always carry a bess with you, lass. It can be used to break more than the hinges off a door.

She crossed the space and grabbed one of the empty candlesticks from the mantel. It wasn't as versatile as a bess, but it would do.

"Get out!" she ordered, waving the heavy silver piece at him. "Get out of our house, and don't you ever dare to darken these doors again or you shall see how much of the Dials still flows in my veins." She waved the candlestick at Lord Lewis and the glowering woman, even as she caught Elinor by the arm and tugged her up, then shoved her toward Minerva.

The lady on the settee rose up. "Oh, move away, Fenton. Good God! She's mad!"

"I'm beyond mad," Lucy told them. "If you ever dare raise a hand to Elinor again —"

"I'll raise my hand to any bitch I want. Including you," Lord Lewis said, lurching forward, but only for one teetering step. Then he froze, his eyes bugging out.

Lucy glanced briefly over her shoulder,

relieved to find the formidable sight of Thomas-William in the doorway, pistol in hand and pointed at the man.

The lady screeched again, but she was silenced by a sharp retort from Lord Lewis. The pair of them edged out of the room and then out the door, all under the watchful, unforgiving gaze of Thomas-William.

But before Lucy could push the door closed, Lord Lewis shook his fist at Elinor. "Don't think this is over, you worthless bitch. I'll be back. I want your sister. You can't keep her forever. The law is on my side."

Lucy had heard enough. She slammed the door shut, then latched it quickly. With her back against it, her fingers still clenched to the latch, she looked up at Thomas-William. "Thank you."

He huffed and said nothing, shaking his head and turning back into the shadows of the house, as if such occurrences happened so often that this one was hardly worth mentioning.

Elinor trembled in Minerva's arms, and they both gaped at Lucy as if they were seeing her for the first time.

As if they had never witnessed such a horror.

She braced herself for the lecture on being ladylike. Of not butting into private business. Of restraint.

So it was of some shock when Minerva said, "Well done, Lucy. Oh, very well done."

If that wasn't enough to bowl Lucy over, Elinor swept across the foyer and took Lucy into her shaky grasp, drawing her into a tight embrace. "Dear heavens, can you ever forgive me?"

"Or I?" Minerva said, crossing the room and putting her tentative arms around the two of them.

Minerva, hugging?

"Whatever are we to do?" Elinor whispered after a few moments. "There is no one to help us."

"No, Elinor. We have each other," Minerva said, stepping back from the other two, as if suddenly remembering her place. Well, nearly. "I think claret and a toast is in order. Isn't that right, Lucy?" she demurred.

Clifton and his old friend Jack Tremont had retreated to a quiet room in White's in order to get caught up without interruption, or, as Clifton said, "Avoid my uncle before he takes it in his head that I should propose this evening."

Jack laughed. "Running from the French? *Tsk. Tsk.* I have heard better things of you.

But in this case, running to ground may be in order."

"Ah, you know my uncle well," Clifton said in all earnestness.

They both laughed.

"So you don't love this chit, but you are going to let your uncle bully you into marrying her?" Jack shook his head and poured a measure of brandy into the two glasses a servant had brought over. "Sounds as high-handed as Parkerton. He used to try every Season to bully me into the parson's trap with some gel or another." Jack shuddered at the memory. "So why marry at all? If you don't like the chit, tell your uncle to bugger off."

Clifton shrugged. "Can't. I need the blunt."

"Hmmm," Jack mused. As the second son, he could understand that problem — for years he'd been perpetually in arrears, his brother, the Duke of Parkerton, holding the purse strings. Luckily for Jack, he'd married Miranda Mabberly, a cit's daughter with a penchant for business. She'd turned around his enterprises, and they now lived quite comfortably.

Yet Jack had the added benefit of being madly in love with his wife, having left his old rakish ways behind and losing his old epithet of "Mad Jack."

Well, nearly. For he'd been a rake for far too long not to recognize the signs.

"There's someone else," Jack said, his eyes narrowed shrewdly.

"Don't be foolish. There isn't anyone else," Clifton lied.

Jack arched a brow at him and studied him intently.

Shifting under his friend's scrutiny, Clifton tried to lie again. "Leave off. There is no one else. When would I have had time in the last seven years to have formed some sort of attachment?"

Jack appeared appeased, for he settled back in his seat. "I suppose not. Why, for a time the only woman I ever saw at Thistleton Park was the butcher's wife."

Clifton laughed. "Was she comely?"

"Hardly. But after a few months, she would become oddly attractive."

They both laughed.

"So what does bring you to Town?" Jack asked. "For I doubt you would have come just at your uncle's behest."

"No, it is some odd business of Malcolm's I'm looking into."

Jack blanched, for he had been with Malcolm the night he'd been shot. He'd tried valiantly to save Malcolm's life, but

there had been naught to do to save Clifton's brother.

Yet Jack carried the guilt of it still.

Clifton caught up the bottle and refilled
Jack's glass. "We all knew the risks. That
night was no one's fault, just a mistake," he
said quietly.

It had taken him some time to reach that
understanding, but how could he not when
he'd seen too many men die over the years?
He'd come to realize the fickle hand that
could be dealt when it came to who survived
and who died.

But Clifton could still see the guilt on
Jack's face and considered another notion.
"I was going through my father's papers
recently and discovered that he had set up a
trust account for Malcolm. Monies separate
from the estate."

"Good of your father," Jack noted.

They both knew most men didn't give
much consideration, let alone blunt, to their
second or third sons, never mind their
natural sons.

"Yes, well, it is a small fortune," Clifton
said. "Enough to get me out of the bind that
I am in. I've tracked the money to an account, but it is still held in trust — for
Malcolm's heirs."

"Which is you," Jack said, raising his glass

in toast to his friend's good fortune.

"You would think, but it has been left to the discretion of Lady Standon. I cannot touch it without her say-so."

"Lady Standon?" Jack muttered. "But why ever would Malcolm leave his money to Lucy?"

A cold chill ran down Clifton's spine. "What do you mean, 'Lucy'?"

"You must have met her. George Ellyson's daughter, Lucy. She's Lady Standon now."

"Lucy Ellyson?"

"Uh-huh," Jack nodded.

"Lucy Ellyson, George Ellyson's daughter, is Lady Standon?"

"Yes, the same. So you do remember her?"

Remember her? *If only Jack knew.* Icy shock settled over Clifton. "Oh, yes, I remember her."

"She married Hollindrake's heir, Archie Sterling. Of course he wasn't the heir then, just a clerk working for some solicitor."

A bit of stray dialogue from long ago flitted through Clifton's memories.

"Naught but Archie, the clerk at Mr. Strout's office . . . he's taken a fancy to Lucy . . ."

"She married him?" he said more to himself than to Jack.

"Oh there was a bit of a hullabaloo over it, especially a few months later, when

280

Archie's uncle — that old drunkard Lord Edward — up and died, leaving Archie as the next in line. Since the marriage couldn't be undone, the Sterlings did their best to bring her up to snuff, but you know Lucy —" Jack grinned. "I think the entire family drew a collective sigh of relief when Archie died in that gaming hell and the title passed to Thatcher." He laughed. "Can you imagine, Lucy Ellyson a duchess?" He shook his head. "Oh, she's given them nothing but trouble as Lady Standon. Too much of her father's temper. She's never been one to suffer fools gladly, and unfortunately, Society is rather overflowing with them."

Well, on that point, Clifton couldn't argue, for he found London Society utterly ridiculous. Yet Lucy's temper aside, why had she married Archie Sterling?

"I'm sorry," he'd managed to say. *"I suppose I should use your married name, but I fear I don't know it."*

She'd shaken her head. *"Lucy will still do, my lord."*

Nor had she told him she was a widow. Or Lady Standon.

His jaw tightened as he remembered how he had teased her about Monday Moggs. *"So if he'd had a title, estates, an income and a stable full of well-mannered horses, you wouldn't have floored him? You'd have let him carry out his nefarious plans?"*

Lucy Ellyson had tossed aside the promise she'd made to Clifton and snapped up Archie Sterling, the eventual heir to a dukedom.

Their interview from earlier glowed in an entirely new light. But it left one largely unanswered question.

"Why would Malcolm have left her his fortune?"

He hadn't meant to say that aloud, but Jack, as it turned out, had his own theories.

"Perhaps he was in love with her. Though I would have thought Mariana, pretty thing that she was, would have been more to his taste. Gads, every man who ever went through that house left half in love with one of them. Glorious creatures, the pair of them." Jack raised his glass in a mock toast.

Clifton sat back, trying to piece together everything Jack had just given him. "Why ever would she have married him?" he muttered more to himself than for Jack's benefit.

"Marry Archie?" his friend replied, mistaking the question for curiosity. "I've wondered that as well. Must have been for a demmed good reason, for Lucy Ellyson was never a foolish bit of muslin."

This pulled Clifton's rising temper into

check, because Jack was right. Lucy had never been a girl whose head was turned by a title or wealth.

"Might have done it out of grief," Jack offered. "Mariana and her father had died. She had no one left, no one to turn to. And there was Archie." He glanced up at Clifton. "I suppose you can understand that one. I thought for sure you'd never come home after Malcolm died. That day you sailed from Thistleton Park, I told Miranda it was most likely the last time we'd ever see you again. Never known a man so lost in grief and heartbreak." He reached over and slapped him on the shoulder. "Glad to see I was wrong."

Clifton nodded his thanks, but his thoughts were awhirl. A cacophony of questions rang a heavy peal over his head.

Why had Lucy not just waited for him?

Why had Malcolm left his money to her?

Even as his anger and suspicion welled up inside him, urging him to march over to Brook Street and demand answers from her, Clifton's pride rebelled, latching onto another of Ellyson's truisms.

Don't ask the question if you don't want to hear the answer.

No, he couldn't ask her. She was the one, after all, who'd broken faith with him, married another. . . . She owed *him* an explanation.

If only he had Malcolm's will in hand, then he might find some clue. . . . If only Strout's clerk hadn't misplaced it . . .

Clifton paused. The clerk . . .

"That's it," Clifton said, rising abruptly to his feet. Oh, why the hell hadn't he thought of it before? The clerk!

"What's it?" Jack asked, looking up from his comfortable chair.

"In the mood for a little investigation, a la George Ellyson?"

Jack's mouth spread into a wide grin and he bounded to his feet. "Will it prove to be illegal or illicit?" Obviously Clifton's contentedly married friend hadn't left his Mad Jack ways completely behind.

"Possibly," Clifton said as he made his way out of the club.

"Far better than meeting up with my brother for another one of his prowsy lectures," Jack declared as he followed, hot on the earl's heels.

As they left White's and waited for Clifton's carriage to be brought around, Jack crossed his arms and kicked at a stone. "You never did say which one of the Ellyson sisters you fancied."

Clifton looked straight ahead. After a few

moments, he said, "Lucy."

"I thought as much," Jack said. "She seems more your type. Fancy her still?"

"No," Clifton lied.

And Jack, being a former rake and ne'er-do-well, knew better than to call him out.

"There must be some solution to all this," Lucy suggested, settling back on the cushion she'd pulled down and set near the grate. "Something amenable to all of us."

"You both could move out," Minerva suggested. Then she grinned at her own jest.

But it might have been the two bottles of claret they'd consumed that had Minerva — of all people — grinning. For after Lord Lewis's departure, they'd raided the kitchen and discovered a small cache of a decent vintage, as well as a plate of biscuits.

Two bottles of claret and a plate of sweets had them fast friends.

"I have no other place to go," Lucy confessed. "My father's house in Hampstead belonged to the Duke of Parkerton. When Papa died, the lease ended. 'Tis why I married Archie."

"The duke cast you out from your home?" Elinor asked.

Lucy nodded.

Her new friend huffed. "If ever I meet the

man, I shall give him a piece of my mind. What a horrid fellow he must be," she declared.

"Indeed!" Minerva concurred.

"I fear I am not only a relic but a pauper as well," Lucy told them.

"What of the contessa?" Elinor asked, then blushed at the mention of the lady who was never named aloud in the Sterling clan. Emboldened as she was, she asked, "Wouldn't she help you?"

"Oh, hardly," Lucy told them. "The last thing the contessa needs is a daughter half her age about. She's too young, she avers, to have a daughter my age! Besides, she's usually up to her ears in debt — especially when she's in between protectors."

"Oh, such a thing! I never knew," Elinor declared before she turned to Minerva. "Why don't you move out? Surely there is some dower house or other such suitable residence that your cousin can offer you, considering the circumstances. You've never been at a loss to tell us how much more superior the Earls of Gilston are, what an ancient lineage they hold."

Minerva blushed. "I've been dreadfully horrid, haven't I?"

Elinor glanced away, for she was still far too much of a lady to be completely honest.

However, Lucy wasn't so restrained. "Beastly," she said before she collapsed into a fit of tipsy giggles, which was then joined in by Elinor and Minerva.

"As for moving home, it is impossible," Minerva said. "My cousin has made it clear that I am a Sterling now, and as such, Hollindrake's responsibility, not his." She paused, and what it cost her, Lucy could only imagine, for then Minerva added, "I have nowhere else to go."

Her honesty sent a quiet chill through the room.

Elinor glanced away. "Nor I."

"Obviously," Lucy began. She shifted and glanced up at Elinor. "But however could your mother tolerate such circumstances. She just sat there!"

Lucy's mother may be a disgrace, but she would never have allowed such abuse.

Elinor shook her head. "Oh, heavens, Lucy, that woman wasn't my mother. That is Lord Lewis's new wife."

"The former Oriable Huthwaite," Minerva supplied. "Low *ton,* really. Very low."

"Agreed," Elinor said, her nose wrinkling. Then she glanced over at Lucy. "No offense meant."

"None taken," Lucy said.

"I will be the first to say that your origins

came in quite handy tonight," Minerva admitted. "Perhaps Bath schools should be teaching alternative uses for candlesticks."

"What I don't understand," Lucy said, "is that if Lord Lewis is your stepfather and that lady isn't your mother, then how can he have control of your future or Tia's?"

"When he married my mother, he gained our guardianship." Elinor glanced away, tears forming in her eyes. She set aside her glass and wiped at them. "It is intolerable. I may have my freedom from him, but my sister does not. And now he means to see Tia married."

"She's but a child!" Minerva protested. "Not yet fourteen."

"Yes, I know," Elinor said. "But it wouldn't be the first time he forced one of his stepdaughters to wed against her wishes. That is why I snatched her out of her school and brought her here to London. To hide her from him, until I could apply to the duke for help. But now . . ."

They all realized that help from His Grace might not be forthcoming, or, at the very least, difficult to obtain.

"We must stop him," Lucy said. Then she corrected herself. "We will stop him." She reached over and squeezed Elinor's hand.

They sat for a while in silence, each

consumed with her own thoughts.

"She truly does have us boxed into a corner," Minerva said in an uncharacteristic bit of cant. "But in your case, Elinor, it might be a good idea to take Her Grace's advice and get married."

"I have no intention of getting married again," Elinor declared. "I have no need of finding myself in another man's bed." Her nose wrinkled in dismay.

"Nor I," Minerva agreed quickly. "I'll not be some man's duty."

Lucy glanced at both of them and realized they were talking about their marriage beds. While she'd never met the first Lord Standon, Philip Sterling — twenty years older than Minerva when she'd become his third bride — she'd heard enough gossip to know he'd been naught but a brute and a lout. Elinor hadn't fared much better with Philip's brother Edward, or, as Sterling family gossip had it, a self-affected drunk who'd fancied his young male companions more than his innocent bride.

No wonder the other two Lady Standons lacked any enthusiasm for marriage.

"It isn't all that bad," Lucy declared. "The duty, that is."

When they both gaped at her, Lucy cursed the claret that had loosened her tongue and her unfortunate tendency to blurt out whatever she was thinking.

Elinor, emboldened by her own glasses, giggled. "Are you going to lead us to believe that Archie Sterling was a good lover?"

Lucy laughed. "Who, Archie? Oh, good heavens, no!"

Then she realized what she'd just admitted.

Elinor's eyes widened. "You've had a lover!" she declared, wagging her finger at Lucy. "A good one."

Rather than looking askance, the two ladies edged closer to Lucy.

"Do tell," Elinor pleaded.

"Yes, all the details," Minerva said.

"No!" Lucy replied, shaking her head furiously.

"Oh, it must have been heavenly," Elinor said, nudging Minerva. "For look how she blushes."

"Was it one of the King's agents?" Minerva asked.

Lucy sat back, her mouth gaping.

"Oh, please, Lucy," Minerva said. "We know all about your father. I suppose there were ever so many daring agents you met. It must have been one of them."

They both sat there, grinning at her like a pair of hungry cats.

And there would be no putting them off.

"Oh, if you must know," Lucy said, "it was. But I cannot say more than that. I won't say more than that."

Elinor nodded to Minerva, who then topped off Lucy's glass.

"Weren't we discussing Elinor's situation?" Lucy reminded them, making a note not to drink any more claret, or she'd be prattling on worse than Mariana ever had.

"Yes, I suppose we must," Minerva said. "Really, Elinor, perhaps, as Lucy suggests marriage might agree, and it would keep that despicable stepfather of yours at bay."

Lucy glanced over at Minerva, for her new friend's unwitting suggestion rang true for her as well. If she was married, Clifton couldn't come after her. He wouldn't dare. . . .

"I was raised to be a duchess," Elinor declared. "Not take potluck with the leftover gentlemen in the duchess's journal."

"Even if it means saving Tia?" Lucy asked quietly.

They all turned and looked at the lone volume sitting where the duchess had left it on the stand in the foyer.

"There is only one way to find out," Lucy said, getting up and crossing the room. She paused for a moment and stared down at the worn cover, at the girlish scrawl written across the front.

Private. The property of Felicity Langley.

So the duchess had held dreams as well, Lucy mused. And found them in her marriage to the man who'd inherited the Hollindrake dukedom.

Taking a deep breath, Lucy picked up the book, then dashed guiltily back to her spot near the fireplace, having closed the door behind her.

They all sat there for a moment, waiting, until Minerva said, "Oh, bother, Lucy. Open it!"

Lucy nodded, counted to three and, letting the Fates and happenstance guide her, opened to a random page.

"What does it say?" Elinor asked, edging down the settee until she could look over Lucy's shoulder. "Oh, goodness. It is Winny Addleston!"

"Not Minny Winny," Minerva said, rising from her chair and coming to sit beside Lucy on the floor. "Goodness, everyone knows he's a great fool!"

"Minny Winny?" Lucy shook her head. "It says nothing like that. Now here, listen to what she writes:

Winston, Baron Addleston, born 1783.

Holdings: Addleston House, an Elizabethan mansion with good pasture land and excellent income from wool.

The baron is known for breeding good hunting dogs and excellent horses. Prefers the country. Kindly temperament, good to the poor in his parish. Needs only to come to Town to find a bride.

Lucy looked up. "Why, he sounds like a decent prospect."

Minerva sniffed. "If you want to spend the rest of your days buried in the country listening to him wheeze."

Elinor laughed. "I daresay he'd wheeze through his duty. Ever so distracting, wouldn't you think?"

They all laughed.

"Find another, Lucy," Minerva urged. "Someone a bit more lofty. Someone with a bit of Town dash to them."

They both looked at her.

"I like a man with some polish to him," she returned unapologetically.

Thumbing through again, Lucy stopped on a random page, hoping the fellow had enough "dash" for Minerva.

Instead, much to her shock, she looked down at a name she knew all too well.

Justin Grey, the Earl of Clifton.

Lucy snapped the book shut. "This is utter folly."

"No, no!" Elinor said, reaching over and snatching the book out of her hands. "That was the Earl of Clifton. Wasn't he the fellow who came around and accosted you, Minerva?"

"Impertinent fellow," she recalled. "And no dash."

"I suppose not," Elinor replied. "Still, he is quite handsome. Such dark hair, and those eyes! So very piercing." She paged through the journal until she got to his entry and began to read aloud:

Justin Grey, the Earl of Clifton

Holding: Clifton House, an old estate situated on the Thames.

The Earl of Clifton comes from a long line of noble gentlemen who have served England faithfully.

"So have most of the nobles in Town," Minerva remarked with a sniff, "but that hardly moves me to believe they can be a good lover."

"No, no, listen to this," Elinor said.

Lucy didn't need to listen; she closed her eyes and saw him. Saw that first day she'd met him, all proper and stiff. When he'd been about to kiss her on the lane, his eyes so dark and mysterious. The night he'd laid her in his bed and made love to her . . .

Meanwhile, Elinor continued to read:

Clifton has displayed a level of courage rarely seen, sacrificing much for his country. He is considered one of the finest men to ever serve the Foreign Office. He deserves a lady of heart and courage (and a good dowry) to help heal his wounds.

"He was wounded?" Minerva said. "He looked quite sound when he was here."

"I believe his wounds are more of the heart," Lucy said. "The difficulties he faced, the perils he overcame."

Her audience nodded solemnly.

"Did he mention what he was seeking?" Lucy asked, trying to sound nonchalant. When both of them looked quizzically at her, she shrugged. "I saw him coming down the steps. Whatever impertinence he displayed, Minerva, it appeared you sent him packing quite efficiently."

"Some nonsense about his brother. His *natural* brother. And how I might know him." Minerva shook her head.

"Malcolm," Lucy said aloud, not meaning to.

"Pardon?" Minerva said.

"His brother's name was Malcolm. And he served as well. He was killed on a beach near Hastings. The local militia mistook him for a smuggler and shot him." Lucy glanced away.

"Oh, the poor man," Minerva said. "What a terrible tragedy."

More than you can guess, Lucy would have told her.

Elinor tipped her head and studied Lucy. "Did you know him? This Malcolm, and Lord Clifton?"

Glancing up at her two new comrades-in-arms, Lucy sensed that tonight they had forged a real bond, one that went beyond the claret and Lord Lewis. They were together in their plight, and she realized just how much she had missed Mariana and the friendship they had shared.

"Yes, I knew them both."

Minerva wasn't just regal; she was also as smart as a whip, and Lucy watched her come to her conclusions. "He was looking for you!"

Lucy held her breath, for Minerva wasn't done. Her expression slowly went from amazement to outright shock, even as she turned her gaze toward the ceiling and then back at Lucy. "Dear heavens above. Mickey."

CHAPTER 11

The next morning Lucy went down to breakfast feeling no end of trepidation. Whatever had she been thinking, telling Elinor and Minerva about Clifton and Mickey, and why the earl could not discover the boy's existence?

Too much claret and not enough common sense, she told herself. She'd spilled her secrets like the worst sort of turncoat agent.

Her father would have been appalled at her behavior.

But in the end, Minerva and Elinor had both agreed to her reasoning and, instead of being dismayed over her revelation, had hugged her close — well, Elinor had — and promised to help her.

We will endeavor to help each other, Minerva had insisted as they had teetered tipsily off to bed.

But Lucy had to wonder if these sentiments would hold true in the cold light of day.

Not that their servants had been informed of the detente that had been forged the night before. Lucy paused on the stairs as the beginnings of an argument between Minerva's abigail and Elinor's maid began in one of their rooms. Something over using the iron.

And down further inside the house Clapp's voice was rising in dismay over something, while even Mr. Otter — calm, sensible Mr. Otter — was having words with the housekeeper, Mrs. Hutchinson, at the foot of the stairs.

"A sensible diet for a young man, madame," he was saying, "does not include a double ration of bacon and eggs. You'll make him gluttonous and a laggard with such fare. Cooked oats and weak tea will serve him much better."

" 'E's not a horse, Mr. Otter," she was arguing back. " 'E's a growing lad with the appetite to match. And I'll tell you right now to mind your p's and q's around me kitchen, unless you want to fancy yourself eating your last supper."

Oh, gracious heavens! And this was only the first morning of their enforced housing.

What would it be like by the end of the week?

Just then the bell over the door jangled, and Lucy looked around for Mr. Mudgett to answer it. But their batman-cum-butler was nowhere about.

And it didn't appear that either Mr. Otter or Mrs. Hutchinson were inclined to answer it as the bell tolled again, this time with a bit more urgency.

Lucy shot a plaintive glance at their housekeeper and cook, but Mrs. Hutchinson was busy wiping her hands on her apron and apparently of the entire business.

"I won't be answering that," she declared. "Probably another of those fancy toffs who've been showing up since dawn. Tired of the lot of them, I am. This house has more flowers than a funeral, and it smells like one as well."

It was only then that Lucy noticed the bouquets, piles of them, stacked on every available space — the receiving table, the window seat; even a cubby designed for bric-a-brac was now stuffed with posies.

Why, every hothouse in London appeared to have been raided.

"My heavens!" Lucy exclaimed. "Who are they all for?"

"Well, take your pick, m'lady," Mrs.

Hutchinson said. "They are all to be delivered to 'Lady Standon.' " She snorted and shook her head. "Don't think one of those witless fellows cares which of you gets them. They've just got marriage on their minds."

"Oh, this is utter foolishness!" Lucy gasped. "Why ever would they think —" Her question came to a halt as the bell rang again.

"Don't look at me!" Mrs. Hutchinson declared. "Quite worn down to my toes what with that fool bell and all the demands I've had to listen to this morning." She paused and glanced over at Mr. Otter with a meaningful arch of her brows. " 'Sides, I've got apple tarts and custards to bake for the young 'un." And with that shot fired, she turned heel and marched toward the rear of the house and her kitchen domain.

This sent Mr. Otter into another volley of sputtered complaints. "My good woman, do you mean to fatten the child for roasting?" He scurried after her, a litany of acceptable fare issuing forth.

She supposed if it was Minerva or Elinor standing here, the poor soul on the other side of the door would just have to continue pulling the bell cord in vain, but luckily for whoever it was, she hadn't their aristocratic sensibilities.

After all, she'd answered her father's door often enough while growing up in Hampstead. Delighted in discovering whatever the other side held.

Always hoping it was him returning to claim her heart, just as he'd promised . . .

The bell jarred her out of that musing, and she quickly wove her way through several large arrangements of blossoms and greenery, flipping the latch aside and opening the door.

Immediately she found a bounty of roses stuffed toward her.

"These are for Lady Standon!" an imperious voice announced.

Another bouquet followed, hyacinths by the heady fragrance, edging the roses aside slightly. "Why ever do you think the fair Lady Standon would take your poor roses, my good man!" another equally lofty voice added.

Lucy did her best to brush them aside so she could see these would-be swains, but another person coming up from behind did it for her.

"Get out of my way," an elderly lady's voice announced. "Gracious heavens, is that you, Percy Harmond?" A cane came between the two men, and a sharp rap on both their elbows had them moving aside, the bouquets going up into the air and falling in a shower of lost petals and blossoms.

Cane in hand, the regal old woman, with a wrinkled face and sparkling blue eyes beneath her gleamingly starched cap and bonnet, eyed both gentlemen as if she couldn't decide which one to knock about next.

Her sharp gaze fell on the unfortunate Percy Harmond. "Good God, man, you've gotten as stout as your Uncle Henry! And probably just as much in debt. Whatever are you thinking? Calling on my niece? Be gone! You as well, Lord George! Why, you look quite ill in that color of waistcoat. Whatever was your tailor thinking? No! No! Don't even tell me it was your idea, for I will think you more of a nitwit than I already do. Nuisances, both of you. Now be gone."

During the course of this berating speech, she'd managed to wedge herself between them on the narrow front steps and then chase them down with her waving cane and round of pointed, and well-informed, insults.

Having sent them scattering like bill collectors faced with a brace of pistols, she then stalked up and past Lucy. "Well, don't just stand there gawking, girl, announce me!"

It was then that Lucy noticed the other lady coming up the steps. "Lady Charles!" she said, surprised to see her mother-in-law. While most of the Sterlings held her in contempt, she'd always found a fond welcome from Archie's mother.

"Announce me, you foolish girl!" the other lady repeated, as Lucy closed the door and turned around.

"I fear I don't know who you are." She glanced over at Lady Charles for help, but all she looked was bemused.

"Why, I'm Lady Standon's aunt, you wretched girl," the little whirlwind announced. "Her Aunt Bedelia. Now move along before I see you sent packing as well." She waved her cane to punctuate her point.

"Of course, madam," Lucy said, a bit taken aback. Over the lady's shoulder she spied Lady Charles smiling, as if Bedelia's antics were part and parcel of being in her company. "I believe your niece is taking breakfast."

Lucy led the way into the dining room, but before she could manage a single word, Elinor spied her in the doorway and said, "Oh, there you are! Did you take it?"

"Did I take what?"

"What she is asking is," Minerva said, glancing up from her plate of dry toast and a single slice of thin ham, "was it you who took the duchess's journal?"

"Aha!" Aunt Bedelia sputtered, coming forward and shaking her cane right under Lucy's nose. "Stealing as well as lollygagging about your duties." The lady peered a little closer at her. "Probably one of Lucy Sterling's ragtag company of misbegotten servants, is my guess."

"Aunt!" Minerva said faintly, rising from her chair, her face paling as if she'd just seen a ghost. "However did you —"

Aunt Bedelia, temporarily forgetting Lucy, now rounded on her niece. "Find you? Well, through no lack of trouble, I might say." She paused and glanced over at Lucy. "Don't you have duties to attend to? Or shall I summon that gadfly Lady Standon — Rosebel, whatever were you thinking, allowing Archie to marry that creature's daughter? Not that men ever consider future expectations when they marry, now do they?" She paused and glanced around the room. "Now where was I? Ah yes, go fetch Lucy Sterling this very moment so I can explain to that ill-bred upstart the importance of keeping respectable servants."

"Aunt Bedelia," Minerva said in a strained voice, her hands gripping at the table edge for support, "that is Lucy Sterling."

Aunt Bedelia didn't even flinch. Instead she sent a withering gaze over at Lucy. "Good heavens! Answering the door?! You are as queer as they say, I will avow that. Now stand up straight, girl." The cane snaked out and tapped Lucy on one side and then the other, until she was standing at attention. "However is anyone to know you are a marchioness if you don't use proper posture. I should know, I was a marchioness — twice!"

Aunt Bedelia, as it turned out, had been married five times. Two marquesses, an earl, a baron and, most recently, a viscount. Viscount Chudley, to be exact.

Marriage was a subject in which she was well versed, and it was marriage she and Lady Charles had come to discuss.

"I cannot help but feel some responsibility for this situation," Lady Charles said after they settled into the receiving room.

"However could you think it is your fault?" Minerva asked, and Lucy had no doubt she had wanted to finish that sentence with a more pointed accusation. *No, my lady, the fault is hardly yours, but that of your meddlesome daughter-in-law.*

Lady Charles waved her off. "I should have done more to see the three of you reconciled, for — and please do not be offended — I have always thought you could be good friends."

The three of them shared a glance, then began to laugh.

"Whatever is so funny?" Aunt Bedelia demanded. "I cannot see that your circumstances are amusing in the least!"

"It is just, dear Aunt Bedelia," Minerva told her, "before last night I would have found Lady Charles's suggestion of friendship utterly ridiculous."

Lady Charles glanced around the room, her gaze falling on the empty bottles of claret. "I see you have cleared the air amongst yourselves."

Aunt Bedelia noticed as well. "Got tippled, did you?"

Elinor raised her hand to her brow. "Not quite so loud, my lady."

"Didn't save any for us," the old lady huffed. "Just as well, we have much to discuss, including your marriages."

"My lady, we have no intention of getting married," Lucy told her. The other two nodded in agreement.

"Not get married! Bah!" Aunt Bedelia shot back. "Of course you must marry."

"Truly, we do not seek husbands," Minerva told her. "We mean to stand together against this injustice."

"Utter nonsense!" the lady said.

"We have had our marriages, my lady," Elinor pointed out. "And do not intend to pursue it again."

"You wouldn't say that if you hadn't made a shambles of your first go round," Bedelia declared. "I had five husbands, and I know a fair sight more about men than any of you."

"I would point out that we had no choice in our husbands. Circumstances as they were," Minerva said delicately.

"But you do now," Lady Charles reminded them. "And I agree with Bedelia — marriage with the right man is quite agreeable. A joy, really."

Lucy thought for a moment of the passion she'd known that one night with Clifton, and she had always wondered if it had been the illicit nature of their affair that had made it so grand.

For her marriage bed with Archie had borne no resemblance to that night.

Lady Charles wasn't done making her case. "It seems a shame that you should spend your lives in this house just to spite the London gossips and the rather unorthodox plans of one marriage-mad duchess."

Minerva groaned. "It's all over Town, isn't it?"

"One look at the foyer should tell you that," Lucy pointed out.

"And are they making wagers?" Elinor asked, hand still on her brow.

"Filled two pages in the book at White's last night according to Chudley," Bedelia advised. "That is why we are here. I went to Rosebel immediately when I heard the news. And we agree there is only one solution: the three of you marry and marry well." Bedelia's eyes narrowed. "The best revenge is always a splendid match."

The three friends exchanged wary glances.

"Mind what I say," Bedelia told them. "By afternoon, every rake, buck and fortune hunter in town will have come calling."

Lady Charles nodded. "As well as every matron with a marriageable daughter, if only to see what she is up against."

"So you must be ready," Aunt Bedelia said. "Now come along, fetch your bonnets and cloaks, we have much to do to prepare you."

"Prepare?" Elinor said faintly. "I don't remember agreeing to any of this."

Bedelia laughed. "Of course you didn't. But you will. And best of all, this will be your choice. No one will force you to marry

309

a man you don't love. That is the joy of a second marriage — it is a matter of your own making."

"Or your third, fourth and perhaps fifth one as well," Lady Charles teased.

"And good choices they were," Bedelia paused, tugging at her gloves. "But you must know what sort you want. Minerva, tell me of the man you would like to marry."

"I don't know, that is to say, I haven't considered —"

"Good God, girl, you've been a widow for nearly ten years, tell me what sort of man you fancy!"

Minerva straightened. "A moral and upright one."

"Good luck there," Bedelia muttered before she turned to Elinor. "And you?"

"A duke," Elinor said. "I will not marry anyone of lesser rank."

"They are mostly mad," Bedelia advised. "But if you insist." She turned to Lucy. "And you?"

"Any man will do," Lucy lied.

Lady Chudley took a step back and stared at her. "Gracious heavens above, Lady Standon! We need to work on your standards. Believe me, any man will not do."

As he walked down Bond Street for his assignation with his uncle, Clifton weighed all the information he and Jack had been able to gather the previous night. He was drawing closer to discovering the connection between Lucy and Malcolm, but now he needed just one more thing before he could solve the mystery.

Malcolm's missing will.

There is more to this, he could almost hear George Ellyson advising. *There is always more to a situation than meets the eye.*

What that "more" could be, Clifton hadn't the vaguest notion.

Like why Lucy had married Archie Sterling. Jack's assertion that she'd done so for "demmed good reasons" had done something to him. It had chipped at his resolve, and he found himself having to shore up his ironclad belief that all she'd ever had to do was wait.

Wait as he'd done all these long years.

Still . . . There was something he was missing. Something he was forgetting.

As he walked down Bond Street toward his appointment with his uncle, he set his jaw, filled with a determination to cry off from any further entanglements with Lady Annella, then get the answers he sought.

All of them.

"Ah!" Penwortham declared when he

spotted his nephew coming down the block. "You have done me proud, my boy. Stewie Hodges bet me a monkey you wouldn't show today, and now not only am I glad to see you but I'm a bit richer to boot."

"Yes, well, about Lady Annella —" Clifton began.

"Lovely girl, good bloodlines, and that enormous . . ." Penwortham went right into his usual litany of the chit's attributes as he fell in step alongside Clifton, that is until he eyed Clifton's attire. "You need a better tailor, my boy. That coat is dreadful."

Clifton glanced down at the plain navy superfine he preferred.

"You need some dash. Some savoir faire. I would have thought all those years on the Continent would have given you some style."

"Uncle!" Clifton said. "Enough. This coat is well cut, and if Lady Annella doesn't like me because of my coat, then she is not the lady for me."

How could he explain to his utterly English uncle that he hadn't been dining in Versailles or lolling about Venice? No, Clifton had spent most of that time in some of the worst gutters and sewers that Europe had to offer.

They came up to the shop where they

were to meet up with Lady Asterby and her daughter, and Penwortham turned to him. "Now remember, be nice to the gel. A little less reserve and a little more charm would serve you well."

Malcolm's exact advice from all those years ago.

He could still hear Lucy's censure of him. *"Mark my words, he is a stuffy, arrogant, overbearing . . ."*

She'd been right. Then again, Lucy wouldn't care about his coat, wouldn't care for his lack of dash. She'd never cared for those things. She'd forced him to discover the entire world around him, not just the chosen and carefully culled environs of Society.

How many times had Lucy's lessons in larceny and cheating saved his life? He'd stopped counting.

And she'll save you again.

He shook off the shiver that ran down his spine and paused beside his uncle in front of the shop. At the curb sat his carriage, waiting for him just as he'd ordered.

Thankfully, his uncle was so consumed with his matchmaking that he failed to notice his nephew's escape route at hand.

"There she is," Penwortham said with a nudge to Clifton's ribs. "Your countess."

But it wasn't Lady Annella that Clifton saw. Nor would Lady Annella ever hold his heart. Not when she stood a little more than five feet away from Lucy Ellyson.

I don't love her still, he lied to himself as he entered the shop. *I don't.*

"What you ask, my lady, I cannot do. Not for all zee duke's money," Madame Verbeck said in a loud affronted voice to Bedelia when she asked, nay demanded, that the lady herself attend to them.

"Whatever is she saying?" Aunt Bedelia asked Lucy, for Elinor and Minerva had fled to the far reaches of the shop. "I never can understand these foreign sorts."

"She has other customers to attend to first. I believe Lady Asterby and her daughter had an appointment for this morning."

"Of all the high-handed . . . ," Aunt Bedelia sputtered, coming forward. "Appointments are for cits. Now see here, Madame, we will be —"

Lucy edged out of her way, for if anyone was high-handed, it was this Aunt Bedelia of Minerva's. No wonder Minerva moved about so much, if only to keep out of the lady's clutches.

For ignoring their protests over getting married, Aunt Bedelia would suffer no

314

delays to her plans for them. She'd ordered them all to come shopping.

"A woman can't go looking for a husband without the right artillery," she declared.

Apparently Aunt Bedelia's third husband had been a military man and had left her with a penchant for strategizing.

Lucy continued to back away from the brewing tempest at the counter and nearly bowled over a petite young lady, all ribbons and delicate curls. "Oh, excuse me," she said as she tried to move around the imperious miss.

But the girl wasn't listening, for she had turned to a woman who happened to be an older copy of her. "Maman, why is Papa so set on this marriage?"

"Because you'll be a countess, you foolish girl."

The girl sighed, looking anything but impressed.

You'll be a countess . . .

Those words sent a shiver down Lucy's spine. Hadn't he promised as much? That he would return for her? Marry her? Make her his countess.

She should have demanded answers from Clifton yesterday when she'd come face-to-face with him. She should have . . .

". . . now remember to smile," the matron

was saying. "This betrothal is all but assured, you just have to catch his eye, and how couldn't you, my little angel?" The woman fluffed at the girl's arrangement of curls and pinched her cheeks so they glowed a bit brighter. "He's enchanted, I'm certain."

"He merely seeks my dowry," the girl said a bit petulantly.

"Yes, of course he does. And if it gets out that the earl is seeking a well-dowered lady to be his countess, then you'll have to do more than just be the prettiest girl in the room. No, better you secure his affection tonight at Lady Gressingham's soiree before the word gets out that he's got pockets to let and wants a bride to fix his straits. It is an honor that he's invited us to attend with him tonight — why, it makes his intentions quite clear." The woman glanced around, her sharp gaze falling on Lucy and her lips pulled into a grim line. She shooed her daughter away. "There's mushrooms enough in Society these days who would be more than delighted to have the Earl of Clifton as their son-in-law," she said with a pointed glance toward Lucy.

"Clifton?" she gasped aloud, then covered her mouth at her unladylike gaffe.

Just then, Aunt Bedelia came bustling

over. "Lucy! There you are. Madame has agreed to show you some silks she just got in from Paris, but we need you close at hand so we can determine which color suits." She glanced over at the matron and her daughter. "Lady Asterby," she said, nodding politely. "Lady Annella."

"My lady," the woman demurred, her daughter making a perfect curtsey, the sort learned in a Bath school.

They did not acknowledge Lucy, but then again, Lucy was used to being snubbed by the *ton.* Not that she cared what this old hen thought of her. She was too staggered by what she'd just learned.

Gilby was broke? And he sought to fix his woes by getting married? To this mealy-mouthed, spoiled chit?

Lucy ground her teeth together and tried to smile, for it meant he would hardly meddle in her affairs if he was about to be wed.

Yet something inside her broke anew at the thought of him entering a loveless marriage.

"Yes, well, come along, Lucy," Lady Bedelia said, catching her by the arm. "Spiteful cat," she muttered under her breath. "Never liked her."

Lucy glanced over her shoulder and took

another look at this perfect vision of elegance, this Lady Annella. Never would she believe that Clifton loved such a creature. Never.

"Is it true?" Lucy whispered to Bedelia, who, she was positive, would know the details of any situation. "That the Earl of Clifton is rolled up?"

"Broke? Oh, yes. His estates are in shambles." Bedelia stopped at the counter and began to hold up the bolts of fabrics Madame Verbeck had brought from the back of the shop. "His father's brother was to watch over the earl's lands, but the poor man died, and there was no one else to manage things. At least not until Clifton returned." The lady glanced across the shop at Lady Asterby and her daughter. "I've heard that he is all but betrothed to that gel, but it will be a poor match for him, I think. But what am I telling you for? I suppose you know Lord Clifton."

Lucy glanced up, startled that Aunt Bedelia would know such a thing. "I-I . . . that is to say."

The lady smiled and patted her hand, even as she set aside a green silk and passed over a blue. "Don't look so shocked. Your father helped the Crown, as did Clifton. In the Foreign Office. I know all about it. My

318

fourth husband was Lord Burnitt. He worked with that horrid fellow over there . . . oh, bother, what was his name?"

"Pymm?" Lucy offered.

"Yes, yes. That's it. Pymm. Dreadful man. He and Burnitt drank together. I fear the bottle did my husband in, and how many times have I wished that it had been Pymm who'd drowned in a glass of gin? But that would have hardly served England's interests and all, now wouldn't it have?"

Lucy didn't quite know what to say.

"Now where was I?" Aunt Bedelia asked — a question Lucy had no intention of answering, for she wanted desperately to change the subject lest this Bedelia be as astute as Minerva and discover the truth. "Oh, yes! The pink or the amaranthus?" she asked, holding both bolts up to examine against Lucy's coloring.

"The pink," a deep masculine voice declared. "As I remember, the lady is utterly enchanting in pink."

Clifton had followed his uncle into the shop and done the unpardonable — he'd walked right past Lady Annella and straight to the one woman he knew could save him.

That, and Jack's words still rang in his ears.

319

"Don't marry the gel if you don't love her. Marry for love, my good man, and you'll never regret a single day of your life."

And having looked from one perfectly coifed miss toward the lady who still claimed his heart despite all his attempts to banish her place there, it had been an easy choice.

"The pink," he repeated, looking from the twinkling light of mischief in the older lady's eyes to the more outraged one in Lucy's.

"I don't believe the choice is yours to make, my lord," she said, looking over his shoulder toward the door.

Oh, you'll not escape me so easily, Goosie, he wanted to tell her.

What he wanted to do was demand answers from her, but he knew those would only meet with her stubborn pride. No, this was like a card game. He needed to tempt her, toy with her, lead her along and raise the stakes until there was nothing left to do but play the last hand.

And with Lucy, it was getting to that final hand that was the dangerous part.

So he took her firmly by the arm. "Madame," he said, deferring to Bedelia, "do you mind if I borrow your friend? We are old acquaintances, and I would like a moment of her time."

"Certainly, my lord," the older lady said,

smiling wickedly at him. "Lucy appears positively delighted to see you." Then Bedelia nudged the scowling lady closer to him, giving Clifton leave to take his captive across the shop.

"How delightful this is, Lucy," he said. "To run into you again so soon after our last encounter."

"Oh, leave off the pleasantries, my lord. Whatever do you want?" She glanced over at Elinor and Minerva, but, much to her chagrin, they only smiled at her.

So much for the solidarity of friendship and standing together.

Why, they looked positively delighted to see her thusly. As if she should be back in the earl's company.

Which she shouldn't be. Couldn't be . . .

"Why, Lucy, such a thing to say to an old friend." He leaned closer and whispered in her ear, "Someone who held you in such close esteem."

She glanced up at him warily.

"I believe you've mistaken me for someone else, my lord," Lucy told him. "Someone who still holds you with some regard." She nodded toward Lady Annella. "I would hate for you to come to a misunderstanding with your intended."

"Oh, I believe what I intend to do next

321

will ensure that there is no misunderstanding between us," he said, moving swiftly to throw Lucy over his shoulder and cart her out of Madame Verbeck's shop and into his waiting carriage.

CHAPTER 12

"I've got her. Drive on, Wort," Lucy heard Clifton call out.

"The bloody hell you do!" Lucy sputtered as she struggled to right herself, for she'd landed face first on the far side seat. "If you think you can just steal me off like this —" Her words came to a halt and her fist froze midair, just before it landed on the Earl of Clifton's all-too Roman, elegant nose.

He'd stolen her off.

Up until this moment, Lucy had been so angry that she hadn't considered what it was he'd just done.

Or realized how hard her heart was hammering in her chest.

For as much as she liked to think she had forgotten what it had been like to be held in his arms, how it had made her every nerve come alive, she remembered now.

How she ached to have him take her in his arms again.

They sat there for a long moment, staring at each other. And Lucy realized two more things about him.

He hadn't flinched.

And he was still the most handsome man she'd ever clapped eyes on.

Ever the smug, arrogant nobleman who'd loved her and left her all those years ago. So she finished what she'd started.

She pulled her fist back and punched him as hard as she could, drawing his cork like the best little scraper.

Because he thought her too much of a lady to actually hit him.

And because he'd stopped at merely tossing her inside his carriage and not come tumbling after her.

No, Lucy wanted to remind him as clearly as she could that she was no lady.

Not when it came to him.

The pain that shot through Clifton's nose and left eye sent a shower of sparks dancing through his senses.

Demmed little vixen.

She'd chopped him like a street bruiser. He put his hand to his throbbing eye and could feel it swelling shut. That, and he could feel the red sticky heat of blood in his nose.

That's what he got for assuming that their past would stay that deadly right hook of hers.

Didn't remember old Monday Moggs, did you, Gilby? he could almost hear Malcolm laugh.

"What the hell was that for?" he said as he dug in his jacket for a handkerchief. He really didn't want to bleed all over this jacket.

He couldn't afford a new one.

Clifton shuddered and stuffed the linen square like a stopper into his nose, then shoved his legs across the carriage to block her escape.

Wily little monkey, she'd taken advantage of his momentary lapse and been about to jump right out of his barouche.

Keep your adversary at his wit's end, her father always used to say. *Upend him until you have the advantage.*

Lessons Lucy obviously still took to heart; never mind the peace accord over on the Continent.

He caught hold of her arm and shoved her back into her seat, which, thank God, she took, her arms crossed over her chest and a mighty glare aimed right at him.

Better her disapproval than that wicked and deadly right of hers.

"Do you know what sort of scene you caused back there?" Lucy's eyes blazed.

"A ruinous one, I hope." Then he had the temerity to grin at her.

"You're stark raving mad! Let me go! Immediately!" she demanded with all the lofty air of a duchess.

He was in no mood to entertain her. "No."

"No?" She shifted.

With only one good eye to watch her, Clifton wouldn't have put it past her to shutter the other one closed if only to effect her escape.

"Did you say *no?*" she repeated.

There was a dangerous note to her question, one that as an intelligent man, an intelligent man who would be sporting an unexplainable black eye tomorrow — well, not entirely unexplainable — perhaps he should take heed of that warning with the same air of caution as one might a tolling bell.

Still, he relied on her father's advice.

Have no cares that your enemy can discern. This is a dangerous game of chance you play.

"I did," he told her as nonchalantly as if he had asked her if she wanted a glass of punch at Almack's.

Well, perhaps not *punch,* per se, his eye and nose stinging soundly.

"How dare you kidnap me!"

"You did teach me the finer points."

"I believe you have forgotten the finer points of taking someone. For I don't remember any lesson that involved plucking a lady out of a crowded shop in broad daylight."

"And here I thought I was being quite ingenious, subtle even."

"Ingenious?" she sputtered. "You think kidnapping me in front of half of Bond Street subtle?" She blew out a loud, very unladylike breath. " 'Tis a wonder you're still alive!"

This was the Goosie he remembered. All bluster and full of spirit.

"Oh, I've managed to keep my head attached," he told her.

"I wonder if it will stay that way," she said. "Have you even considered whether Lady Annella, that china figurine of a betrothed of yours, is going to have you now?"

Jealous, Goosie?

"Won't she? We'll see," he mused. "Mark my words, she'll attend the Gressingham's ball with me tonight. You watch and see."

"I'll watch you get refused before all of Society," Lucy said back in that smug sort of way of hers.

Oh, so she thought to up the wager, did she? He changed the play a bit.

"Perhaps I have no intention of marrying her."

Was it him, or did her eyes spark at this news?

"But everyone says —"

He waved her off. "Listening to gossip, madame? I thought you above such pursuits."

She pursed her lips together.

"I would never have married her."

"Why not?"

"Because I doubt she would have been able to give me what I want from you."

Then he upended her, just as he'd been taught to do.

What he didn't expect was to find himself undone in the process.

Lucy told herself later that she'd put up one devil of a fight.

But that was dissembling at its worse.

The moment Clifton had tugged her into his grasp, his lips poised to claim hers, she'd been lost.

She would have willingly surrendered without firing a shot.

But to her chagrin, he just held her there, so close their breath mingled, so close it wasn't hard to imagine, difficult to remember how it would feel to close that gap between them.

Her heart hammered in her chest — why wouldn't it be, she was already furious with him — but how easily those emotions turned traitor against her.

Left her shivering with needs so long unmet.

His fingers, strong and warm, curled around her chin so he looked her squarely in the eye.

Lowering his voice to a whisper, Clifton said, "Goosie, I need you."

Lucy stilled.

"I need you." His statement sent a raft of desires down her spine.

And I you, Gilby, she wanted to say and throw her arms around his neck, press her lips to his.

But there was something to his dark gaze that stayed her temptations, kept her holding herself in check, as if he was waiting for her to leap into the fire.

So she held herself still and waited. Waited for him to continue.

And he did, smiling at her, the lion of his domain, the predator assured of his supremacy. "I need you, Goosie. Not some chit who can curtsey and pour tea, but one with your, shall we say, more larcenous talents."

He hadn't wanted to kiss her? He wanted her to steal something?

Why, the arrogant, presumptuous —

Lucy laid both her hands on his chest — had it been her imagination or was his heart pounding as well — oh, bother his heart! She shoved as hard as she could to escape his grasp and scrambled over to the other side of the carriage.

Not that he didn't grin at her as she'd fled.

His eyes, the ones that she'd never been able to truly read, now said something all too clearly.

Coward.

She squared her shoulders. Even if she was guilty as charged.

"If you haven't noticed, my lord," she said, straightening her skirt and bonnet, all of which had fallen askew, "the wars are over and my skills, such as they are, are no longer necessary or available."

"But I need them," he told her, leaning forward and smiling at her.

He needn't grin so. She was quite immune to his charms. She was . . .

"I'm not in the business anymore . . . I can't . . . I won't," she told him, unwilling to say much more for fear her desires would get the better of her.

Thankful he hadn't kissed her, for then

she would have probably agreed to anything.

"Aren't you even curious?" he asked.

She sighed and let herself ask the question she knew she was going to regret. "What do you want, my lord?"

"I need you to find a lady for me," he'd said.

Her pride ruffled. A lady? She sat up and stared at him. He wanted her to find him a lady? "Isn't kidnapping me enough?" she said more diplomatically.

Aren't I lady enough for you, my lord? her pride clamored.

"Well, it has proved to be rather diverting," he said.

She pretended not to hear him. But that became impossible with his next utterance.

"Actually, I need you to help me determine which Lady Standon Malcolm was having an affair with."

This brought her gaze ripping back to his, and once again, she found herself drowning in those dark eyes of his.

He thought Lady Standon had been Malcolm's lover? She tightened her lips together so her mouth wouldn't fall open in shock. It wasn't so much that he had the entire affair muddled, but that he'd gotten this far in just a day.

"An affair? With one of the marchionesses? Impossible," Lucy scoffed as nonchalantly as she could.

Besides, for once she was telling him the truth.

"Not at all. One of them was connected to Malcolm. *Intimately.*"

The word came out like a caress, and she ignored the way her senses awakened, as if beckoned by a siren.

Oh, if you only knew, Lucy wanted to say, but again stayed her tongue and said nothing, letting him continue to reveal his hand.

Clifton leaned back in his seat. "When my father died, he left Malcolm a small fortune. Monies unentailed to the estate, so he was free to give it as he saw fit. And as it turns out, Malcolm left it all in a trust, which is apparently under the control of Lady Standon."

Lucy had played enough cards not to let this shocking news change the wager.

But still, a trust?! Malcolm had left a fortune to his heirs? How could this be?

"I don't see how —" she said more to herself than to him.

"No, no, there is more," he said, cutting her off. "The monies have never been touched. At least as far as I know."

Slowly, ever so slowly, she raised her gaze to his to measure what exactly he was asking. What he was revealing . . .

How much he knew.

"What does this have to do with me?" she dared to ask. *Besides everything.*

"Well, it has everything to do with Lady Standon. At least one of them." He paused and looked up at her. "I need to determine which Lady Standon was connected to Malcolm and how."

Now it was Lucy's turn to sit back, her hands clutched to the leather of the seat. "How do you know all this?" she blurted out without even thinking.

"Honestly, I shouldn't know that much. Mr. Strout has been absolutely unwilling to discuss the matter. Wouldn't give me the least bit of information about Malcolm's will." He paused. "You know how he is — your father used him, didn't he?"

"Yes," she replied. "Papa trusted him implicitly." *And so did I until this moment.*

Why, that lying, self-serving bastard. Malcolm had left a fortune to her for her use? Strout had never said a word.

"But if Strout refused to tell you —" she said, leaving her query dangling out there like a lure.

And he caught it quickly. "Oh, he refused to tell me. Claimed Malcolm's will was explicit and would not share the contents with me. Confidentiality and all." Then he sat back, once again the smug, self-assured man who'd stepped into her father's house. "But his clerk was another matter."

Lucy closed her eyes. The clerk. Of course. She'd met the man. Thin and pale, over-worked and underpaid.

Just as Archie had been.

A fact that obviously hadn't gone un-noticed by the earl. "Apparently Strout is as parsimonious with his pay as he is with his client's secrets." He flashed a smile at her. "All it took was a —"

"Beefsteak and a few pints of ale," she muttered, sinking lower into her seat. "Yes, of course. You filled his belly and then muddled his good senses."

Why wouldn't he have? Her father had taught him that. And blast him to hell, Strout being a penny-pinch of a bastard had made the task all that much easier.

"Yes, exactly," Clifton said. "Once that half-starved fellow was fat and happy —"

"He sung," she provided.

"Yes, just like that little canary your sister kept."

Lucy only wished she could stuff Mr. Strout's idiot of a clerk into a gilded cage . . . and withhold the bread crumbs — for he'd all but led the earl right to her. Bet-

334

ter yet, she was of half a mind to send around for Rusty and Sammy and have them ensure that the pale little man never spilled his employer's secrets ever again, beefsteak or no.

The only saving grace was Clifton's obvious stuffy notions. Apparently it was too much for him to consider that she, Lucy Ellyson, might in fact be a marchioness. A lady, in title and deed.

Certainly not worthy of a second look or chance, of being his countess.

Her father's warning from all those years ago echoed through her thoughts as if she stood in the map room in Hampstead.

"... I won't bandy this about, any more than I will see your heart broken. As much as you fancy this man, he will never have you. Not in a way that is honest and noble. He cannot."

She heaved a sigh as discreetly as she could and looked back up at Clifton. Immediately she wished she hadn't. Did he have to be so handsome? Did the sight of him have to make her heart waver and her resolve as tipsy as she'd been last night?

Oh, not that she didn't see the changes in him.

Where before he'd had a air of insurmountable confidence, an air that the world was his simply by the very rank of his birth, there were cracks in his stony façade.

There were lines around his eyes that hadn't been there before. A wary light to his glance. A bit of grey at his temples. He'd gone into the war full of duty and obligation, but obviously he'd seen the other side of it.

A dark world of deeds and errands that most agents rarely talked about, not even in their reports, and she'd learned of it only as her father had lain dying, delirious and lost in his past, confessing his sins as his fever had grown, as if she'd been a priest to grant him forgiveness.

So the trenches had touched Clifton as well. How could they have not?

And added to that had been the loss of Malcolm. He and Malcolm had been more twins than half brothers. As if the entirety of their personalities had been placed in two halves. Funny, reckless Malcolm and serious, top-lofty Clifton.

And now he needed her help.

Her help. Oh, the irony of it.

For a moment, as Clifton had kidnapped her, her heart had gone wild, beating with a tremulous rhythm. *He's here. He's back. He remembers his promise.*

He wants to apologize.

When Clifton had raised his gaze to hers,

taken her in his arms and nearly kissed her, she, being the romantic fool, had thought he would ravish her into succumbing to him once again, believed he intended to make amends.

Would beg for her forgiveness.

And quite frankly, he'd have to beg to gain it. At the very least, he'd have to display a respectable amount of groveling . . .

And kissing . . .

She did have her standards after all. Despite what she'd told Aunt Bedelia.

But then he hadn't. He was here because he needed her help. Not her heart, not her love.

She tried not to think of the consequences, of getting herself any further mired in any of this, but she needed to know everything he knew.

If she was going to upend him.

"Is that all he told you? This canary of Strout's?"

"Yes, unfortunately. Apparently Strout hasn't the confidence in the man to let him know where he keeps the key to the safe."

"Truly?" she mocked. "How untrustworthy of Mr. Strout."

So there they were. What he truly wanted from her. Her ability to open Strout's safe. Without this hidden key.

Clifton looked directly at her, in a measured way that made Lucy shiver. "So you can see why I need you."

I need you.

That was all her foolish heart heard. *He needs me.*

To steal for him. To lie for him. To do his dirty work.

But not how you want him to want you.

She shook her head. "And then what? Am I to accost the other Lady Standons as you did Minerva the other day?"

"No, no, nothing like that. I will admit, that was a miscalculation on my part —"

"Truly?" she asked sweetly, smiling with that wonderful expression of noble condescension that was the Duchess of Hollindrake's specialty.

"Yes, rather. But you have to admit, I haven't been in Society for some time. I fear my manners are a bit lacking."

Lucy bit her lips together for fear that what she wanted to say would come bursting out.

If your manners were a bit lacking, we wouldn't be just sitting here talking. You wouldn't have kidnapped me for some tête-à-tête. We'd be tangled up, kissing, making an utter disgrace of polite manners.

He continued on, oblivious to the nature

338

of her thoughts. "— I just need you to make some inquiries, discreetly of course, to discover what her connection to my brother might be, and most importantly why she has control of his estate."

"Why ever do you need to know all this, my lord? Whatever does Malcolm's money have to do with you?"

And then she remembered the gossip from earlier.

He had pockets to let, and she knew him to be too proud to go begging by means of marrying an heiress.

And once he got Malcolm's money?

Oh, it may not be Lady Annella, but he'd be looking for his lady love very soon. Hadn't that always been his plan?

"I will have to consider a lady's bloodlines . . . Her education should be impeccable, and I will have to examine her suitability, her countenance, the way she holds herself in public . . ."

An image of some graceful Original entwined with Clifton danced through Lucy's stormy thoughts. Because, just as her father had warned her, Lucy wasn't good enough for him.

Any more than she should have been the Marchioness of Standon.

Lucy Ellyson, the daughter of a thief and

the infamous contessa, was who she was, all she'd ever be.

But that didn't mean she was a fool.

Sitting up straight, tipping her head to stare at him down the tip of her nose, she said, "What you really want, what this scandalous stunt was about, is that you want me to get that will for you. To steal it."

He didn't bother to say a word. Clifton just gave her a single nod.

She drew a deep breath to steady her trembling arms, the fury growing inside her. "So, let me see if I have this correct. You want me to help you steal money from a widow?"

He took her air of confidence as some misplaced admiration for his outrageous request. "Exactly. Goosie, you are just the one for the job."

Oh, if he only knew.

"Set me down," she said, pointing at the door of the carriage. "Set me down now."

He ignored the chill in her voice. "Lucy, you must help me, you are the only one who —"

Lucy stopped listening, for all she heard was her father's warning ringing in her ears.

"You'll always be the daughter of a thief . . ."

"— you see how it is, don't you? I'd wager every last farthing I have that Malcolm's will is in Strout's safe. I'll never get that lock open. You know it, and I know it. You're the best one for the task. The only one."

She shook her head, shaking off the way his smooth coaxing tones appealed to her heart. Left her leaning toward him. Left her wishing . . . "No!"

He sat back and gaped at her. "No?"

Lucy leaned forward and poked a finger into his solid chest. "No!"

Then, moving with the speed of, shall one say, a thief, she caught up his walking stick and rapped it as hard as she could to the ceiling. The driver reacted immediately, pulling the carriage to a quick stop.

And the moment the carriage jerked to a halt, she was out the door, hurling his walking stick back at him so he had to duck out of the way. In those precious seconds, she strode to the curb, shaking her skirts out as she went.

"Damn him, damn him to hell," she muttered, ignoring the looks of the shocked bystanders on Bond Street.

Oh, yes, this was just exceedingly perfect. Her adventure was being witnessed by half the gossips of the *ton.* The duchess would hear about this display before her afternoon tea, and Lucy would wager that she would be packed off to the Scottish hunting box by suppertime.

If she was allowed even that roof over her head.

But by now her temper, her infamous temper, the one that had gotten her into this mess in the first place, had the better of her, and she didn't care if the Duchess of Hollindrake sent her to the wilds of Nova Scotia.

For it was the same wrong-headed, obstinate, misguided faith that had urged her to brazenly tell her father that the Earl of Clifton loved her and would return for her.

"Lucy, for God's sake, why won't you help me?" Clifton asked from the door of his carriage.

Hands fisted to her skirts, she ground her teeth together before she said, "Because, you great pompous ass, I'm Lady Standon."

CHAPTER 13

"What do you mean you aren't coming with us to Lady Gressingham's soiree tonight?" Aunt Bedelia complained when Lucy came downstairs to explain that her megrim would prevent her from attending.

An ailment, more specifically, by the name of Clifton.

"You must attend," Elinor told her. "We all agreed. We would come out in Society together and make a united front. If you remain at home, it will only add to the rumors."

There was a moment of strained silence in the foyer, for Elinor was speaking all too clearly about Clifton's scandalous behavior in Madame Verbeck's shop.

Which had been mentioned by nearly every caller they'd had that afternoon, inquiring about Lady Standon's "unfortunate encounter."

"Yes, your absence will only serve to fuel

343

the gossip," Minerva added.

Lucy had been able to convince her friends that Lord Clifton's actions had been but leftover grief from his years on the Continent. "Battle madness," she'd told them.

Let all of Society think the earl around the bend, Lucy had mused. *That ought to help his marriage prospects.*

Aunt Bedelia had waved her off and declared the earl a menace to decent women. "He should be locked up!"

That would be convenient, Lucy had thought when the lady had pressed for the Watch to be called, but she'd demurred only because she'd known Clifton was already engaged for the evening — escorting Lady Annella to the Gressinghams'.

And that was all she needed — one night with him out of the way.

"Lucy, couldn't you rally, just for this evening," Elinor pleaded softly.

"No, no, I fear not," Lucy said, wavering on her feet. She'd never had a headache in her life, so she hadn't the slightest idea how to appear too delicate to go on, but she did her best. "I do believe I might be more ill than I thought."

She collapsed onto the settee and covered her face with the back of her hand.

Really, all she had to do was think about Clifton marrying that mealy-mouthed Lady Annella and she did feel quite queasy.

Still, that didn't appease her guilt when she saw the look of concern Minerva and Elinor were sharing. They thought her quite stricken.

"Well, Aunt," Minerva said, "it would be a greater disaster if Lucy were to faint in the middle of the soiree. Imagine the speculation that would surround us then."

"Yes, yes," Aunt Bedelia agreed, wagging a finger at her niece, the feathers in her turban bowing in kind. "Point well made, Minerva." She turned to Mrs. Clapp, who stood hovering by the doorway. "Take your poor mistress upstairs and have Mrs. Hutchinson brew her a nice cup of chamomile. It does for both megrims and other upsets."

"Certainly, Lady Chudley," Clapp told Minerva's overbearing relation, hustling over to Lucy and lending her a hand to rise from the sofa. Clapp viewed the formidable Aunt Bedelia with a heroic state of awe. "A cup of tea and I shall sit with her myself, my lady."

"Oh, no!" Lucy protested a little too enthusiastically. The other women paused and stared at her. She slumped over a bit and clung to Clapp. "It is just that I don't like to leave Mickey unsupervised. Dear Clapp, doesn't our little darling need a bath this evening?"

"Yes, but —" Clapp protested.

"Oh, I would be ever so much more rested knowing that he is clean and properly tucked into bed."

So he doesn't get up and come looking for me, she didn't add.

Besides, she knew that giving Mickey a bath would wear Clapp down to her last bit of worry, and the old girl would then drop into her bed and sleep until the dawn.

Which is exactly what Lucy needed.

The ladies began to file out the door, with Aunt Bedelia herding them with the sharp eye of a border collie. But that didn't mean she still didn't have Lucy under her watchful gaze.

"Lucy, you will attend the Burton ball tomorrow night," Aunt Bedelia told her as Lucy made her careful way up the steps, keeping up the appearance that she was about to be overcome at any moment. "There will be no more of these megrims, my girl. No matter how convenient they prove."

With that, the lady swept out the door, and before Mr. Mudgett could close it, she was already chastizing Elinor and Minerva as if they were a pair of ungainly debutantes. "I don't know if that primrose color suits you, Elinor. I think you would do better in a fine shade of blue. Minerva, whatever were you thinking, buying those gloves? Thankfully, I always carry a spare pair."

Lucy hurried up the rest of the steps, leaving Clapp in her wake.

"Lucy, you musn't overtax yourself. Remember what Lady Chudley —" she chided when she caught up with her. "Oh, heavens, what are you doing?"

Lucy had stripped off her gown and was in the process of pulling on a pair of black breeches. "Now, Clapp, don't you fret, but I haven't any megrim or ailment, but I fear I have a bit of business to attend to this evening and you must keep my disappearance a secret."

Clapp's hand covered her gaping mouth as Lucy ducked into a grey shirt and then a black coat. She tugged a black cap over her hair, then bent to haul a pair of soft boots out from under her bed.

"Oh, my lady, none of this bodes well!" Clapp protested.

"No, my good Clapp!" Lucy assured her, hauling the woman into a hug. "It is our future I am after. I've a fortune to claim."

347

■ ■ ■ ■

For after Lucy had gotten over her anger at Clifton, she had realized he had also given her a ticket out of the duchess's prison.

If Malcolm had left a fortune, she wasn't about to miss the opportunity it would afford her. Perhaps she could even purchase the house in Hampstead and return with Mickey and her servants to the place and life she loved.

The earl's plan — for her to steal the will — was perfect, except she had no intention of including him in such a caper. If Malcolm's will was in Strout's office, then she would steal it while Clifton was occupied with escorting Lady Annella to the Gressinghams' ball.

With the rest of proper Society.

Lucy, for one, was done with propriety.

Rolling through the streets of London, she sat next to Thomas-William, trying to appear as innocuous as just another servant going about their master's business, but inside she was buoyant with the prospect before her.

"I don't like this, Miss Lucy," he said for about the twentieth time.

"I would think you would find this a bit

more entertaining than spending the night listening to Mrs. Hutchinson complain about Mr. Otter's dietary restrictions."

Thomas-William rolled his gaze upward, for that much was true.

"And," Lucy said, continuing her argument, "when was the last time you had a good old adventure? When the last time you went housebreaking?"

"Bah," he scoffed. "Likely end up getting hung."

"What? Are you afraid of getting caught? Has your advanced age caught up with you and left you incapable of a simple burglary?"

His brow furrowed into a thick line. If there was one thing Thomas-William didn't like to be reminded of, it was his age — not that he'd ever revealed exactly how old he was. "It's that pair you sent for. I don't trust them."

"What? Rusty and Sammy? You know as well as I that they are the finest around," she said in all confidence.

"Aye, but can you trust them?"

Now it was Lucy's turn to blanch. There was that.

Oh, Rusty and Sammy were a knock-up pair of ken crackers, but they were also used to making off with everything that wasn't nailed down, and Lucy couldn't have that.

"That is exactly why I need you, Thomas-William. I daresay you are the only man in London they fear. If you tell them not to steal as much as a penknife, they will abide by your orders."

He snorted, as if he no more believed her flattery than he had any confidence that Rusty and Sammy could keep their hands in their pockets once they'd gotten the door to Strout's office open.

Lucy sat back in her seat and tried not to feel overly smug. Oh, wouldn't the earl be furious then.

Serve him right. And go far in taking that arrogant smile off his face. The one he'd worn after he'd kidnapped her.

Well, tonight the tables would turn.

"There it is," Thomas-William said with a slight tip of his head as they drove past the building.

She remembered it well. "Does he still keep his offices on the ground level and live above?"

"Aye. And the clerks are in the attic. According to one of the lads who works down the street, Strout bought the building a few years back."

"He owns the building?" Lucy made no effort to mask her surprise.

"Aye, and the ones adjoining," he said,

having spent most of the afternoon doing the necessary surveillance. "Bit odd, don't you think? Seems rather rich pickings for a fellow like him."

"However could he afford to own so much property, and right here adjacent to Lincoln Fields, no less?" she murmured, glancing over her shoulder at the row of proper houses and shops that ran down the street.

"Thought as much myself," Thomas-William said.

"And if Mr. Strout didn't deign it important enough to let us know of Malcolm's will, what other secrets do you think he might be hiding?"

Thomas-William's brow furrowed again, for he could see the suspicious wheels turning inside her thoughts. "Now, Miss Lucy, we aren't going to spend any more time inside that man's offices than it takes to open his safe and get what we need."

"I know, but there is something not right about all of this."

"Remember your father's advice," Thomas-William whispered as he handed her down. "Don't take the next step if you don't know what you'll find."

She nodded in agreement, though she was thinking of another bit of her father's wisdom.

Like a dog who bites, a thief rarely steals just once.

Thomas-William was right, of course; they must get in and out quickly and undetected. But she couldn't shake an undeniable sense of ill ease. Something wasn't right about all this.

He turned the cart down another street and then into an alleyway that meandered behind the houses. He pulled it into an empty mews and jumped down. After leading the horse around so it now pointed out the alley — just in case they needed to make a hasty exit — he tied the animal to the hitching post with a light hand.

She glanced up as two figures slid out of the shadows. *Speaking of dogs who bite.*

Her father's former cohorts said not a word in greeting, professionals that they were, but Sammy couldn't resist reaching over and giving her a light chuck under her chin.

He winked at her and smiled broadly.

Lucy hadn't seen the pair in at least two years, and it warmed her heart to have them flanking her as they all stole down the alley.

Thomas-William nodded at the door ahead.

Sammy moved forward and pulled a bess from the sleeve of his coat. In the blink of an eye, he had the door pried open. She turned to Thomas-William in triumph. *See, I told you.*

His brows arched. *This isn't over yet. Not by a long shot.*

Rusty moved inside, lighting a glym, the sort of small lamp favored by housebreakers and others in the lawless trades. He held it up to reveal a stairway on their right and a long hall on the left.

They all turned to Lucy, for she'd been to the office on numerous occasions — both on errands for her father, then after her father's death, when Mr. Strout had given her the bad news of her father's less-than-plump estate, and finally with Archie.

She pointed at the hall. It ran from the alley all the way through the house to the front door, where clients entered. The first room off the front door led into the clerk's office, and from there they could get into the private domain of Rupert Phinneas Strout, Esq.

Lucy went first, moving as her father had taught her. If she hadn't known her compatriots were right behind her, she would have thought they'd deserted her, for they moved with the same stealth.

They entered the clerk's office, where everything sat in tidy piles and at right angles on the desk, not a single paper askew.

Nothing amiss save for the fact that Strout didn't pay him enough to keep his mouth shut, she mused. Though she did find some pleasure in the fact that Clifton's investment in beefsteaks and ale (which he could probably ill afford) were about to be her boon.

She pointed at the formidable set of double doors that led to Strout's office. Once again Rusty and his bess went to work, opening the door with nary a creak of the hinges.

When they were all inside the large room, Thomas-William closed the door, and Rusty lit another glym, so they could get the lay of the land.

"We must find the safe," Lucy whispered.

From across the room, the great chair behind the desk whirled around, and an all-too-familiar voice said, "How convenient for you, Goosie. I've already gone to the trouble of locating it."

Luckily for all of them, Thomas-William reacted first.

His hand shot out and covered Lucy's mouth before she gave them all away.

Her muffled yelp barely registered, but that didn't have every body in the room stilled and five pairs of ears straining for any evidence that said their presence had been given away.

"Tsk, tsk," Clifton whispered, rising from the chair. "What was it your father always said? 'Silence is golden, especially in thieves.' How unlike you to forget such sage advice."

She peeled Thomas-William's broad hand off her mouth and glared at him. "You rotter! What the devil are you doing here?"

"Aye, guv'ner," Sammy said, reaching inside his pocket and pulling out a pistol. "What game is this?"

"No game," Clifton told them. "I am after the same thing her ladyship is. The truth."

For he'd known when he'd given Lucy all the information he had, provoked her by kidnapping her, nearly kissing her, and reminding her of the arrogant man he'd once been — the one she'd despised — that she would do everything in her power to cross him.

And play her last card.

All the while, he would be waiting for her, winning hand at the ready.

"Truth?" Sammy asked. He turned to Lucy. "Said we was after a fortune."

"We are," Lucy told them, facing Clifton with the determination he'd always admired about her. No one could have missed the resolute determination in her pledge.

"I've spent the entire day wondering why my brother would let such a fortune tumble into your hands," Clifton said.

"Perhaps you'd like to leave and finish your pondering," she suggested, nodding toward the door.

Even in the meager light, he could discern the blazing gleam in her eyes, the fire behind her sarcasm. The way her mind was replotting her course. "Perhaps you'd like to enlighten me and save me the trouble."

She snorted. "Not with my last breath."

He leaned closer and whispered in her ear so only she could hear him. "We could take another turn in my carriage and see if you change your mind."

She shivered but held firm. "Not unless I can push you beneath the wheels first."

"Move along, guv'ner," Sammy said. "This here is ours."

"Not really," Clifton said. "Black Britch was quite clear about the creed: He who finds it first."

"Aye," Rusty agreed warily. "But if you found it first, why haven't you made off with it?"

Clifton leaned against the desk, his arms crossed over his chest, his walking stick dangling from one hand. "For the simple reason that I can't get the safe open."

Lucy smirked. "Terrible problem that. Now leave, so we can take what you're unable to gain."

"I still have right of claim," he told her.

Her eyes widened. "Right of —"

"Oh, he has you there, Goosie," Sammy whispered over her shoulder. "Right of claim gives him the first skimming."

"The Creed of Thieves?" Lucy nearly choked.

"Ss-sh-sh!" her compatriots whispered.

"Oh, yes, the noble Creed of Thieves," Clifton repeated, "for I daresay Rusty and Sammy won't go against it."

They both nodded in agreement, albeit reluctantly.

"Well, you'll find Thomas-William and I have no such loyalties," she said, crossing her arms over her chest and taking a wide stance that mirrored his own. "And if you are dead, neither will Rusty and Sammy."

"I thought it might come to this," he told her, and in one quick movement, he tossed up his walking stick. It rose to within inches of the ceiling before he stopped it, the top hovering just within rapping range.

"If you refuse to help me, I'll summon Strout down here. I daresay he'll insist on calling the Watch and rewarding me for capturing the thieves who dared to steal from him," Clifton told them. "What say you, Lucy? Will you open the safe for me, or shall we see what sort of generous mood Strout might be in?"

He watched her jaw work back and forth. She looked as murderous as she had earlier, when he'd kidnapped her, when he'd taken her in his arms and held her close enough to kiss her.

Oh, how close he'd come to plundering her lips, but his pride, thank God for his pride, had held him in check.

But what he hadn't thought of was the way he would spend the rest of the day and this night haunted by the feel of her, the scent of her hair, the curve of her hips and press of her breasts against his chest.

She'd reawakened every longing he'd ever had for her in those few moments. Every realization of how much he loved her.

Had loved her, he tried to correct himself as he stared once again into her furious gaze.

The one that suggested he had best watch his back for the next fortnight or so if he ventured outside the confines of his house.

But he would worry about that after she got the safe open and he'd managed to amass enough pieces to this mystery that he could discover the truth.

Or, at the very least, an inkling of it.

"I'll open it," Lucy agreed. "But I get Malcolm's will." She paused and cocked her head. "No questions asked."

He nodded in agreement. She could have it once he was done with it. Not entirely what she thought, but then again, she hadn't been all that clear, now, had she?

About keeping her vow to him. About waiting for him.

"Where's the safe?" she asked.

"Under his desk. The floorboards are quite ingenious, though not entirely insurmountable."

Rusty moved around the desk and eyed the boards that now sat piled up next to the safe. "Nice work, guv'ner. Haven't lost your touch, I see."

"Not at all," Clifton said. "I do owe you gentlemen a debt of gratitude. I've put your lessons to use on more occasions than I can number."

"Oh, go on with ya," Sammy said, waving him off like a blushing debutante at Almack's.

Lucy's gaze rolled upward, then she made a soft *harrumph* and pushed past the lot of them. "A light, Sammy," she said, pointing to the spot she wanted illuminated.

Ever the bossy, formidable Goosie, Clifton

mused, resisting the urge to grin at her. "Can you open it?" he asked, kneeling beside her, his shoulder brushing hers.

They both jumped a little, for the contact, as always, was electrifying. Revealing. Too much so.

"Must have had a demmed good reason . . ." Jack's words whispered past him.

"Of course," she said, shrugging off his question as if it had been too foolish to even ask. Could she open it? Did birds fly?

"That's my girl," he said softly, reaching over and brushing a wayward strand out of her eyes.

For a moment they both stared at each other, Clifton lost in the memory of what it had been like to loosen her glorious dark hair and watch it tumble past her smooth shoulders. "I've always admired your skill and your confidence." He reached for her again, and this time she swatted his hand away and tucked the lock back under her cap, hiding it from him.

"You delighted in shocking me back then," he teased quietly, wishing he could pluck that demmed cap right off her head.

"No more than you liked ruffling my feathers," she whispered back.

She glanced at him, this time without that murderous gleam, and the sweet memories of those weeks long ago wove between them, knocking cracks into the mortar and stone that he had built in their place.

Then, as if she found the intimacy of their position too much, she turned her attention to the lock. She found, however, that it remained stubborn to her efforts.

"Oh, heavens, why couldn't Strout have been as cheap with his locks as he is with his clerk's pay," she muttered. "He would have to go to the expense of buying a Swiss safe."

"Come now, Goosie," Clifton said. "You're the finest dubber in the city. You can open it."

"Too bad you didn't bring the little monkey along," Rusty whispered. "Still a bright one with the picks, is he?"

Lucy stiffened and shot her old felonious friend a black look.

"Who's the little monkey?" Clifton asked.

"No one," Lucy said quickly. "A thief. He would have been a liability," she shot off, as if trying on one answer, then another.

But Clifton wasn't about to press the matter; there would be time later for answers.

There is always more than meets the eye . . .

Meanwhile, Lucy continued to work at the lock.

"I saw a safe like this in Geneva a few

361

years back," Clifton said, nodding at the iron box before them.

"Did you get it open?" she asked, her brows furrowed as she studied it.

"No. I could have used you that night."

That and so many others . . .

He shoved that wistful notion aside.

But she, smart little minx that she was, had heard the note as well. "You thought of me?"

Was it him, or did she sound surprised? "Yes, Goosie. I thought of you."

More than he cared to admit.

"How would I have known?" she said as she went back to work. "You never wrote. Never sent a word."

"But I did," he protested.

There was a little *harrumph* from where she was bent over the safe, her back to him, but he didn't need to see her face. She didn't believe him.

"I sent you a flower with every dispatch. A pressed blossom. I thought you'd know what they meant."

She stilled and glanced over her shoulder at him. "There were never any flowers. Just reports."

"So you thought I'd forsaken you," he said, more for himself.

"What else was I to think?"

But before he could say more, there was a definite *click* from the safe, followed by an echo of *clunks,* the tumblers aligning. She paused for a moment, a slow grin lifting her lips. Then she turned the latch and began to pull the heavy piece of iron up and open.

Clifton reached over and lent her a hand, and the moment their fingers twined together, his hand covering hers, it was as if the entire interlude in the carriage sparked between them.

She tried to bat his hand away, but he kept his hold on her.

He wasn't ready to let her go. Not now that he'd found her again.

And the notion left him breathless.

Together they heaved the iron door open the last few inches. He caught up the lamp and held it above the opening, the rest of the crew crowding around to take in the sight before them.

Even Rusty, the best cracksman in London, let out a low whistle. "I thought you said this fellow was naught but a solictor."

"He is," Lucy said, sitting back on her heels and shaking her head.

"Looks like a regular smuggler's hoard," Sammy said, nodding at the bags that bulged with coins. And there wasn't a one of them that didn't suspect they were full of sovereigns. "Never seen so many flymseys in all me days," he said, nodding at the banknotes stacked next to the gold.

On the other side of the safe, account books sat atop account books, along with folded and sealed papers bound with black cords.

"Wills," Lucy whispered.

"Wills?" Clifton asked back. "How do you know?"

"My father's will was done up thusly. Arch—" She paused for a second. "The clerk said Strout always did the wills with those black cords and seals because it made them easier to find."

"So many?" Clifton tipped his head and studied them. "All locked up and hidden away. Whatever for?"

Lucy glanced over her shoulder at him. "I don't like this. There is something altogether wrong here."

They looked at each other, and whatever differences lay between them unraveled, for they shared the same curiosity, the same drive and desire to uncover the truth of a matter, the intimate details that would tell the entire story.

It was why they had suited so well to begin with.

"I agree," he said. "Why do you think Mr.

Strout keeps so many wills locked up in his safe?"

She shook her head, then reached inside and pulled out a handful. "Shall we find out?"

It didn't take long to discover what the esteemed and trusted Mr. Strout had been doing over the last two decades or how he'd amassed his fortune.

The man who had served as solicitor to so many of England's agents before they had gone abroad had taken advantage of their trust. Of their tentative fates.

Darby Bricknell and a dozen or more names that Lucy recognized had entrusted their last bequests into Strout's hands, and the man had repaid them by not honoring a single dying wish.

Properties that were to have gone to loved ones, distant cousins, and friends were still in Strout's hands, the rents — according to the numerous account books — filling Strout's personal coffers.

Clifton's anger knew no bounds, but it was the packet of correspondence and a will in particular that nearly had him forgetting their vow of silence.

For it had to do with Lucy.

As she was busy reading one of the wills,

he eased into a corner with a glym at hand and quickly scanned his purloined discovery.

Her father's estate had been trimmed down to the bare bones by Strout's shady dealings.

Worse yet, there was a letter inside from Strout's clerk to the Duke of Parkerton reminding His Grace that upon George Ellyson's death the lease on the house in Hampstead had ended.

Does Your Grace want the offices of Mr. Strout to find a new tenant, for it is doubtful the current resident can pay the current rate for such a fine house?

And the signature on the letter?

Archibald Sterling, Clerk

The scurvy little rat had set in motion Lucy's eviction, and moreover her marriage to him. Oh, Clifton could just see the fellow coming to Lucy with the news of her pending eviction and a solution to her woes.

Marry me, Miss Ellyson, and you'll never want for a home.

And if that wasn't enough insult, Strout had received a fee for finding new tenants.

And where had he been? Clifton cursed

the demmed Fates. For he'd been too far away to help. And he'd known this might happen, for hadn't Lucy told him so all those years ago?

"The old duke granted Papa the use of the house during his lifetime, but when he dies, the house goes back to the estate."

And Strout, the very devil, had given Archie a clear field toward marrying her, having stolen all of Ellyson's money beforehand.

Well, Archibald Sterling was most likely roasting in hell, but that didn't mean Strout wasn't around to pay his dues.

"I'll see him hang," Clifton muttered as he discreetly stowed the documents inside his jacket.

Just as Goosie had taught him to do all those years ago.

Lucy glanced up and for a moment drew back at the evil light in Clifton's eyes.

Good heavens, he looked ready to march upstairs and hang Strout from the rafters. And as much as she wanted to do the very same thing, she was just as happy to consign the solicitor's fate into Mr. Pymm's devious and evil hands.

He'd find a spot that was as near to hell on earth into which to cast the fellow.

She reached over and touched the earl's arm, letting the warmth of her touch warm the chill that appeared to have taken hold of his heart. "Well, if he is to hang, then let's make short work of the task." Then she nodded at the evidence before them.

They went through the books, one by one, and marveled at the extent of his crimes.

"Look here," Lucy said, handing over the will she'd been reading. "Darby's betrothed was to have five hundred pounds, paid fifty pounds per annum until she married." She shook her head and rolled the paper back up. "She never did, you know. Has faithfully carried his memory all these years, and here is Strout, cheating her out of what she is due. She's no idea that Darby held her in his heart right up to his dying day."

"She'll know of Darby's love now," Clifton told her. "We'll make sure of that."

We. It was a word with too many implications for Lucy to imagine. *There is no "we,"* she wanted to tell him, but somehow so many things had changed in the last few hours.

It was as if they had rediscovered the ties that had brought them together. Reminded them how alike they were. How much they held in common.

Lucy still couldn't believe he'd thought of

her all these years, sent her flowers to make sure she'd known. Where had all those tokens gone?

She sighed. Her father, most likely. Doing everything in his power to put an end to what he'd seen as a disastrous alliance.

What would he say now? she wondered. Oh, she could just imagine.

You haven't told him all, Goosie. What of that little secret you possess, the one slumbering away in a narrow bed back at the house on Brook Street?

Would Clifton be furious to discover Mickey? Shun the boy because he was base-born? Or would he welcome the child into his heart, into his home? Certainly Malcolm had always been welcome, but would Clifton's wife be as open-minded as the previous countess?

Lucy didn't know, couldn't know for certain. But one thing was true: she'd guard the boy with her life, as she had since the day he'd been born.

And as they closed the last account book, Clifton shook his head at the collection of villainous evidence. "I must say Strout is, if anything, meticulous."

"Why ever do you think he kept these records?" Lucy asked as she sorted the last of the wills and handed them over to Clifton.

"It ain't easy to remember a lie," Sammy said, sounding more sage than one could think. "I keep a record of the houses I've cracked so I don't waste me time robbing a place that ain't got the silver no more."

Lucy conceded the point with a nod to Clifton.

There it was. Strout, ever the thief, had kept a record so as not to dip into the same well and run the risk of it noticeably drying up. Or his being caught.

"But if he kept everything," Clifton said, "where the devil is Malcolm's will?"

Lucy held herself still and lied. "Perhaps it is as Strout claimed, lost." She glanced over at Thomas-William, who thankfully had his gaze fixed on the ceiling, for she had to imagine he was the only one who'd noticed her slipping it up her sleeve. "You'll have time to look closer when you come back at first light with Pymm and the warrant."

Clifton hardly looked convinced, but there was naught more they could do but put everything to rights and close up the safe.

They had decided to leave everything where they had found it, a suggestion that had left Rusty and Sammy sputtering over the foolishness of leaving so much money behind — that is, until Clifton informed them the money was intended for widows and orphans.

A notion that completely escaped Sammy. "Guv'ner, everyone wants to help them widows and orphans, but no one is ever going to give me a handout."

There was no arguing that, but just then Thomas-William, who had said nothing up until this moment, pointed at the door. "Off with you. Both of you."

It was enough to send Rusty and Sammy scurrying out like a pair of rats.

Lucy and Thomas-William went to follow, but Clifton loitered, taking one more look around the shadowy room.

"Come along, my lord," Lucy whispered. "There will be time enough later to tear the place apart board by board."

He nodded and followed her out.

She felt guilty leading him like this, but she had her reasons.

It matters not that he sent you flowers. That he didn't forget you. It is all different now, she thought, knowing that the real trick was going to be escaping the earl once they were free of Strout's offices.

But as her luck would have it, when they got to the alley, they found Sammy holding a tall, scrawny fellow, one hand clapped over his mouth, the other curled around the fellow's chest.

Clifton took one glance at him. "The clerk."

"We caught him coming in," Rusty explained. "Can't have him squawking about like a right fine chicken, so I says we should slit his throat."

The fellow's wide-eyed gaze fell on Lucy, as if imploring her to help him.

"It will leave a mess," she told them. "Can't have that." Then she glanced over her shoulder at the earl. "Do you think he could be of some assistance?"

While the clerk nodded furiously, for it appeared he'd probably agree to sell his sainted mother's life at the moment, Clifton tipped his head and eyed the terrified man. "Might. I could take him to Pymm. He'll know what to do."

CHAPTER 14

It took some time for Lucy and Thomas-William to return to the house on Brook Street, for they'd given their horse and cart to the earl so he could carry off Strout's clerk.

Just before he'd driven away, Clifton had looked ready to say something to her, but then he'd turned on his booted heel and climbed into the cart.

What had he thought to say to her? Lucy trembled as her imagination ran wild.

Come with me, Goosie. Spend the night in my arms.

She shook off such thoughts, but it was nigh on impossible to dismiss them when she still could feel the brush of his hand over hers as they'd passed papers back and forth.

The times she'd caught him watching her. Studying her. As if he'd been looking at her once again.

Taking a second measure of her.

Somehow, during the course of the evening, the tables had turned between them. As they'd gathered evidence and compared notes of their case against Strout, she'd realized they had reached an accord, a peace of sorts.

But what could that mean?

Nothing! she admonished herself. *Nothing at all.*

So what had he been about to say?

She hadn't the least idea, and had only been able to watch him drive out of sight, into the inky streets of London.

Left on their own, and dressed as she was, Lucy and Thomas-William were hard-pressed to find a hackney willing to take them up, but Thomas-William finally found a carter who agreed to go out of his way to Mayfair, though it took all of Lucy's ready coins to convince the fellow.

When they arrived the house on Brook Street sat dark and quiet, and Lucy breathed a sigh of relief that Minerva and Elinor had not yet returned from the Gressinghams' ball.

She'd made it back to the house none the wiser.

Or so she thought as she made her solitary way through the halls, Thomas-William having gone off to his room.

She entered her room, relieved to find it entirely cast in shadows; not a single candle burning, for she'd always found the dark strangely comforting.

She stood with the door to her back and gave way to the musings she'd tried to ignore the entire way home. Like how her body ached for Clifton's touch. His kiss. How she longed to revisit that long-ago night in Hampstead.

One more night with the earl . . . then she'd be off and away with Mickey and her household, and Clifton could go about his business of finding his proper countess, none the wiser.

"What the devil were you going to say to me, Gilby?" she whispered into the night.

"Why don't you just ask me?" came a reply.

And then there was the strike of a match. In that tiny flicker of flame, she watched the earl reach over and light a single candle before he blew the match out and tossed it in the grate.

Even in the shadows, even in the meager light, she knew what he'd been about to ask back there in the alley behind Strout's house.

And her answer . . . oh, she'd known it all along.

She was like the match he'd held, ready to burn with fire, lacking only a single strike to set her ablaze.

A single kiss.

She crossed the room without a word and threw herself into his arms.

And reignited a passion she'd thought forever lost.

Clifton had expected an explosion of another sort.

But this — Lucy, his Lucy, in his arms, her eager lips claiming his — was enough for him.

At least for now.

For he wasn't fool enough to think that all the misunderstandings and broken promises between them could be swept aside so easily.

Yet this brazen woman in his arms, her acquiescence, her eagerness, was a start, and one that reawakened him.

It wasn't the way his body responded to her, for it did — he was already rock hard and losing any bit of sense he claimed — but it was as if something he thought long lost suddenly flashed to life.

And he knew exactly what it was.

His heart. For he'd never stopped loving her. Could never forget her. And that was what love was. Something far beyond the ken of reason, far beyond the anger and grief with which he'd lived all these years.

For here was the balm and the light of his life.

She brought him to life like no other.

His scandalous, wonderful Lucy.

Lucy felt the shift in his attention. It was as if at first he'd been hesitant, but suddenly Clifton became only too impatient, hungry, like a man starved.

His hands tugged her shirt free from her britches and roamed up beneath the muslin, touching her, claiming her. Pulling her close.

But it wasn't enough.

He plucked her shirt off, sending the few buttons scattering across the floor. For one frantic moment she remembered Malcolm's will concealed there, and she was able to let it fall quietly to the floor, where it was quickly buried and hidden away.

Her britches followed, leaving her in her chemise and drawers, but not for long. Once she was naked, he caught hold of her and set her atop the dresser, sweeping it clean before he set her down, sending her comb and brush scattering.

Lucy reveled in the strength of his arms, of having him take her . . . without asking, without begging her permission.

Clifton just took what he wanted. And he wanted her.

Perched as she was, she sat eye to eye with him, her legs wound around his hips. She pulled him right up against her.

His taut manhood strained beneath the tight buckskin breeches he wore, and she dragged him closer still, so she could feel him right up against her. Her body seemed as hard and taut as his, eager for him. For what he, and he alone, could give her.

He leaned over and took one of her nipples in his mouth, sucking hard and pulling from her waves of desire.

Lucy arched back, her hands on his hips, tugging him ever closer.

All those years — never mind how long it had been since he'd loved her — came back to her as if it had only been last night.

Pulling her legs from his hips, he leaned back, and Lucy moaned at the loss of him — the loss of that hard, tempting manhood pressed against her — but not for long.

"Ssh, Goosie, you'll wake the house," he teased.

Lucy didn't see anything amusing about it. "I want you, Gilby."

Clifton grinned up at her, then leaned over and gave her what she wanted.

His hands caught her thighs and opened her to him, then he leaned over and swiped his tongue over her sex.

Lucy moaned, deep and loud.

"Good God, woman, you are going to wake Mayfair."

"I'll be quiet," she managed to say. "But demmit, Gilby, do that again."

And he obliged her, running his tongue over her, exploring her sex with long, sultry swipes, then taking her into his mouth and sucking her as he had her nipple.

Lucy's body came alive. Oh, how had she forgotten what this felt like, this throbbing, dangerous need. She wanted to cry out and awaken all of London.

Take me. Please take me. Give me . . .

And then she reached her crisis, that burst of waves, that tempest that took her from a tightly wound knot of need and darkness to the freedom and fire — like a match being struck and bursting into light.

"Oh, yes, Gilby! Yes! Oh, yes!" she managed as quietly as she could, clinging to his shoulders and barely aware of being whisked into her bed — that is until the earl tumbled atop her seconds later, gloriously naked, and covering her with the heat of his body, his hard manhood thrusting between her still quivering thighs.

Lucy knew that the passion still holding her in a dreamy thrall was only the beginning, and oh, how her body was still eager for more.

For she knew what "more" meant, and she opened herself up to him and let him fill her, take her in one hard stroke.

Now it was Lucy's turn to grin, for the earl groaned loudly as he filled her, as he began to move within her, as he sought his own release.

And all too soon, his desires were hers as well, and they both chased after them — seeking the rewards that lovers pursue in the embrace of night.

"Lucy," Clifton whispered sometime close to dawn, with her nestled tightly in his arms.

They were both spent and tired, but neither was sleeping, and he sensed that now was the time.

To clear the air and settle the matters between them.

So they could start anew before the sun rose when he would need to leave to finish the business with Strout.

"It is nearly morning, and I must go," he said.

She stirred and glanced up at him with half-open eyes. "Stay," she whispered, reaching for him and pulling him close.

"I dare not."

"I'll make it worth your while," she said, opening the coverlet in invitation.

"I must be gone before the house stirs," he said, then winked at her. "Before Minerva is up. I dare not risk another encounter with her."

Lucy laughed, then covered her mouth. "Oh, bother, I suppose you must." She arose as well and began to help him gather his clothes in the faint light.

"I know why you married Archie." His words stilled her, but he pressed on. "I know about the house, the eviction. His part in all of it."

She rose up and faced him. "If you knew, why didn't you do something?"

"I just discovered the truth last night. At Strout's."

She tipped her head and stared at him. "How?"

"There was some correspondence."

Lucy tipped her head and studied him for a moment. "You must be mistaken. Archie had nothing to do with any of that. It was all Parkerton's doing."

Clifton leaned over the side of the bed,

caught up his jacket and pulled the papers from his pocket, offering them to her.

She moved to the window, where the light was better, and quickly read through the pages. "That rotten, conniving bastard," she muttered after she'd finished.

"Which one?" Clifton asked. "The duke, Strout, or Archie?"

"All three." She tossed the papers aside. "Well, I can't hang Archie," she conceded. "And I suppose I must leave it to Pymm to take care of Strout. But if I ever have the ill fortune to run into Parkerton, it will be an interview he won't forget."

"Not if I get to him first. I almost fear for the Parkerton line." He reached for her and held her close. "I am so sorry," he said. "I should have been there. I should have stopped them. Seen to it that you were cared for. I just thought —"

"That I would be there," she said.

"Yes. Stupid of me."

"I thought you would come back," she said quietly. "But you never did."

He let go of her, his face serious. "I longed to, but my orders were always the same — stay put," he told her. "Though Malcolm was able to go back and forth, much to my chagrin. I sent a note with him once, when he knew he would be able to come to

Hampstead."

"When?"

"A year after we left. Malcolm was sent with information for your father. When he returned he said he'd seen Mariana, but you were gone."

"Papa must have known he was coming and sent me on some errand to keep me from receiving any communications from you."

"He knew of us?"

Lucy nodded. "He caught me coming home from your inn that night."

Clifton whistled softly. "Malcolm said he'd given the note to Mrs. Kewin."

Lucy closed her eyes and groaned. "Oh, no, he didn't! Mrs. Kewin, bless her soul, couldn't remember where we kept the sugar pot most days. She probably took your note and tucked it in her pocket and that was the end of it."

"I didn't get back to England until . . . well, I was on the same ship as Malcolm," he said, turning from her.

"When he was lost," she said.

"Yes. I came straight to Hampstead — after — only to find you were already married and the house let to strangers."

Lucy's eyes filled with tears. "And now you know why," she said, nodding toward the papers scattered on the floor. "Mariana died first, then Papa and Mrs. Kewin within a day of each other. It was so very terrible, the house was so empty. And then Parkerton's notice arrived. I had a sennight to come up with the money for the lease or leave." She paused and glanced away. "I should have found some way to raise that money. I should have waited for you. I am so sorry I failed you."

Failed him? Ridiculous. If anything, it was the other way around.

"I thought you'd heard of Malcolm's death and my part in it and knew . . . knew I was what you always suspected, a failure. Unworthy."

She stepped back from him. Gaping. "You? A failure? Hardly!"

"Lucy, Malcolm died because of me," he said, the words tumbling out of him. A confession he'd never uttered aloud.

But had haunted him all these years.

She shook her head. "I heard what happened on that beach. It took some time, but I heard. You were nowhere near."

"No, I wasn't, I was still aboard Dashwell's ship." He paused and considered his words. He'd never spoken of that night, not even to Jack. He hadn't wanted anyone to know the truth.

Then Clifton drew a breath and confessed what he'd never told anyone.

"Malcolm was so eager to get ashore. We only had a few days before we were slated to go back, but with each delay to get ashore, we were losing time." He reached over and tussled her hair. "I had planned to come to you. I was going to get a special license in London and come straight to Hampstead so we could be married."

She gazed at him. "You were going to marry me?"

"Of course, foolish Goosie. I had promised, and . . ." He paused. "I loved you."

"I didn't know," she said. "It had been two years since you'd left, and not a word of where you were. You don't know how many times I searched Papa's map room looking for some note, some dispatch that held your name." She bit her lips together, tears welling up in her eyes.

"Malcolm insisted on going ashore first and setting out to London ahead of me. To add to it, Templeton was there. He was eager to get to his wife, so we played cards for the one available seat in the longboat."

Lucy gaped at him. "You cheated!"

"Aye, I did. Templeton isn't all that good at cards, so he was out almost immediately, and it was down to Malcolm and me. It was my deal —"

"And you decided to give yourself the winning hand," Lucy said.

"Yes, in my haste, I didn't do a very good job of it, and Malcolm caught me out." He shook his head.

"So he took the seat." Lucy's voice grew wistful, and she gazed up at him. "It could have been you that night."

"You don't know how many times I wished it had been."

"It wasn't your turn," she said. "And think of the lives, of the work you had left to do, the work you've done tonight."

He ignored the truth of what she said. "I failed and Malcolm died because I was desperate, willing to go to any lengths to get to you."

"Yes, and if it had been you on that beach, would Strout's deception have ever been discovered? Or what of Marseilles? Don't think I don't know how you aided Larken there. Or any of the other matters you've handled over the years."

"There would have been someone else. Some other fool."

She shook her head vehemently. "No, those deeds were yours and yours alone to do," she paused. "Just as last night was ours to discover. *Ours,* not anyone else's."

"You sound like your father," Clifton told her. "Is that more of his advice?"

She set her jaw, then reached up and cradled his face in her hands. Given that it was Lucy, she didn't hold him with a gentle, caring caress — her hands were strong and firm. "Demmit, Gilby, you will see the truth of this. My father always maintained that the work he'd done on the Continent, all those years in the field working for the Duke of Parkerton weren't meant for the honors and the rewards — they were only important in the sense of what they prepared him to do — his real work, if you will."

Her words finally struck a light in the darkness inside him. Like a lone flicker of reason.

"Preparing agents," Clifton said, feeling a light begin to brighten.

"Yes, exactly. Think of all the men he trained — Templeton, Jack, you, Malcolm, Darby. His earlier heroics were just lessons for him to impart when the struggle was far more desperate, far more important."

"But Goosie, I am only one man. What does all that have to do with me?"

She huffed a loud sigh and threw up her hands. "Everything, you great fool. If naught for all your training, the lessons and experiences you gained, do you think Strout's thievery would have been discovered?" Her green eyes burned with determination.

And something else. Pride.

"Perhaps not," he conceded.

"Gilby, the events of our lives are set in motion by a hand greater than ours — and we are never given a task that we cannot, do not, have the powers to conquer."

"But I couldn't have done it without you," he whispered, leaning over and kissing her brow before he continued dressing. She followed suit, catching up her wrapper.

As he bent to pick up his shirt, his back to her, a rolled-up packet of papers fell out.

"What the devil?" he muttered as he leaned over to pick them up.

For it was a will. One of the wills from Strout's office, to be exact. And then he looked again at the shirt in his hands and realized it was the one she'd been wearing the night before.

And he would have wagered his last grout that this was Malcolm's will.

She'd smuggled it out of Strout's office last night and had meant to keep it from him.

Clifton closed his eyes, the fire of her deceit burning away the love he'd confessed to her this night. It burned and raged out of control, leaving him shaking with fury.

Then he paused, tucking the will in his coat pocket and turning around to face her. "There is only one thing left undone, Lucy."

"Yes, Gilby?" she said in a cozy, well-sated little voice.

"I still don't understand why Malcolm gave you guardianship over his estate."

Before his eyes, he watched her still.

But he needn't have asked her, for the answer to his question, the very reason for Malcolm's secret, came bounding into her room.

The door plowed open and into the room barreled a young boy.

The little monkey, Clifton guessed.

"Lucy, Lucy, I thought I heard voices —" the child said before he stopped and cast a wary gaze at Clifton.

The earl studied him as well. And there, staring up at him, was a pair of dark eyes so like his own, a face he had both never seen and hadn't seen in years.

He turned to Lucy, and even in the dim light, he could see she'd gone as white as a sheet.

But he didn't think for one second he would get the truth from her, so he turned back to the boy. "Who was your father, lad? Who was he?"

Lucy's horror had left her speechless. She'd never meant for him to find out.

At least not like this.

"Who was your father, boy? Tell me?" Clifton thundered.

She'd forbidden Mickey to ever speak of the matter. To never reveal the truth. For she'd reasoned, and rightly so, that if the truth of his parentage was discovered, the Sterlings would have sent him off packing to the Grey estate.

Mickey stared up at the face so like his own, and his gaze narrowed, as if he had guessed the truth as well.

"Malcolm Grey, sir," the boy answered. "Did you know him?"

Clifton staggered back, not even looking at her, his gaze still fixed on Mickey.

"You're Malcolm's son?"

"Aye, my lord," he said.

Clifton shook his head, then turned and marched out of the room.

Oh, good gracious heavens! He thought she'd had an affair with Malcolm.

Lucy dashed after him. "Clifton, you must hear me out. You must listen to me —"

He paused on the stairs and shook a finger

at her. "I will hear no more of your lies. Your deceit, madame! You are no better than Strout or that shiftless, spineless man you married."

All through the house, Lucy could hear the creak of beds and the squeak of hinges as the doors adjacent to the stairwell opened. Oh, how perfect. Now the entire household had ringside seats from which to witness this scandalous row.

"Would you cease your bellowing and listen to reason!" she shouted back at him.

"From you? I doubt you know what reason is. Or have you managed to steal it from someone who actually possessed it?" he fired back.

Lucy sucked in a deep breath and tried to frame a retort, but it was too late; he'd turned and was going down the stairs two at a time.

"That boy is my nephew, and I won't have him raised by the likes of you!" he declared from the foyer. "I'll be back with my solicitor. Have his things packed and ready." Then the front door slammed shut, rattling on its hinges.

"His name is Michael!" she said after him, slumping down on the stairwell, her legs giving way beneath her.

In a moment, Elinor and Minerva were

on either side of her.

"He means to take Mickey from me!" she cried, sobbing into Elinor's shoulder.

"We won't let him," Minerva told her, glancing over Lucy's shaking shoulders to look Elinor directly in the eye. "We will not let him."

Elinor nodded in agreement.

"I fear he is past listening to reason," Lucy continued. "I've made a dreadful muddle of this."

"Never fear, Lucy, he'll listen to reason," Minerva told her, patting her on the shoulder. "He'll listen. We'll see to that."

CHAPTER 15

Some hours later, Minerva and Elinor sat in the darkened confines of the duke's carriage outside the doors of White's.

"Minerva, if we are seen here, lurking about on St. James Street, we'll be the scandal of the Season." Elinor slumped lower in her seat.

"I tell you, he'll be here soon enough, and then we can be gone," Minerva assured her. "Lucy would do the same for us."

This notion brightened Elinor's resolve. "I suppose she would. Who would have thought she could be such a dear?"

"No, who would have thought it," Minerva agreed. For indeed, if anyone had suggested that she would go to these lengths, putting her reputation on the line for the likes of Lucy Ellyson Sterling, she would have sent the fool packing.

For that was exactly what they were doing — perilously close to ruining their reputations, for no woman of a good name dared set foot on St. James Street, the storied home to most of the most refined and exclusive men's clubs in London.

But this was where Clifton's butler had told them his master was going — "to his club" — before the proper fellow had closed the door in their faces.

And so to the club Minerva and Elinor had raced. And now they waited.

They had snuck away as Lucy had sat waiting for the solicitor the duke had promised to send over to aid her. For if they'd revealed the true nature of their plot, she would have stopped them.

"Do you think he will listen to us?" Elinor mused.

"He will," Minerva said, pulling a pistol out of her reticule.

"Dear heavens, Minerva! Where did you get that?"

She held the piece gingerly, then glanced over at Elinor. "I stole it from Thomas-William's room."

Elinor glanced at the gun and then up at Minerva. "Bravo!" Then she glanced out the crack in the curtains. "There he is! At least I think it is him. He has a shirt on now."

"Scandalous man," Minerva muttered, her hand on the latch, for there indeed was

Clifton coming down the block. "Though I imagine he suits Lucy to a tee."

They both held their breath as he drew near, and when he was right alongside the carriage, Minerva swung out and shoved the pistol into the earl's back.

"Get in the carriage, my lord, and I promise not to shoot," she told him.

"Lady Standon?" he said, glancing over his shoulder at her. "Do you even know how to fire that thing?"

"My lord, I haven't the least idea if it's loaded, but are you willing to find out?"

An hour later, a shaken, but intact, Clifton emerged from the Hollindrake carriage. He made his way into White's, where he was met by the solicitor he'd summoned to meet him there.

It had been a full morning, what with helping Pymm arrest Strout, sending around for the solicitor so he could gain custody of the boy, and finally, being kidnapped by not one of the Lady Standons but two of them.

Good God! If it got out in the Foreign Office circles that he'd been nabbed by a pair of dowagers in front of White's, he'd never hear the end of it.

Not that he thought Minerva or Elinor were about to natter on at their afternoon calls as to how they had spent the earlier part of their day.

As it was, he'd sent the solicitor packing, for he'd had quite enough of wrangling and legal matters for one day. Why, he was just thankful the profession was barred from admitting ladies, for he rued the day the likes of Minerva Sterling would ever be given a chance to argue a case. Her words still rang in his ears.

"You arrogant fool! You never gave her a chance! When was she supposed to tell you about your brother's child? When, sir?"

Before he'd had a chance to make an answer, any answer, Elinor Sterling had been right there.

"Malcolm loved Lucy's sister, Mariana. Left her with child. And Lucy has guarded the lad since the day he was born. And now you dare to impugn her, when she has cared for him, kept him —"

"— much to the consternation of the Sterlings," Minerva pointed out.

"And at risk to her own reputation, mind you, because just like you, most of us assumed he was hers. Why, she's put her own happiness behind the welfare of that child over and over just to ensure that he stays with her."

Minerva wasn't finished either. *"And why would she have told you? By any accounts, in her eyes you had disavowed her love, never come back and were all but engaged to another! What else was she to think?!"*

Clifton shook his head, sifting through everything he'd learned. She'd guarded Malcolm's child. Raised him as her own, and buffeted all of Society's rules and sneers to keep him with her — because he was all she had left of the life she'd loved.

In Hampstead, in the country.

Now it was his turn to lament. *Malcolm, if only you'd told me about Mariana. About the child. I would have done all I could for them.*

Why his brother hadn't told him, he knew not, and now he would never know.

"Clifton!" came an affable greeting.

The earl looked up to find Jack coming down the stairs.

"How goes our little business?" Jack winked and gave him a nudge.

It was then that Clifton noticed the man at Jack's side. It was easy to tell they were brothers, for the man was of Jack's height and build, but the resemblance stopped there; Jack's companion was dressed to the nines, in a resplendent jacket of the latest fashion, boots polished to a gleam, his hair cut precisely, as if it were trimmed each morning.

And capping it all off was a glorious

cravat, tied in one of those most envied arrangements and embellished with a dia-
mond stickpin.

The fellow gazed over at Clifton through
a lorgnette, and his brow raised at the
crumpled state of the earl's jacket and what
was probably the shadow of a beard.

"Oh, there, where are my manners," Jack
was saying. "I don't know if you've met my
brother, His Grace, the Duke of Parkerton."

"This doesn't appear to be the best time
for introductions, Jack," the duke intoned.
"Your friend looks in need of some attention." The duke shook his head in dismay,
then waved his hand for Clifton to move
out of his way.

Clifton raised his gaze and looked at the
duke. Stared at the man who'd had a hand
in all this mess. "You owe a lady an apology."

"I owe no ladies any such thing — and if I
do owe some unfortunate creature of *your*
acquaintance a few words, I doubt she is a
lady. Now out of my way, sir," the duke
repeated, drawing himself up to his most
imperious stance.

"Oh, good God," Jack muttered, stepping
back, shaking his head. "This isn't going to
end well."

Clifton's eyes saw not the duke but Lucy

being forced out of her home. Lucy having to marry Archie Sterling to keep herself and Mickey safe. Lucy thinking him lost to her — worse, that he'd never cared for her.

In much the same fashion in which Parkerton would regard anyone not of his lofty realm. Beyond his consequence.

So Clifton gave the duke a lesson in common eloquence.

He leveled a doubler into the duke's side. The air left the man in a loud *whoosh*, and Clifton finished him with a right solid facer, the Duke of Parkerton landing in a very inelegant sprawl on the very fine and elegant marble floor of White's.

Jack took a few, slow tentative steps over and glanced down at the unconscious figure of his brother. "Oh, that was a truly fine muffler, Clifton. Excellent hits. You don't know how many times I've longed to do that." He glanced up at Clifton as he added, "But you do realize, he'll insist on having your membership revoked."

Summoning a few of the servants to help, they managed to carry Parkerton off to a quiet room. With a bottle of White's best brandy and a beefsteak at the ready, Jack revived his brother.

"What the devil!" Parkerton sputtered as

he came to. "What happened?"

"Clifton floored you," Jack told him, pressing a beefsteak to his swelling eye. He glanced over his shoulder to where Clifton stood in the shadows. "Shuttered you good, I fear."

"I have a black eye?" Parkerton said, his fingers brushing aside the steak to test the spot. He winced and took the cut of beef from Jack, settling it on his injury himself. "I've never had one."

"Oh, go on with you," Jack said. "Of course you have. Every lad gets a black eye once."

Parkerton glanced up at him. "No, Jack. I was never allowed the freedoms you had." He blinked his one good eye and glanced around the room. "And who exactly are you?"

"Clifton," Jack reminded him. "He's a friend of mine."

"Which one of your friends?" Parkerton asked, one brow arched. "One of your old friends" — referring to Jack's more nefarious past — "or one of your more recent acquaintances?"

Clifton straightened. "He knows?"

This question was directed to Jack, who nodded.

The duke straightened up and shook his

head a bit, as if sweeping out the last vestiges of Clifton's facer. "So I take that to mean you are one of the gentlemen from the Foreign Office who from time to time *visited* Jack."

As in used the secret caverns and smuggler's passageways at Thistleton Park to slip in and out of England on their way to the Continent.

"Yes, Your Grace," Clifton said, bowing slightly.

"Good God, no wonder they sent you," the duke said. "You've got a bruising punch."

Clifton bowed again.

"I believe you mentioned something about a lady," the duke said.

"Yes, Lucy Ellyson."

"Ellyson? That name is familiar." He tapped his chin. "How do I know that name?"

Jack's eyes widened, and he shook his head at Clifton. *Nay! Don't tell him.*

"Wasn't that some fellow our father raised up?" he said.

There was a slight groan from Jack, and he just shrugged in reply.

"And this Lucy creature?" the duke asked.

"His daughter," Clifton said.

"Jack, will you quit looking like you are

about to be ill," Parkerton ordered. "You look paler than the time you had to inform me Great-Aunt Josephine wasn't dead."

"It's similar, I fear," Jack admitted.

The duke stared at him. "What are you saying, or rather, not saying?"

Jack shuffled a bit. "Our father used to recruit thieves and nobles alike for the Foreign Office. He would send them to school, train them himself, and then take them with him when he would go on tour on the Continent to help him spy for England."

Clifton thought it might have been kinder to just land another doubler into the duke's middle, for now the lofty duke turned quite pale.

"Our father was a spy?"

"An excellent one," Clifton added, much to the dismay of the duke, who waved him off.

"Yes," Jack told him. "Ask Aunt Josephine if you don't believe me."

"Oh, I'll save myself the pain of that interview and take your word," the duke said wearily. "This news only confirms my long-held suspicion that I am the only member of the Tremonts not inflicted with madness."

Jack grinned.

"And this Ellyson fellow? Was he one of our father's noble gentlemen?"

Clifton and Jack shared a glance.

"From that look and your silence, I garner the answer is no," the duke said.

"Yes and no. Ellyson was a thief who picked your father's pocket and your father had him sent to school and then —"

"Used him in the King's service," the duke finished, putting a much more palatable gloss on the subject. "But there is more to this?"

The earl nodded. "Your father gave Ellyson the use, during his lifetime, of a house in Hampstead, where he continued to . . . continued to . . ."

". . . serve the King," Jack said. "Training others. Myself included."

"He lived there with his daughters and performed a noble service, despite his less-than-honest origins. Yet when he died, Your Grace ordered —"

The duke waved him off. "I have to imagine my steward ordered the daughters evicted and —" He pointed to his swollen eye.

Clifton nodded. "My apologies, Your Grace. I fear my temper —"

"No apologies. This Miss Ellyson must be quite a lady."

"She is," he and Jack said in unison. Then Clifton added, "She is Lady Standon now."

That regal brow rose again. "One of those dowagers that is the talk of Society, I gather?"

Jack nodded.

"If you would but consider giving her back the use of the house," Clifton suggested, "I would be most grateful — it would free her from the confines of Society and give her a chance to make a life of her own choosing."

"And I suppose you are of a hope that she will choose you in this new life?"

"Yes, though I doubt it. I've rather made a mess of things," Clifton admitted.

"Your temper, I gather?" the duke said wryly. He struggled up to his feet. "I will call on Lady Standon immediately and make my amends."

Clifton and Jack shot each other wry looks.

"What? Can I not call on the lady?"

Jack shook his head. "Not looking like that!"

The duke looked down at his rumpled cravat and creased coat. "I suppose not. A new suit is in order."

"No!" Clifton said, shaking his head.

"Definitely not," Jack said, starting to pull off his own coat. "Take mine."

Parkerton regarded his brother's offering

with disdain. "Wear that? I'll look like my steward!"

"Exactly," Jack said.

"Excellent notion," Clifton said. "Um, Lady Standon isn't much for Society and has even less regard for Your Grace."

"Why ever not?" Parkerton asked as he found himself being divested of his coat and having Jack's more serviceable one pulled on.

Jack paused for a moment, a calculated light in his eyes. "Do you want it bantered about town that you were seen calling on the Standon dowagers? Every matron within a hundred miles of London would take it as a sign you are looking for a new wife."

Parkerton shuddered at the notion.

"More to the point, Lucy Ellyson isn't one with a regard for titles and rank. And you did have her evicted," Clifton told him. "And I learned that right hook from the lady herself. I'd hate for you to have a matching set —" He tapped his own black eye to make his point.

"Ah!" Parkerton said, raising a hand to his own swollen eye. "Good advice."

So it was, an hour later, that Lucy found herself in the receiving room seated before a man who claimed to be the Duke of Parkerton.

"You don't look like a duke," she said skeptically.

"Madame, I will have you know I am the Duke of Parkerton," he said with an imperious air.

Lucy tipped her head and eyed the fellow. "With a shiner?"

The man drew a deep breath. "Courtesy of the Earl of Clifton. We had an encounter, shall we say, at White's this afternoon."

". . . if I ever have the ill fortune to run into Parkerton, it will be an interview he won't forget."

What was it Clifton had said?

"Not if I get to him first."

And so he had. Her mouth dropped open, and she raised her hand to cover it when she remembered she wasn't supposed to gape at guests. And most certainly not dukes.

The duke politely ignored her gaffe. "He and my brother Jack suggested that I come in this guise so as not to draw attention to my visit, and so that you would be more amenable to my offer."

"Offer?" she said faintly, as she was still struggling to believe that Clifton had given the duke a shiner. And in White's, of all places.

"Yes, an offer. In light of your father's esteemed service to the Crown, and since it was my father's wish that he be compensated, I am giving you the deed to the house in Hampstead."

"You are giving me the house?"

"Yes. I regret that I did not know of the agreement between our fathers, or I would have extended the lease. Today has been quite enlightening," he said, touching his eye. "I also called on Hollindrake before I arrived, and he has arranged for your dowry to be released, so you will have an income to live on. You are free to make your own life now."

"My dowry? I've never had a dowry," she said.

"You do now," he said, smiling, then winced at the pain of it.

"Would you like a beefsteak for that eye?" she offered.

Parkerton looked up at her and smiled. "My lady, you are a regular bruiser, aren't you?"

"So I've been told," she admitted.

"Would you permit me to make a suggestion for your newfound freedom — without fear of discovering how much of a bruiser you truly are?"

Lucy laughed. "Of course, Your Grace."

"Repay the earl for his service to the Crown by granting him your heart —" He held up his hand to stave off her protest. "The man, I understand, made a grievous error of judgment —"

She snorted rudely at this.

"Yes, so it seems," the duke agreed, "but I would guess that you love him."

"And what makes you think that?" Lucy asked.

"Because you haven't flattened me for daring to suggest such a notion."

They both laughed.

"Go to him, Lady Standon. He wants the same things you do. His country life and a marriage of love. He is in the park near the Serpentine. Tell him all is forgiven and live the life you've always wanted."

She rose and was about to leave in all haste, then she paused and glanced over her shoulder. "If I forgive the earl, do I still get to keep the house in Hampstead?"

For Lucy was still her father's all-too-practical daughter.

Elinor arrived at the house, just as Lucy was leaving.

"There is too much to tell," Lucy said in

a rush, "but I am to have the house in Hampstead, a dowry and the earl!"

Elinor watched her go and wished Minerva hadn't stopped to call on Lady Charles, so she could have seen the spark of happiness in Lucy's eyes.

In this good humor, Elinor entered the house only to find a strange man coming out of the receiving room and, at the same time, Tia dashing down the stairs.

"Oh, Elinor, thank goodness you're home," she said in a rush. "Isidore is having her pups, and I fear she is having a time with it. I know not what to do!"

This stopped Elinor, for usually one of the stable hands handled these matters. "Neither do I. Oh, poor Isidore!"

And they both turned to the stranger in the hall. Elinor assumed it was the solicitor they'd asked Hollindrake to send, but the man hardly had a townish look to him and seemed to have a country air about him. "Sir, have you any experience with dogs?"

"A bit," he said in a rather haughty manner.

Well, he needn't be so high in the instep, Elinor mused. After all, he wasn't much above a steward. Nor should he stare at her so. For it gave her a warm shiver down her spine.

She stole another glance at him, and it surprised her that she found him quite handsome.

How unfortunate he wasn't titled.

"Would you mind assisting us?" she asked. "This is Isidore's first litter, and she's one of the finest greyhounds I've ever owned."

"I would be honored, my lady," he said, bowing to her.

And as he rose, Elinor glanced at him again and realized that he was quite tall and well fashioned. In a common sort of way, yes, but she couldn't help but feel a bit of blush rise on her cheeks as he looked at her.

"Do you do business for the duke often?" she asked as they made their way up to the closet where Isidore had hidden herself.

"Do I do what for the duke?" he stammered, looking every bit taken aback.

"Business?" she repeated. "You are a man of business, I assume."

After a pause, he nodded slowly. "Why, yes. Yes, I am."

"Excellent! Do you have any connections in Society?"

"A few," he demurred, bowing his head.

Elinor nodded. "Would you mind looking into a matter for me?" she added. "Discreetly. I can pay you, of course."

"I would be honored to be of service to

you, but I don't know who I am helping," he said as they knelt before Isidore and her growing litter of pups.

Tia stepped right in and made the necessary introduction.

"This is my sister, Elinor, Lady Standon, for the time being," the girl said, grinning. "Until she marries her duke."

Lucy hurried toward the park, not caring about the stares and comments that fluttered behind her like fallen leaves.

It was a bright, sunny day, and being February, the air was crisp. To her, it could have been the first of May and the flowers could have been blooming.

But when she got to the Serpentine, there was no one about, and not a sign of Clifton. Her heart sank. Had Parkerton led her afoul?

Not if he wants to live, she mused, her hands fisting to her sides.

Just then, a bit of movement caught her eye, a figure slipping out from behind a tree. *Clifton.*

How she had missed him all these years. And they had been kept apart for far too long.

She rushed to him, and he to her.

"Will you forgive me?"

"You? Will you forgive me?"

They both laughed, and Clifton brushed her tousled hair out of her face.

"What of Mickey?" she asked anxiously.

"Oh, you cannot imagine my joy at finding him! Malcolm's son! Gads, Goosie, he's the spitting image of his father."

"Aye," she agreed. "But you'll find he has Mariana's penchant for trouble."

Clifton grinned. "Then he will be our joy — and a good example for our children to follow."

Lucy's heart swelled — at the thought of a home with Clifton, and children laughing and playing around them.

"I've never stopped loving you," he said.

"Nor I, you," she whispered back.

And then he kissed her. Slowly, deeply, his lips tender atop hers.

It was his pledge, Lucy knew. His promise.

But their interlude was interrupted by shouting from a rider nearby.

"Clifton! You devil! Is that you?"

The earl looked up. "Asterby," he muttered.

"You wretched cur! I will see you tossed out of White's — though I don't think it will be much trouble, considering what you did to Parkerton."

"Nice facer," Lucy said, beaming up at him.

He chucked her under the chin. "I was taught by the best."

"Do not ignore me!" Asterby said, pulling his horse to a stop before them. "You low-born dog!"

"Sir, if this is about your daughter —"

"My daughter?! Of course, you fool, this is about my daughter! She's gone and run off with Percy Harmond — that no-account Tulip! They've married. How he came up with the blunt for a special license, I'll never know, but he did and he's gone and married my daughter!" Asterby wagged a finger at them both. "If you hadn't treated her so disgracefully, I wouldn't be saddled with that idiot for a son-in-law."

Lucy choked back a fit of laughter, thinking of the angelic Lady Annella, all the while plotting her own escape from her parents' machinations. "Perhaps it is a love match, my lord," she suggested.

"A wha-a-at?" Lord Asterby blustered.

"A love match," Lucy repeated. "Perhaps your daughter simply wanted to marry a man she loved."

"Marry for love? What utter nonsense! Love is about duty and obligation!"

Lucy looked up at Clifton. "Is it?"

He shook his head. "Not for us."

"Oh, bah! It is like trying to talk sense to a pair of hedgehogs. What the devil is wrong with the world these days?" Asterby blustered before he rode off.

"Duty and obligation!" Lucy shuddered as Clifton took her by the hand and began to lead her home.

"Oh, don't discount the importance of those notions, my future Lady Clifton," he told her imperiously. "For your first order of business is to marry me, then you are obliged to produce an heir."

Lucy pulled to a stop and spied a wicked gleam in the earl's dark eyes. "Then I suppose we will have to work on that, er, obligation immediately," she told him solemnly. "It will take a dedicated effort on your part."

Clifton bowed before her. "Ever at your service, madame. Ever and always."

Lucy grinned as he swept her into his arms again. "As you should be."

ABOUT THE AUTHOR

Elizabeth Boyle has always loved romance and now lives it each and every day by writing adventurous and passionate stories that readers from all around the world have described as "page-turners." Since first being published in 1996, she's seen her books become *New York Times* and *USA Today* bestsellers and won the RWA RITA® Award and a *Romantic Times* Reviewer's Choice Award. *How I Met My Countess* is her thirteenth title for Avon Books. She resides in Seattle with her husband and two small sons, or "heroes in training" as she likes to call them. Readers can write to her at PO Box 47252, Seattle, WA 98146, or visit her on the web at *www.elizabethboyle.com.*

We hope you have enjoyed this Large Print book. Other Thorndike, Wheeler, Kennebec, and Chivers Press Large Print books are available at your library or directly from the publishers.

For information about current and upcoming titles, please call or write, without obligation, to:

Publisher
Thorndike Press
295 Kennedy Memorial Drive
Waterville, ME 04901
Tel. (800) 223-1244

or visit our Web site at:

http://gale.cengage.com/thorndike

OR

Chivers Large Print
published by BBC Audiobooks Ltd
St James House, The Square
Lower Bristol Road
Bath BA2 3SB
England
Tel. +44(0) 800 136919
email: bbcaudiobooks@bbc.co.uk
www.bbcaudiobooks.co.uk

All our Large Print titles are designed for easy reading, and all our books are made to last.